The Devil's Doorbell

16 Tales of The Darkest Romance

**Compiled & Edited by
Xtina Marie**

A HellBound Books Publishing LLC Book
Austin TX

**A HellBound Books LLC
Publication**
Copyright © 2019 by HellBound Books Publishing LLC
All Rights Reserved

Cover and art design by
HellBound Books Publishing LLC

www.hellboundbookspublishing.com

Printed in the United States of America

Contents

Foreword

Two of my absolute favorite genres to read are horror and romance. Ahhh, I can just about feel the chills running down my spine. It's almost as if the fingers of the devil himself were lovingly caressing me. Let's face it, horror and romance belong together!

For some time now, HellBound Books Publishing has had an idea to compile a darkest romance anthology. Submissions were sought and the results were outstanding! The task of selecting the stories that would make the cut was heartbreaking—they were all so good. Within these pages, you will read 16 spine tingling tales of darkest romance brought to you by some of the best in the horror community.

So, we had the idea, we had the stories—now we needed a name!

"The Devil's Doorbell". Slang for the clitoris. Who knew? Certainly not me!

While researching the origin of this entertaining euphemism, I came across some pretty funny stories, although not nearly the explanation I had been looking for. One delightful question I read was asking; if the clitoris is the devil's doorbell, would that make the vagina hell? I know many men would could completely agree.

Then I got to thinking, maybe the origin can be traced back to the Bible itself! I mean, there are plenty of verses in there that talk about how succumbing to the strange woman is a direct pathway to hell. (Shout out to my girl, Mary Magdalene!) Check it out for yourselves. Proverbs is especially worried about these interesting—cough!—I mean, evil women.

Love is a beautiful thing. Finding true love is amazing. When you add a touch of darkness to that love—well, what you have then is just pure unadulterated bliss. Enjoying a decadent slice of rich chocolate cake while on your diet. It's so good, so damned good—yet unbelievably bad for you.

I suggest pouring a glass of wine, lighting a few candles and curling up beside your loved one once you've picked up this entertaining anthology. And when you've stumbled onto the good parts, don't forget to ring my doorbell—err, oh you know what I mean!

Enjoy!

-Xtina Marie

HellBound Books Publishing LLC
2019

The Devil's Doorbell

Visions of Blood
Madison Estes

He had the dream again, the one with the redhead that always made him wake up aroused, with wet, sticky sheets clinging to him. He thought they were premonitions at first. Of course, the fact that he could touch her without searing pain gave him reason to doubt that, but still, he longed to believe it was a preview of something that could be.

It was the dreams that led him to an escort website. He usually just browsed, imagining he was a normal guy who could set up an evening with one of the call girls and then have sex with them however he liked. His desire for more than just naked videos brought him to the point of bringing a call girl to his house. He picked a redheaded woman that looked similar to the girl from his dreams. They had the same emerald eyes and dimples; he'd always had a thing for dimples.

They wouldn't have to leave his house, but he still dressed up for the occasion. There was no need for her to know he was an agoraphobic slob who worked from home and lived in his pajamas. After he showered, he changed into a pair of jeans and a grey, button-up shirt. He ran a comb though his short brown hair and put on cologne even though he didn't intend for her to get close enough to smell it. He made his bed and hid things he felt a twenty-two year-old man shouldn't display in his bedroom: his Star Wars collectables, his Pokémon cards, and his middle school trophies. Unsure of what to do after that, he paced in his living room. He jumped when the doorbell rang. He took a deep breath and answered the door.

"Hi," he said. He swallowed hard as his eyes raked down her body. She wore a black cocktail dress with a sweetheart neckline that accentuated her pale breasts. Her crimson hair was pinned up on the sides. The scent of roses and jasmine wafted his way as she took a step closer. Her smile made her seem approachable and sweet. She was beautiful, and the thought of letting someone into his house, let alone someone he was about to see naked, was nerve-wracking. His palms started to sweat.

"Hi, my name is Natasha. It's a pleasure to meet you," she said. She extended her hand. He pretended he didn't notice it.

"I'm Dylan. Please come in," he said. He opened the door wider and stepped back. She frowned at him rejecting her handshake, then shrugged and stepped inside.

"Sorry about that," he said as he realized he had offended her. "I have this thing about touching people. I'm not really into it."

"Oh, okay. I get it."

"I seriously doubt that you do."

"I've dealt with all kinds of sexual preferences and kinks. I doubt you could shock me."

"That's good because I'm just going to be watching tonight." He dropped the polite smile as his icy blue eyes roamed over her again. Her smile vanished as well, and in that moment while she appraised him, he recognized her. His mouth opened in shock. She didn't just look similar to the girl from his dream; she *was* that girl.

"You don't exactly look like your picture," he said, trying to hide his surprise as his heart pounded. "Not in a bad way, just different."

"It's an old picture." She smiled and perked her voice up as she asked him, "Should we get started now?"

***

He tried to convince himself he was projecting his fantasy onto Natasha. It made sense. His dreams were what drove him to inviting an escort into his home. It would make sense his mind wanted to turn Natasha into that girl. She was the closest he'd ever get to fulfilling that dream.

As Natasha pulled her top down, her full breasts bouncing as she shimmied out of the bottom half of her dress, he found that he didn't care to analyze his subconscious dreams, or fantasies, or whatever they were. The fact that Natasha either was or looked like the girl he'd dreamed about having sex with was just a bonus. It added a surreal spin to the situation, but he found that he wanted to just go along with it instead of question it and ruin the experience.

Natasha crawled onto the bed and began to play with her breasts, the pink nipples perking up as she rolled them between her expert fingers. Her fingers trailed down her abdomen, and he imagined it was his own hands grazing her skin. Her small fingers slithered between her legs and into her hairless mound. The pale lips reddened under her ministrations. She let out a low groan. She looked up, locked eyes with him, and crooked the index finger that was not buried inside her, beckoning him onto the bed.

"Wouldn't you be more comfortable next to me? We don't have to touch. You can just lie next to me. Might get a better view."

It was tempting, to be close enough that he could imagine doing things to her that he'd done in his dreams. He longed to smell the floral perfume she'd worn for him mixed with the smell of her arousal that he could only imagine from his position in the chair across the room. He could watch every expression flicker across her face up close while he jerked himself off beside her. He could even come on her, if she allowed. The image of his cum dripping off her breasts caused him to cave in to her offer. He reclined on the other side of the queen-sized bed and pulled himself out. He poured some of the lubricant on the nightstand into his palm and began to slide his hand along his shaft.

"Are you sure you don't want me to touch you?" she purred. "It would be my pleasure."

"No touching," he said.

"I bet I could make you feel really good if you'd let me."

Her persistence began to annoy him. He didn't care to explain his condition, not while he was rock hard and starting to get into the fantasy. He shook his head.

"Just keep going. I like watching you."

She watched his hand moving up and down his shaft, and her tongue darted out as she licked her lips. Her voyeuristic gaze so similar to his own sent a jolt of pleasure through him. Being desired was a foreign concept, not because of his appearance, but due to his self-imposed isolation. Her hungry gaze travelled from his eyes to his large, jutting cock, her pouty lips and eyes asking him wordlessly why he wouldn't let her play with it. He bit his lip as she started to rub her clit faster, shaking the bed with the force of her motions, until they were both gasping and trembling on the edge of release.

He came first, her name leaving his lips like a prayer. He was close enough to her that he could roll over on his side as he peaked to shoot his cum onto her sweet little body. Her eyes shut and she moaned out his name, coming right after he sprayed upwards onto her stomach and chest.

He glanced over and saw where his cum had landed. Pride swelled inside of him, the thought of his cum spread out on this beautiful woman. She smeared it with her fingers and then lifted them into her mouth, tasting him.

"Not bad," she said. He groaned.

"Now there is something else I want to taste," she said. He opened his mouth to object as she leaned in. Imagining that she was going to kiss him, he turned his face away. He was unprepared for her assault on his neck. As soon as her teeth pierced into his flesh, he screamed, trying to push her off. She pushed him down with her hands, and he surrendered, weakened by the agony of the pain shooting through his head. It felt like shards of glass crammed into his skull.

She had another man pinned down beneath her, except she was riding this man as she attacked his neck. Dylan couldn't tell if the man was crying in pain, pleasure, or both. When she pulled away, blood dribbled down her face and neck. She wiped the blood off her chin with a satisfied smirk. She kissed him with her still-bloody lips, and the man whimpered.

The next vision was worse.

She cradled the body of a woman limp in her arms. Natasha wept in this vision, her nails digging into her thighs as she choked back sobs. There were two crimson holes in the dead woman's neck. Both oozed blood.

"Oh my God, are you okay?" she asked when Dylan came to minutes later. Drool spilled from his mouth. He'd ended up on the floor at some point. His temples throbbed, and his hypersensitive body trembled. Out of the corner of his eye, he saw her about to put a comforting hand on his back.

"Don't touch me. Please don't touch me," he whimpered.

"I don't know what happened," she said in a helpless voice. "I just kissed your neck, and you had a seizure."

He laughed, rolling over onto his side. The white carpet rubbed against his arms as he turned, burning his already sensitive skin.

"I have seizures whenever people touch me. And visions," he added the last part in a hushed tone. "And that was not just some kiss on the neck. What the fuck are you?"

"If you really have visions when people touch you, I might ask you the same thing," she said coolly. She crossed her arms over her chest. He noticed she was still nude, but the frightening visions he'd seen subdued any desire.

"I'm a psychic. What are you?" he repeated. He noticed his neck was wet. For a moment he thought it was his own saliva, as he often slobbered all over himself during a seizure, but when he touched his neck he saw his hand was coated in blood.

"I'm a vampire," she said in a calm tone.

"Well," he said, as her words began to sink in. "If this is how you treat all your clients, I'm surprised you have any customers left."

"When I drink enough blood, it creates memory loss. Something to do with vampire saliva and the way humans respond to it. I didn't get that chance with you though."

"Lucky me," he said. "I get to remember this experience for the rest of my life, however short that may be," he scoffed. He sat up and crawled back in his bed, resting his throbbing head against the pillow. He needed his pain pills badly, but he wasn't about to mediate himself while a predator remained in his house.

"I'm not going to kill you. Give me some credit here, when you started seizing, I could have just left."

"I kind of wish you had left," he said. "I'd rather not have any more visions of you killing people."

"I've never killed anyone," she said. She picked up her clothes and started getting dressed. Dylan sighed in relief, thinking maybe he'd get lucky and she'd just leave him. If she really wasn't a killer, what else could she do? It's not like anyone would even believe his insane story about a vampire prostitute if he tried to report her to authorities. He couldn't even get most people to believe he was psychic.

Yet the image of her sinking her fangs into the man from his first vision lingered in his mind. He shivered. "That's not what I saw in my vision."

"And what do you think you saw?"

"You were drinking some guy's blood in one vision, and in the second one, you were crying . . ." He paused, realizing if she was weeping than perhaps she wasn't the one who'd killed the woman. Or perhaps she had, if she'd lost control of whatever sinister urges she lived with. "You were crying while you held some blonde woman in your arms."

"Vanessa?"

"I don't know her name. All I know is that she had two holes in her neck. I'm not a detective or anything, but I'm thinking that means death-by-vampire."

"You'd be correct, but it wasn't me. Do you think you could show me who killed her, if I touched you again?" She reached her hand towards him, and he almost back flipped off the bed to avoid her touch.

"No, it doesn't work like that! If someone touches me, I see random visions of their life. Usually the worst of it. But . . ." he hesitated, not sure if he wanted to get dragged into this. Her hopeful green eyes implored him to continue. He sighed in defeat. Damn her and the sweet way she was looking at him. A predator like her had no business looking so innocent. "If you take me to the place where you found her body, I could give you a description of who did it. Maybe even a name."

"Thank you," she said, almost leaning down to hug him before she pulled back. "Sorry," she said.

"It's okay," he sighed. He rubbed his throbbing temples and shook his head. "Just do me a favor. Don't ever touch me again."

***

"A grey-haired man, long nose, brown eyes, thick eyebrows, ring any bells?" he asked. Natasha shook her head. Dylan had been touching random objects all around the alleyway where Natasha had found her friend's body. He touched the walls and the concrete beneath their feet. Dozens of small-time crimes flashed in his mind: low-level drug deals, petty theft, and hookers blowing customers and pimps. He tried to focus on the murder, zooming in on Vanessa's scared face, trying to sink into her mind in those last few moments of her life.

She ran down the alley, thinking if she could climb the gate before he got to her, she'd be able to enter the side door to the club and reach her friend Natasha. No one fucked with Natasha. Her middle-aged stalker was much faster than she'd expected, more athletic, more lethal. One moment she was running, the next she was up against the brick wall with his teeth in her throat. She managed to choke out his name before fainting from blood loss.

"Alex."

Dylan repeated the name, and Natasha's eyes widened.

"You know this person?" he asked. She nodded.

"An old friend," she replied. "Well, used to be an old friend. We parted ways due to. . .philosophical differences. It's complicated."

"He wanted to kill people and you didn't?"

She shrugged. "Okay, maybe it's not that complicated."

"Do you know how to find Alex?" Dylan asked. He tucked his hands into his pockets and tapped his foot. He wasn't sure if it was a good idea to offer to help her find this guy. Alex was dangerous, and he wasn't sure he wanted to get in the middle of this feud. Yet he felt invested in seeing it through, possibly due to the connection he'd felt with Vanessa during his visions, or perhaps it was more basic than that. Maybe he was just smitten with a pretty vampire, even if he couldn't do anything about it thanks to his condition.

"I can find him," she said. "In fact, he's coming back into town in the next few days. He does business with a friend of mine. For now, anyway."

"Ah, I see," he said. "Well, I guess this is where we part ways."

"Is it?" she asked with a playful smirk. "Don't you want to see where this goes?"

"Excuse me?" he asked, taken aback—although admittedly flattered—by her forwardness.

"Don't you want to see this killer brought to justice? Don't you want to know your visions made a difference?" Her voice was gentle but there was a desperate urgency underneath, as if she didn't want to go through this situation alone.

He opened his mouth, about to tell her he really didn't give a shit about his visions or justice, when it occurred to him he never derived much comfort from the things he was able to accomplish with his "gift" of the second sight. In fact, he spent most of his life avoiding using his abilities due to the unpleasant side-effects. He thought that seeing this through to the end, finding some good resulting from his curse, might help him accept what he was. It could help him make peace with it.

"Maybe you're right," he said, surprising himself. "What the hell. Why not?"

***

They went back to her place so she could take care of some business, confirming that Alex would be returning to town shortly. Dylan pretended to be on his phone, but was secretly watching her and exploring her cozy house. Her décor was bright and cheerful for a vampire: floral paintings, yellow walls, and statues of cute animals everywhere. The exact opposite of what he would have expected. The only odd thing was that she had a bed instead of a couch in her living room. "I don't have a lot of company," she explained. "So I use the living room as a bedroom and the bedroom as a study."

"And by 'study' you mean a sacrificial alter to Satan?" he jested. "Or what about a kinky BDSM playroom?"

"You wish," she said. She rolled her eyes and disappeared into the bathroom. Dylan snooped through her stuff before he grew distracted by the subtle pain returning to his temples. He decided he could trust Natasha enough to take a few of his pain pills while in her presence. The kitchen sink didn't work and her refrigerator was empty, so he knocked on the bathroom door to see if he could get some water from the sink. She didn't respond.

He heard the shower going when he entered the restroom, but he needed water for his sedatives, and he'd already seen her naked. It wasn't like she was a prude. He meant to be in and out, but couldn't help stealing a glance as the clear glass did little to conceal the naked woman on the other side. He stopped and stared at her form, watching the soap bubbles trickle down her breasts and stomach, pooling between her thighs. His mouth watered at the sight of her hand slipping between her legs while her other hand fondled a rosy nipple. A whimper escaped her, and he dropped the pill bottle in his hand.

"Crap," he said. He bent over to pick it up, a blush rising to his cheeks. "I didn't mean to watch, I just came in here to get water for my pills, I swear."

"It's okay," she said. Her laughter echoed in the small space. He hurried out of the room, his face hot and the crotch of his pants much tighter than before. He lay down on the bed and tried to steady his uneven breathing.

Fog drifted out of the bathroom as she stepped out a moment later. Her cheeks were flushed in a pleasing way. Her wet hair was pulled to the side, draped over one shoulder. She dropped the towel dramatically. Water droplets slid down her body. A small one darted between her breasts, then down to her belly button, then lower into the place he wanted most to touch her. Dylan's eyes were glued to her. She smirked in response, revealing her dimples. He exhaled and bit his lip.

"Come on. Now you're just being cruel," he said, shaking his head.

"Weren't you willing to pay five hundred dollars to see this the other night?" She quirked an eyebrow and gave him an amused smile.

"Yeah, but. . ." He rubbed the back of his neck and glanced down. "Sometimes it's more frustrating than enjoyable, to see something you want so much that you know you can't have. And I didn't want you as much then as I do right now. So please, just don't."

Heaviness filled the air. Her eyes flickered with sadness. "I'm sorry," she said as she picked up the towel and covered herself.

"It's okay. I'm used to not getting what I want." He chuckled bitterly. His blue eyes darted to the side. The tent in his pants wasn't going down despite the depressing turn the conversation had taken. "Uh, I might need to go take care of this."

He sat up and prepared to enter the restroom to take care of the problem that had developed in his pants when she stopped him with a single hand gesture. She raised her palm and gestured for him to lie back down.

"What if there is something I can do?" she asked. She moved a step closer to him, not enough to set him on edge, but near enough that his heart began to flutter in his chest. "Not quite sex, but something that might help with that?"

His eyebrows rose and he smirked. "Like what?"

"Hang on," she said. She went to her closet and brought out a clear, plastic box. She set it on the bed next to him and opened it. Various toys were inside: dildos, vibrators, small plastic rings, and various other devices.

"Whoa, you got a whole sex shop in there," he said.

She shrugged, pulling out a large, flesh-colored dildo.

"I'm thinking you take care of me, and then I'll take care of you, with this," she said. She gestured to a slender, green toy with a hole in the side. It had round bumps on the inside and outside, presumably for helping the user maintain a grip. Dylan would have never guessed it was sex toy based on its appearance.

"Oh, I've seen this before. At PetSmart," he quipped. She laughed.

"You have not!"

"Oh no, I have. In the dog toy isle."

"I hope not. It's a Hand Job Stroker."

"No, I'm pretty sure it's a dog toy. I'm not having sex with a dog toy," he said. He picked up a plastic replica of a vagina and examined it with curiosity.

"That's a Fleshlight," she said. "I thought you'd be familiar with that one."

"I know what it is, but what exactly are we going to be doing with these things?" His voice lowered. He rubbed the growing bulge in his pants and bit his lip as he waited for her answer. Her devious eyes met his curious ones.

"Close your eyes," she said. "Relax. I want you to imagine this is your cock I'm touching, your cock I'm tasting."

She put a beige colored dildo in her mouth, teasing the shaft with the tip of her tongue. She dipped her head down, taking more of the silicone shaft into her mouth. Her tongue darted out. She licked the head in long, slow strokes. His hand slipped into his boxers and wrapped around his cock, mimicking the movements as he imagined her mischievous mouth wrapped around him. She set the dildo down and picked up another device.

"I want you to put this inside me," she said, placing a pink, full-service vibrator next to his hand.

"Why that one?" he asked, a little out of breath.

"It's the longest one, about eight inches, so there is less chance of you accidently touching me." She flipped a switch at the bottom, and the device shook in her grasp. "Plus, it vibrates," she added with a wink.

She lay down on the bed. He followed her instruction, sliding the vibrator inside her as she spread her legs for him. An array of euphoric expressions danced across her face. Her emerald eyes enchanted him, the way they held steady under his penetrating stare.

His heart raced as her pussy clinched, pulling the toy deeper inside her, and therefore bringing his hand closer to the swollen, reddening lips between her legs. He let out a small groan as he longed to replace the small external vibrator with his tongue, to fill her wet hole with his fingers and cock. Most agonizing of all, the potent scent of her arousal hit him, an unforeseen pleasure that went straight to his cock. Unable to wait any longer, he pulled himself out of his boxers and began to stroke his shaft in pace with the thrusts, imagining himself buried deep in her.

He started panting as her sweet moans grew louder. The wetness between her thighs began to slide down the toy, closer to his hand. Unsure if her juices could cause him pain and visions, he thought he might have to stop; he let out a frustrating groan she must have mistaken for pleasure, for seeing him so turned on by her own arousal brought her over the edge. She arched off the bed and threw her head back, nearly bumping against him as her body stiffened. Her toes curled as she fought to avoid closing her thighs. Her pussy drenched the toy as she came, and he begrudgingly relinquished his hold on the toy to avoid the juices he wanted to taste. She shut her thighs then, and held the toy in the vibrator in place with her hand as the last tremors of ecstasy shot through her. She removed the toy and collapsed onto the bed with a contented sigh.

Disregarding whatever Natasha had planned for him, Dylan decided there was nothing more he wanted in the world than to once more see his cum on her satiated body. She looked up at him with a lazy smile and nodded, granting him permission.

"You made me cum so hard. It felt good. If you want to finish now, then come for me. Come on my pussy."

Her sultry voice coaxed him into finishing on her. The sight of her soaked cunt gleaming and the knowledge that *he* had made her come, had driven the toy deep enough and fast enough to get her off brought him to orgasm. He pumped his shaft furiously and shot his load over the entrance of her pussy, coating every inch of it in his semen. His thighs ached from clinching so hard, but he felt more sated than he had in ages. He plopped down beside her and released a breathless laugh.

"Well, I guess the dog toy will have to get fucked another day," he said. She snorted, and wiped the residue between her legs with a tissue she retrieved from the nightstand. She tossed it in the wastebasket and lay next to him, inches away. Inches that could have been miles.

They lay side-by-side, watching one another. He gave her a weak smile.

"What is it?" she said with concern in her voice. Her eyebrows furrowed, and she almost reached up to stroke his cheek before she remembered and withdrew her hand. "What's wrong? Did you not enjoy it?"

"I did. Oh God, I did. I just. . ." He laughed, shaking his head. "I just really wish I could kiss you right now. Or even hold you."

She reached down and pulled the purple blanket up to his chin, then set her head on top of his chest. He winced, afraid the material might not provide enough of a barrier, but nothing happened. He felt the weight of her head, and her arm coming up to rest on his torso. He relaxed into the embrace.

"I think this is the best I can do," she said.

"Thank you, Natasha."

"My pleasure," she added. He could feel the movement as she nuzzled her face into the coverlet. Although he wanted to run his fingers through her ruby hair, wanted to kiss her full lips, he settled for the feeling of her weight on top of him, appreciating that it was the closest thing to intimacy that he could ever expect to have.

***

The next day they waited in Natasha's car for Alex to return to his warehouse. The often busy street was slow that day.

"I want you to stay in the car," she instructed him.

"No problem," he said, tucking his hands behind his head and reclining in his seat. "I have no desire to play the hero."

"Good," she said. "Just let me know if he brings any back-up."

"Will do."

He waited about an hour before he checked in with her. He would have checked in earlier, but he didn't want to seem afraid, or clingy, or anything else that would make him seem lesser in her eyes. His psychic curse made him feel pathetic enough. She responded that she was fine, and he left her alone, until one of his migraines started to build. He knew a vision was impending—the severity of the pain alerted him to the inevitability of a premonition—and he feared the worst. He called her again and got no response.

"Damn it," he murmured. Ignoring his promise not to play hero, he got out of the car and ran toward the warehouse. Before he made it to the entrance, he felt a new wave of pain like scorching metal burning his chest as an arm wrapped around him and a pair of sharp incisors penetrated his flesh. He collapsed before he could make out any one defining detail from the dozens of bloody visions that flashed through his mind.

***

Dylan woke up tied to a chair. The man from his visions sat across from him, his sharp fangs protruding from his mouth. Dylan grunted in discomfort.

"Natasha, come here, unless you want me to drain him dry!" Alex yelled. The man went on taunting her about all the horrible ways he planned to kill him.

"Oh please, you're a cartoon villain. Save the monologue and kill me now," he said.

"Oh no, I like an audience," Alex said with a smirk. "I'll wait until Natasha decides to rescue you—"

A large dagger stabbed through Alex's chest. Blood spewed onto Dylan's face. The tall vampire could not even glance over his shoulder before Natasha pulled the blade back and stabbed him again. He turned around, wounded but not incapacitated, and lunged for her.

Natasha pulled her dagger out and retreated. Within moments, she was gone.

"You want to hide? I bet I can lure you out!" Alex threatened.

Alex stormed over to Dylan, pulled him by his hair and sunk his fangs into his neck. Dylan screamed as visions of Alex's former victims flooded his mind. Hundreds of bloody faces flashed within seconds. By the time Alex released him, Dylan was in and out of consciousness due to blood loss. When he came to, Natasha was beside him.

She leaned in close to him, her breath like a soft caress on his cheek, and in his half-delirious state, he wondered if she was going to kiss him. The thought terrified him, but excited him against all logic. Kissing meant pain. He knew this, and yet he found himself wishing for it anyway. He thought if he could feel her lips for even a few seconds before the pain kicked in, it would be worth it, but he doubted he'd even get that much.

Instead she appeared to be rubbing her wrist against his lips. Visions flashed before his eyes as the familiar aching blasted through his temples: *Natasha as a child playing with her siblings, being turned into a vampire by a strange man, being forced to drink blood against her will, then groaning in pleasure as she gave in and drank from some man's neck.*

"Stay with me, Dylan. Please." The blood from her wrist poured into his mouth. She squeezed the flesh around the self-inflected wound, coaxing more into him.

Natasha adjusting her dress as she rang his doorbell. Natasha panicking as he went into seizures and fell off his bed. Natasha looking at him before she went inside the warehouse, wondering if she should send him home.

"Drink, damn it," she cursed. The pain echoed and amplified in his skull. More visions of her flooded his mind. *The cruel smirk of the vampire who turned her just for his own amusement. The kindness Vanessa showed*

Natasha when she discovered what Natasha is, a far more understanding reaction than Dylan had shown at first. Natasha killing Alex just moments ago, equal measures of pride and vengeance as she slid the knife into his chest again, and then decapitated him afterwards.

Dylan shared her pride for a moment, knowing his vision had aided her in the task of ridding the world of a monster, and even if he died, he could go knowing he'd used his ability for something good. As the feeling of contentment settled in, everything else faded to black.

***

He woke up in Natasha's bed. She slept in just a t-shirt, curled into his side, no blanket between them. Her soft arm rested on top of his. After taking a deep breath to steady his nerves, he nudged her awake. Her eyes fluttered open and she smiled.

"Good morning," she said. "Glad to see you're okay."

He ran his thumb against her cheekbone as the realization sank in. He could touch her now without pain or visions.

"How is this possible?" he asked. He brushed her hair out of her face.

"I don't know. Maybe because you died and came back?"

"If I'd known all I had to do to touch you was die, I would have done it a lot sooner."

She rolled her eyes and playfully slapped him on the shoulder.

"Hey, I'm serious. It was worth it," he said. She smiled and wrapped her leg around him, then rolled on top of him.

"Any pain?" she asked.

"No. This is amazing. Kiss me," he asked with pleading eyes. She leaned down and let her mouth hover over his, a delicious tease of what was to come.

As he ran his fingertips under her shirt and over her pink nubs, his mind went blank. The only thoughts that seemed to matter were those of an ancient, innate nature, the kind that made him feel like he might die if he wasn't joined with her soon. He helped her remove his clothes, and then they were nude and pressed against each other, just like in the dreams. He closed his eyes and ran his fingers along her arms. He leaned up and kissed her neck.

"That feels so good," she moaned, the vibration in her throat ringing against Dylan's lips as he sucked there. Her voice made the sweetest sounds he'd ever heard as she whimpered for him. He attacked her with more fervent kisses along her pale neck. She shoved him against the mattress and grinded her hot core against his cock. He let out a strangled groan, bucking against her but not into her.

Dylan thought if he ever had the chance to have sex, he would savor every single caress and kiss, but in his excitement, he got carried away. He was greedy for her, desperate for more skin contact. He wanted no part of her left unexplored, and he wanted to feel her on every inch of his skin. His hands roamed across her stomach and round chest. They moved without thought, her soft skin hypnotizing his hands to travel without his command. His hips rutted against her. He wasn't conscious what part of her he was rubbing against, as long as it was her warm flesh against his. His head was buried in her neck, licking and sucking the salty skin. Her pulse throbbed under his mouth, but the desire to feed on her was overwhelmed by his rising need to bury himself into her.

"Slow down," she laughed. He moaned in response, halfway between lust and frustration.

"Oh God, I can't," he said, rubbing himself against her inner thigh.

"You're going to come before you even get inside of me," she teased.

"I'm sorry. You're right."

"It's okay," she said, stroking his hair. "It's your first time. This is about you."

"Yeah, but it's our first time together, so it should be about both of us." He circled the pink nubs of her breasts. They hardened beneath his gentle but firm touch. He squeezed her pert nipples, leaned into her neck to leave a trail of breathless kisses, his mouth parted as he panted between each one. She shivered in response to the breath on her neck.

He rolled on top of her and switched their positions. He gazed at Natasha as though he needed to memorize every detail of her and forever imprint her in his mind. He locked eyes with her, and they shared another heated kiss before he slid two fingers inside of her. She sucked in a short gasp of air, and her pelvic muscles contracted as she became accustomed to the feeling of him inside of her. He pumped his fingers in and out, his thumb pressing down on her clit, before sliding another finger into her opening.

"I'm ready," she told him, gripping his hard cock and positioning him at her entrance as he hovered above her. "Are you?"

He nodded, placing his hand over hers and guiding himself into her slick heat. He groaned as he entered her. She was tighter and hotter than he expected. He bit his lip and fisted the sheets, trying to regain control. He'd never had full control of his body before, and he was determined to find that control that had evaded him his entire life.

When he felt calm enough to continue, he rocked his hips. Natasha grinded her hips against him, coaxing him to go faster. Their bodies intuitively found a rhythm. Dylan propelled faster within her as she vocalized her pleasure with louder and more frequent moans. Her every expression and movement excited him, made him fuck her harder as the sight of her becoming more aroused made his own body respond the same way, sending him into a frenzy. He verged on the peak of desire, kept at bay only by the insatiable craving to watch her reach her ecstasy first.

"*Dylan*!" she screamed, clinching around him as she came hard. Her nails dug into his shoulders. He grunted. Although he felt pain, his mind could not process the source. The sensations of pain, pleasure, and the unforgettable vision of her coming underneath him and howling his name, were enough to send him over the edge. Dylan tossed his head back as he spilled himself inside her, his hands kneading into her hips as he pounded into her. He shuddered, pleasure enthralling his every nerve ending. He collapsed next to Natasha after it faded, basking in the feeling of their bodies so close to one another. Dylan panted, staring straight up at the ceiling in a daze.

"Are you okay?" she asked with a content smile. She entwined her fingers in his and squeezed.

"No," he panted. "That was too much. I think I'm dead now. Or deader."

She snorted. "You can't get much deader than us."

"True," he said. "God, that was amazing. I mean next time I want to go slower, but that was. . .wait, there is a next time, right? I'm not being presumptuous?"

"There better be a next time," she smirked, running her hand along his arm. He trembled. Being touched was still so new and foreign. His heart thrummed in excitement and anticipation of what new things she would do to him. As she continued to run her soft fingers against his skin, he realized that for the first time he didn't know what was to come, and that mystery was a gift in and of itself.

Tremors
John Leonard

For the last twenty-five years, Alice Hadley had worked as the night auditor at Rachael's Roadhouse, a shabby motel with a grill and bar on US Route 1 in the village of Chester, Virginia. From her small, cramped office that smelled like moldy flowers and wet cigarettes, she balanced the day's receipts, set wake-up calls, prepared the bank deposits for the following morning and occasionally checked in the weary guest who invariably found that the nicer hotels on this stretch of road were all booked up.

Nothing much had changed in her life over the last twenty-five years. She sat at the same desk, drove the same 1979 Pontiac Catalina to and from work and wore her hair in the same fashion. In many ways she felt that life had just passed her by like so many of the cars up and down US Route 1. She felt stuck, trapped in a never-ending cycle of boredom and pain.

When she graduated high school in 1976, the possibilities seemed limitless. She was voted home coming queen and "most likely to succeed". She dated and eventually dumped her "hunky" quarterback boyfriend for a biker she met at the bar at Rachael's. Bobby Miller. Bobby the Biker. It was a wild and wonderful fling; riding on the back of his motorcycle, the wind blowing through her long blonde hair as they went from place to place, working where they could, partying where they couldn't and all without a care in the world.

Life was her oyster.

Until 1981.

When the tremors started.

The diagnosis was multiple sclerosis. MS. Dizziness, fatigue, sensitivity to heat and light, lack of coordination, sudden onset of paralysis and cognitive difficulties. It was an "individual" disease the doctors said. She could be symptom-free for weeks, even months but inevitably the symptoms would reappear.

The first time she woke up and couldn't move a muscle in her body was the most terrifying moment in her life. Thankfully the paralysis was not a frequent occurrence and over the years she dealt with it calmly when it occurred. The tremors and slurred speech killed any hope of a social life. But it was the constant pain, the "pins and needles" sensation she experienced throughout her body that was the worst. She heard another patient say that it was like being constantly bitten by fire ants. Sometimes she would cry for hours because the pain was so intense, other times it was barely perceptible.

But it was always there.

And not just the pain but the fear and anxiety that at any moment her speech could slur, her tremors could become violent and noticeable or that she could be trapped in a state of paralysis for days; maybe even for the rest of her life.

Her disease was too "heavy" for Bobby the biker. One day he just up and left. No note. No goodbye. She never saw or heard from him again. But she remembered that last look on his face; it was one of deep concern.

As devastating as his departure might have been, it was surprisingly easy to get over him; she had the pain and worry to contend with every day.

So for 25 years she hid herself away from the world, too afraid, too ashamed and too embarrassed to truly live.

She was adding up the receipts from the bar when Diane Smythe, the owner, manager and bartender extraordinaire of Rachael's walked into her office while clearing her throat.

"What's up, Diane?" she said, not looking up from her adding machine.

"We're hiring a new desk clerk and I need you to train him."

The click-clack of the adding machine ceased abruptly and Alice slowly turned to her boss.

"Why?"

"Alice, look honey, you know I love you. You *know* that. But your condition is getting worse."

Alice's lower lip began to quiver every so slightly. "N-no itsssss n-not," she managed to blurt.

Diane crossed the room and threw her arms around Alice, hugging her fiercely. Tears streamed down her cheeks. "Honey, I know it's not easy. Lord knows I know. You know I know. But I have a business to run."

She started to pull away but Diane kept her arms around her, feeling the first signs of tremors begin wracking Alice's body.

Diane took her face in her hands and brushed away Alice's own tears. "Honey, what if something happened to you while you were here alone? What if you had a fit of paralysis and someone decided to jump over the front desk and rob us blind? I'm doing this as much for you as I am for me, okay?"

Even though her long-time boss and friend's words stung, Alice could still see the logic in her decision and the reasons behind it. She was getting older and the MS was getting worse. The Avonex and Betaseron drugs helped to curtail her symptoms but without them she would probably have to be hospitalized.

"D-Diane, I'm s-so s-sorry that I…"

"Don't you worry about it, honey. You have a job here for as long as you want. But just think about it. Wouldn't it be great to have someone here with you every night, looking out for you? Learning from you?" She laughed and said, "Someone you can boss around?"

For the first time a long while, Alice smiled through the pain. It warmed her aching heart to know that she had such a dear friend and concerned employer in Diane.

"You did say 'him', right?"

"I did indeed, and he starts tomorrow night. His name is Anton. He's from up north somewhere. Have a good night, Alice," she said as she left for the night.

The click-clack of the adding machine began again.

The next evening, just as the gray shadows of dusk started elongating into an inky blackness of night, the bell from the front desk sounded. Alice got up from her cluttered desk with wobbly, aching legs and hobbled to the lobby. A man wearing a crisp white shirt with a black tie beneath a battered leather jacket was standing confidently on the other side of the desk. He was turned toward the parking lot so she did not get to see his face but for that split second he resembled Bobby the Biker. But that couldn't be; this man had not aged a bit.

The man must have heard her shuffling because at that moment he turned around with a smile full of bright white teeth. They gleamed like little white knives fresh from the dishwasher. The breath caught in her throat. It *was* Bobby.

But…it wasn't Bobby. His hair was shorter, fuller and had a healthy sheen. His face was rugged and handsome like Bobby's but the facial structure was off just a bit. His eyes were an even deeper shade of blue and there was something simmering behind them, something hidden, something dangerous. But it didn't matter.

At first glance she would have bet her last dollar that it was her Bobby. But of course it couldn't be Bobby because Bobby would be older than she was now, and the way Bobby lived—his drinking and smoking—they would have taken a toll on his body over the years but it was evident that this young man was vibrant, muscular even through his oversized jacket.

"Excuse me," he said in a voice like a cool evening breeze, "I didn't mean to startle you miss, but I was looking for Alice Hadley."

It took several moments for her to recover but she finally found her voice. "I'm Alice. H-how c-can I help you?"

If it were possible, the man's smile turned brighter and wider. "Pleased to meet you, Alice." He offered his hand across the desk. "I'm Anton Macrae."

There was an uneasy sensation in the back of her mind, a wriggling thought that something wasn't quite right about Anton but she swatted the idea away as if it were a buzzing gnat.

With a matching smile, somehow devoid of pain, Alice took his hand as if it were a glass of cool water and she a desert nomad.

***

The next two weeks were marvelous. Anton showed up for work on time every single evening, ready and eager to learn from Alice. He followed her around the motel grounds like a puppy, hanging on her every word. Never once did they argue, never once did she have to correct him. When the going was slow and customers were few and far between, they would sit in her cramped office and talk quietly about anything and everything.

One of the things he told her was that he owned and drove a motorcycle; a brand new Harley-Davidson Dyna Lowrider. She could just imagine him on that bike riding down the highway. Young. Confident. Sexy.

One evening he asked her what it was like living with multiple sclerosis. It was the most personal thing anyone could ever ask her. She could have spent the better part of the evening telling him about it but instead she just said, "It's not so bad." And lately that was the truth. He looked at her long and hard then and she got the distinct impression that he could see through her lie and deep into the core of her pain.

The similarities between Anton and Bobby were enough to make her feel like a giddy school girl.

She had become so preoccupied with training Anton and looking forward to each evening when he would arrive for work that she could not remember the last time she felt the effects of her disease. It was like she had been dipped in magical waters. When she passed a mirror or caught her reflection in the glass she seemed less like herself and more like how she was before…before Bobby left.

After three weeks Anton's training was almost complete. If she had to miss a day of work or—god forbid—something worse, Anton could fill in admirably. Even Diane was ecstatic with his progress.

For three weeks she had Anton all to herself, but the more he learned from Alice, the more Diane would want to meet with him on this or that matter—matters to which she was not privy.

There was a time when Diane would tell her stories about the customers from the bar and the motel's guests until the wee hours of the morning. She would talk about the trucker who hit a deer on the road and was so shaken up that he had to pull over and get a drink. About the guest in room 102 that clogged the toilet with so many maxi-pads that she had to call a plumber. It irked her that for 25 years, she knew everything that happened at Rachael's Road House. And now that Anton was here, Diane was probably telling *him* these same stories, taking *him* into her confidence and excluding Alice, the diseased, old woman.

But as much as she wanted to get upset at Diane and even at Anton, she could not bring herself to do so because the absence of pain was such a stroke of good luck that she did not want to jinx it.

Then one night, Anton was late for work. He had never been late. A boiling pit of anxiety suddenly opened in her stomach. Sweat broke out on her upper lip and she felt that sudden sensation in her legs. Was that the first stirrings of that all familiar pain?

She paced the lobby like an expectant father. Ten minutes late now. She re-checked her figures from the afternoon receipts. Fifteen minutes late. She emptied the ashtrays in the lobby and dusted her office. Twenty minutes late now. The crease in her forehead became deeper and deeper until it felt like her head was being squeezed by giant, unseen hands. Thirty minutes late. She was about to call Diane over at the bar when the phone rang. The coincidence left her shaking and weak.

It was Diane.

"Hi sugar, how you making out?"

"Anton's late. He hasn't called or anything."

"Oh he's not late, honey. He's helping me over here at the bar. My back's been bothering me lately and I asked him to take the empty kegs out back.

The pins and needles came flying back. The fire ants came on so suddenly that she could barely hold the phone to her ear. And it wasn't just the pain.

It was jealousy. Hot, searing jealousy.

"Really?" she replied contemptuously.

"Why? Do you need him for something?"

Through the phone she could hear the bar patrons as they drank their cares away. She could hear the smile in Diane's voice and worst of all, she could hear Anton's laughter in the background.

"N-n-noooo. Th-th-that's okay." She hung up the phone and scuttled back to her office; her sanctuary. With shaking hands she swallowed her dose of Avonex. She was on the verge of tears when a noise from the lobby broke through her pity.

"Alice?"

It was Bobby. No, not Bobby but Anton rather.

"Alice, are you back there?"

She did not want him to see her like this. He would know in a moment what she was thinking.

"I'm coming back."

She heard him leap over the front desk and cross the hallway to the back office all the while doing her best to wipe the puffiness from her eyes and to suppress the shaking from her aching hands.

Then she felt a hand on her shoulder. Normally she would have lit up like a Christmas tree from his touch but there was something off about the feel of his hand on her body. She knew it was Anton because he always smelled faintly of his motorcycle but the hand on her shoulder felt like a cold fish and it sent an involuntary shiver up her spine.

"Alice, are you all right?"

She wanted to answer him, to say the things that were on her mind and in her heart but she was afraid that she'd stutter and make a complete fool of herself. And she was also more than a little afraid at the moment. He had crossed the parking lot in just a few seconds and then he leaped over the front desk as if he were an Olympic gymnast. Simple things, maybe, but done with a speed and grace that was equal parts amazing and otherworldly.

And the uneasy feeling of his touch on her shoulder was beginning to freak her out.

"I'm sorry," he started. "I should have told you I was going to be with Diane. Should have told you that I was going to be late." His hand slipped limply from her shoulder to the small of her back. She could feel his clammy breath in her ear as next he whispered, "I should have told you where I've been all these years."

She turned around and faced him then because his last confession was not in Anton's voice but…Bobby's.

What she saw then held her like the fleeting moments of paralysis her disease would visit on her. It was like a diseased dream she couldn't wake up from. The man in her office had blood on his face. It was caked with the stuff. Bits and pieces of flesh and gore hung from between his teeth and blood dripped down the front of his ever-present Led Zeppelin t-shirt.

It was Bobby all right. From the way he held himself, to the length of his sideburns and the very clothes he was wearing; it was most definitely Bobby. But unlike any version of him that her reeling mind had ever conceived.

"B-Bobby?"

"It's me, babe." He kneeled down so that they were at eye level with each other. The coppery scent of blood washed over her. Alice felt the bile rise in her throat. "Anton was just a way to get around, like a suit you put on when you want to dress up." His hands were smeared with blood as well and he touched her face with a bloody finger. He was trying to be tender; she could sense that, but the horror of it all just made her want to throw up.

And just like that, she could feel the MS take hold of her body again. The pain was back. The anxiety was back. And it gripped her like a cold, wet rope. Heavy and unmovable.

"It took me a while but I've found a way to take away your pain, to make you into the woman you once were," he whispered in her ear. "It requires a helluva lifestyle change but I think you'll find it's worth it."

His words floated in her ears like slimy mushrooms left in the sun too long. She wanted to look away from him, to find the strength to stand up and run, but the tremors wracked her body with increasing intensity. She thought of Diane. If Bobby had been with her just moments ago then was it her blood on his lips?

"D-Diane?" she asked in brittle voice.

He reached past her onto her desk, withdrew a few tissues from the dispenser and began to wipe his face. He looked at the bloody bits and the crimson stains against the sterile white of the tissue and shook his head. "I never liked her," he said absently.

"B-B-Bobby h-how c-c-could you?"

"I did it for you, babe," he said with a toothy grin that looked more like it belonged on a shark's skull.

Her vision dimmed. She was losing control. The tremors became so intense that it felt like she was rafting on a raging river. She couldn't even hold herself up in her chair. She slumped to the floor with Bobby's elongated face swimming in her vision like a bloated, cancerous moon just before she blacked out.

***

When she awoke, the sun had long since set. She was still in her office at the motel but the lights were off in the entire building. Normally she could detect the glow of Rachael's neon sign reflected off the windshields of the cars in the bar's parking lot, but it was as if the whole world had been swallowed by the night.

Yet oddly enough she could see perfectly.

Still lying on the floor, she could see the individual perforations of the water-stained ceiling tiles. She could read the titles of the books in the shelf across the room.

She sat up slowly, an awful, yet familiar taste in her mouth.

"Welcome back, Alice," Bobby's voice hissed from the darkness.

With a quickness her diseased muscles were unaccustomed to, she stood bolt upright to find her Bobby sitting confidently in her desk chair, smoking a cigarette.

"What's going on, Bobby? What have you done?"

"Something wonderful." He glanced at his watch for a moment before continuing. "You'll see what I mean in about…five minutes."

"What? Damn it. What?" She turned on him with clenched fists, a deep-seated rage boiling through her bones. Any other day of her life she would have cowered in fear, any other day she would have been paralyzed with grief and anxiety. But not now. Not if he had really killed Diane.

The truth of the matter was that she felt more energized and stronger at that moment than she could ever remember feeling. And as thrilling and invigorating as that was, it was also unsettling because it was not in her nature to become this angry at anything except her own disease. It was her disease that turned her into the woman she was. It was her disease that kept her behind that desk, night after night.

"Is it really, Alice?" he said, seemingly answering her unspoken thoughts. "Isn't it more a case of the fear of your disease controlling you that you hate the most?" He stood up from her chair, taller that he should be, thicker, wider than she remembered. "It is your fear that you hate."

He had a point. She could see that now. Even if he could somehow read her mind, as freaky as that was, she knew he was right.

He walked in circles around her, faster than she thought was possible but somehow she did not become dizzy or disoriented.

"I am truly sorry it took me so long to come back for you. Believe me. But you have no idea where I've been and what I've had to do to get here."

With a strength and quickness she never knew she possessed, she reached out and put a hand on his chest, stopping his pacing. "What exactly did you do to me, Bobby?"

He smiled then, a cold, reptilian smile with impossibly long incisors that snaked below his bottom lip. "I have my own disease, Alice. And it is extremely contagious."

"What?" she said incredulously.

"I searched for years in some of the most horrible, despicable places you could ever imagine but I finally found it." He shrugged and blew a ring of smoke in her direction. "And you'd never believe where I found it either." He shook his head and smiled, remembering something he chose not to share. He stood up then and spread his arms wide. "But the bottom line is that I'm back now. And what's more, you're carrying *my* disease inside you now."

Although she felt as strong as an ox, she backed away from him in disgust.

"No reason to freak out, babe. We share the same affliction now."

"And what is that?"

He shrugged. "Call it what you will. I just know that in about three minutes, you're going to have to do something you might find repulsive. At least at first anyway."

She had no doubt that Bobby was serious. She could feel it in her bones. A thrumming, electric current snaked through her veins. There was something different about her. She knew that now. And she was ready to believe that whatever he did to her had released her from her fears. Released her from the sad, sorry life she had carved out for herself over that last 25 years. She flexed her arms, clenched her fists and she thrilled to the power simmering in her body. She could almost sense the wrinkles in her skin fading. She could imagine her body fat melting away.

And it was good.

A strange, delicious sound reached her ears then. With a new set of instincts, she glided more than ran to the window that looked out over the parking lot.

A lone hitchhiker walked despondently along the shoulder of the road. She could tell it was a woman. She could…smell her. And she was menstruating. She knew that it was not possible to know these things but nevertheless she also knew it to be true. And the scent of the hitchhiker's blood was like an uncorked bottle of wine. The bouquet was pungent and mouthwatering.

But at the same time Alice was repulsed by these observations. She turned back to Bobby wearing a defeated look on her face.

Bobby shrugged again. "What can I say, babe? It was the only way."

Alice turned back to the hitchhiker. She was repulsed and captivated at the same time. She put a tentative hand up to the glass as the woman passed by the window. A gnawing, burning pit in her stomach opened and she longed to be near the woman.

Suddenly, Bobby was by her side and he put his hand on her shoulder again only this time it was warm and loving and full of the future.

The hitchhiker had lung cancer. She had been a smoker for many years and her disease was eating her from the inside out. It was almost as if the tumors were blossoming flowers in the woman's lungs and she could smell them, sense them. Alice could not say how she knew this, only that she did.

And suddenly she was hungry. Hungrier than she had ever remembered being. It was as if there was a hole inside her that had to be filled and the only thing that could fill that hole was what was inside that hitchhiker.

Bobby leaned close to her. "Go to her, babe." He took her face in his hands. "You need her and she needs you."

Alice kissed him then. It was long, hard and deep and it was the most satisfying thing she had ever experienced. At least for the moment anyway. Because after she flew from Bobby's arms and out into the parking lot like the proverbial bat out of hell, she killed the hitchhiker without a moment's hesitation and gorged herself on the blood and tissues of her dying body.

The tumors were especially tasty.

She could hear Bobby's insane laughter from inside the motel as the tremors started again. They wracked her body in ways she would have never thought possible.

Only this time, they were tremors of pure, crimson pleasure.

The Dungeon Wraith of Altersberg
J.N. Cameron

The train drops us off in the valley, and we make our way to a *gasthaus* called The Thirsty Soldier. I introduce Janett as my sister to the barmaid. The aroma of steaks sizzling from the kitchen causes my stomach to roar, and I order food with our drinks.

An elderly gentleman sits near us in the common room and introduces himself as Herr Hofmann. He chews the stem of a briar pipe and pretends not to ogle Janett's cleavage. He orders a stein of *roggenbier* that smells like oven-fresh pumpernickel when it arrives.

We strike up a conversation with him while Janett drinks a *helles*, and I devour a plate of peppery Angus beef chunks in brown sauce. Eventually, Janett asks Hofmann about the ruins.

"The bones of that old monastery can still be found high up Altersberg massif, but just below the krummholz!" Herr Hofmann points his pipe stem to the north. His silver beard wags as he speaks. "A carriage trail leads there, but it is treacherous. It will take a full day if you have the right guide and reliable transportation."

Before returning the pipe to his mouth, he spits into the corner. Our table is near the central fire pit, and the flames dance over the crackling oak like golden elementals. Above the fire, a pall of grey funnels its innards up into the maw of a wide, brick chimney.

"Could you arrange a carriage for us?" I ask.

He sizes us up for the twentieth time that night while taking a deep drag from his pipe. His eyes once more pass over Janett's chest, and he asks a question in return.

"You say your surname is Armbruster. Where are you from?"

"We are from New York. Our grandparents were from Munich."

"Well, the Munich Armbrusters are good people. I will arrange for my grandson to drive you. He knows all the trails in the massif, and his coach is comfortable. Would fifteen gulden be fair?"

I try not to look at Janett for a sign of approval. Instead, I take out a small notebook and a pencil from the inside pocket of my jacket. I act as if I am making calculations. I scowl a bit and then nod my head in agreement.

"Will he return for us the next evening?" I ask.

The old man's eyes widen.

"You…you will spend the night?"

"Yes," I reply. "We came prepared to stay at least one night in the ruins. It is necessary for our research."

"I assume that you already know of the local tales?" He taps his pipe empty on the table.

"Yes, we do."

"And do you believe them?"

"We will be cautious, dear sir," Janett assures him. "We do not take the legends lightly."

"Well, I doubt I could stop you if I tried. I will tell my grandson to bring you back when you instruct him."

"Then we have a deal. Fifteen gulden." I hold out my hand and Herr Hofmann shakes it. His grip is powerful from a lifetime of labor. "Could he meet us at first light?"

"He will be waiting. Now, I bid you both goodnight."

Hoffman stands with the help of a cane, and the maid comes and walks him to the front. She helps him into a fur overcoat before seeing him outside and quickly shutting the door to keep out the biting winds.

Janett and I are not alone, but we might as well be. The maid returns to the kitchen, and a plump, middle-aged man in the far corner snores soundly with his face on the table in a pool of beer. Janett scoots down the wooden bench until she is close enough that I can feel our thighs touching.

She helps herself to my stein and drains its warm, foamy contents. Then she leans in and whispers. Her roseate lips touch my ear. Her breath is hot. Her dark locks brush over my shoulder, and the sensation of her so close is arousing. But I control my feelings. I know our true mission. I know the importance of keeping our relationship as professional as possible.

"What an actor you, are Hans Armbruster," she giggles. "You almost even had me convinced that you are my sibling." She grabs my hand and pulls me up as she rises from the bench. She speaks louder now. "Come, brother! It is time that we retire to our room. We have a long journey in the morning!"

Soon, Janett is asleep, and I lie on my pallet at the foot of her bed. On the floor next to my right arm is my only weapon, my trusty Henry 1813 Navy. The barrel is loaded and the hammer cocked. It is the very same pistol that kept me alive through the Battle of Lake Erie.

The air is crisp, and we are both snuggled deep under layers of heavy, plump quilts. Orange coals glow in the small fireplace, but do not seem to emit any warmth. I listen to Janett's breathing. It is soft and gentle.

It is a frustrating night, as is every night spent near her. There are times when I am tempted to approach her bed. I wonder what her reaction would be to my advances. I imagine her naked flesh against mine. Would she open her arms, or would she reject me?

My thoughts soon turn to shame at my own base desires. I know that any lustful actions on my part are forbidden by our employers, the Art Conservation Society (A.C.S.). Aside from being exceptionally unprofessional, it might jeopardize our entire expedition. Eventually, I find the resolve to drive the sin from my mind and fall into a deep, dreamless slumber.

***

As it turns out, Herr Hofmann's grandson is the driver of the local *burgermeister*. And the local *burgermeister* is currently abroad on business. Ansgar Hofmann arrives in a four-wheel, covered coach that is high quality, yet utilitarian. It is pulled by a team of four stout *Holsteniers*, all dark or mahogany bay, and has a lantern atop the outside of each side door. While we eat a breakfast of boiled eggs, white sausages, and honey-buttered rolls, Ansgar ropes our trunks to the top and rear racks.

The mountain roads are winding and treacherous, but the interior of the carriage is a comfortable, black leather. Only fifteen minutes into our ride, an endless overcast veined with ricocheting lightening covers the sky. When the storm starts, the downpour is so heavy that we cannot see more than a few feet outside.

Wind and raindrops manage to get through the doors, so I pull the canvass storm flaps down and tie them shut. It is dark, and Janett sits next to me and unfolds a blanket over our laps.

"Our driver says that it will take seven to eight hours. Perhaps we should try to nap," she suggests. "We will likely be awake and searching the ruins most of the night."

Janett sleeps, but it is hopeless for me. With the heat of her ample body pressed against my side and her head on my chest, I am wide awake. I lean my head back on the soft leather and close my eyes. I think of the treasure we hunt.

Our sources within say there is an original Hieronymus Bosch somewhere in the catacombs. Depending on its condition, the painting could be worth a fortune of anywhere from $40,000 to $60,000. But our sources also say the painting has an undead guardian. It is rare that ghouls, wights, or nosferatu become attached to works of art. When it happens, the A.C.S. sends Janett Marie Bancroft.

By the afternoon, the sky is still dark but the rain has stopped. The road, if you can call it that, hugs the side of sheer cliffs. At points, it straddles the massif ridges and tilts dangerously to one side or the other. Horse hooves and coach wheels slip in the mud of the escarpments.

We enter a mountainside woods that goes on for hours through twisted, malignant-looking evergreens until we reach the crumbling walls of what was once home to The Mendicants of the Bleeding Mother. The many roomed, medieval monastery has long been destroyed. All that remains are a maze of broken walls and scattered granite underneath blankets of a bright nitrous-green ivy.

Ansgar helps us find a dry corner in the ruins to make camp, a place that still has enough roofing over two intersecting walls to provide cover. After unloading our trunks, he agrees to pick us up the following evening. And then he leaves.

"He was in a hurry to get out of here, wasn't he?" Janett says as a remark more than a question. After we set up the wedge tent and unpack the trunks, she strips off her coat and dress to put on her hunting leathers. I try to be a gentleman and not watch.

***

The old map we have is precise, and it only takes ten minutes of picking our way through the rubble to find the opening into the catacombs. But the opening is where our map ends. Like a dromos of ivy at the base of a pile of crumbled granite, the tunnel gives way into a steep angle of descent.

Janett is behind me with her blunderbuss in both hands. She wears a Springfield 1817 flintlock on one hip and her cutlass on the other. I keep my pistol tethered within reach around my neck by a long lanyard. I hold my sixteen-inch Bowie in my left hand and a miner's oil lamp in the other. As Janett's manservant, my job is to help her search for the artifact and stay clear when she dispatches the undead guardian.

This is not our first venture traipsing through dank dungeons in search of art and monsters. But a career in this field is different than others, in that it can be dangerous to rely on past experiences. The creatures we tend to deal with exhibit evil genius and have a variety of offensive and defensive capabilities. What works in banishing one revenant may not work on the next, and instead might make it more powerful. That's why I leave the real work to the expert.

After a descent of a quarter mile, the tunnel spills into spiraling stairs chiseled down through layers of a coarse-grained conglomerate and an obsidian-veined rhyolite. The air grows much colder.

My lamp flickers from drafts blowing from even further below.

The stairs end at a fork, and it is my suggestion that we split up. Janett agrees. I light a torch for her, and she offers to take the eastward tunnel while I take the westward. We decide to backtrack and meet up at the same spot in thirty minutes.

The westward tunnel levels out and winds through a series of chert and basalt layers before becoming encased in granitoid once again. The floor is bare and clean, and the usual archeological signs are missing: no shards, bones, or petrified wood. After walking due west for over ten minutes, I come to a large archway of clay brick. The top half is covered in spider webs.

I flick open my lighter and hold it up. The webs burn away, and dozens of tiny spiders scuttle from the burst of flames.

I step through the archway.

The air here is as still as the grave, and the silence is incredible. My own breath seems loud, so I try holding it as long as I can. My heartbeat is like a war-drum, banging out a roaring, erratic cadence.

I turn in circles as I walk, holding the lamp out and revealing the chamber. Tattered frames of ancient paintings line the brickwork, and chests of rusted rubble and dust-crusted baubles spill open under them.

That is when I hear a rustle of movement in the northwest corner, up, as if on the ceiling. I turn and hold the lamp up.

Nothing is there.

The yellow flicker of lamp light causes shadows to waiver and undulate, closing in around me. Now I hear movement from behind, in the southeast ceiling corner. I turn again.

I hold up the lamp. Nothing.

"Is anyone here? Janett, is that you!" I shout. My voice sounds muffled, almost as if I am shouting underwater.

The distinct sound of movement is behind me once again, in the northwest corner where it originated.

I turn again and raise my light.

A skeletal form hovers below the ceiling. Tatters of rotten cloth dangle from its limbs. It opens its mouth in a hiss and reveals two long, twisted incisors. I step back.

I trip on something and fall. I drop the lamp. A flash of red explodes across my vision as my head hits the floor.

Darkness.

I hear Janett shouting as she fights. Her blade whistles through the air several times. The movement ceases.

I awake to find myself on fresh satin bedding. Candles are lit in the room, and there is no sign of struggle.

I start to sit up and realize that I am naked under the sheets.

"Don't move," she says from behind, and I turn to look.

Janett is no longer wearing her hunting gear. She wears a long, white bedgown of thin lace that reveals her pink flesh underneath. She seems to glide as she moves across the room.

On the wall behind her is the painting.

"Do not sit up! You hit your head before I saved you. After I killed the creature, the painting appeared. It was hidden by sorcery."

I obey her and rest my head back on a thick pillow. She walks over until she stands above me. I am acutely aware of the diaphanous material she wears, the curves of her legs and ample buttocks, and the swell of her belly and breasts. My erection gives me away.

"I see you miss me!" She giggles and then pulls her gown off and kicks my sheet away. I try to reach up and grab her hips, but she grabs me by the wrists and then straddles me.

She moans as she takes me in. She begins a gentle rocking, back and forth.

I am lost in what seems a hazy miasma of sensuality. The heat and wetness of her sex gripping mine is ecstatic. I keep my eyes closed, focusing on the pleasure, on her tightening with each stroke.

When I open my eyes, she is watching me with a strange glare. Something is not right. It is her eyes. They are not Janett's eyes. They are the same size and the same color, a bright hazel, but what is behind them is different. It is a different person.

Something breaks in my mind like a rope snapping.

A light enters the doorframe behind us. I turn my head. It is Janett, but she is dressed in her hunting gear. I look back and find a desiccated corpse sits on my lap and grinds into my crotch. It is a sour, stinking thing with a sunken nose and withered lips around its fangs. Thin bits of long hair hang from its scalp.

I scream, and the lich starts clawing at my chest with black, jagged fingernails.

I try bucking it off while fighting away the claws, but my swollen phallus is stuck, still clutched by the putrid hole. The demoness wails and rips at my skin with wild motions. My weapons are nowhere within reach, so all I can do is hold my arms over my face for protection.

Janett wastes no time and rushes to my side. She points her blunderbuss at the creature and pulls the trigger. A cone of sparks and silver pellets blasts from the trumpet-like weapon. The explosion is deafening and causes dirt to fall from the ceiling. The ghoul's head, neck and shoulders are disintegrated.

"Shall I pull it off, or let you finish?" Janett teases.

"Pull it off, please," I reply without smiling.

Janett tugs at the smoking remains of the corpse until it comes loose, and then she tosses it into the corner. She takes my lamp, pours some oil onto the heap of leathery skin and bones, and then lights it on fire. From a possibles pouch on her belt, she pulls out a pinch of ground sage and belladonna. She sprinkles the mixture onto the fire, and a stream of green flame shoots up.

"The demon will not return." She traces an index finger on the outer edges of the Hieronymus Bosch. She pulls out a magnifying glass and inspects the linen fibers. She leans in, and her nostrils widen as she sniffs.

"Safflower oil and walnut," she says.

"It's authentic?" I ask.

"It certainly is. This was the guardian's burial chamber. She protected the painting in life and in death. I will come back once I get you to the tent."

She returns to my side and helps me back into my clothes. The satin cushions and sheets are now rags of decay. She gently kisses one of the deep scratches on my chest before pulling my shirt over my head.

"Wait…was that a real kiss?" I ask, "Or am I still hexed?"

She smiles. It is the most alluring smile I have ever seen.

"You decide the answer to that later. I will help you to our tent. You may prepare a bed for us to share for the night. Of course, I will have to boil some water first and clean you thoroughly and bandage your wounds. Would you mind that?"

"Not at all."

Artificial Death
Arista Cyrene

Ricky Bowman was searching the classifieds, same as he did every day, seeking a job and a new place to live ever since that asshole Smith he had recently worked for lied to him and then canned him. Ricky couldn't afford the apartment he was currently living in, not with being unemployed. He had a little money saved up, so if he could find somewhere less expensive maybe he could make it last long enough until he found some work, even if it meant washing dishes at the crappiest joint in town.

The jobs were all the same as yesterday. Most of them required a degree, which he didn't have, and the others he had already applied for, including one for a maid. The hotel didn't think he had the legs for the job.

The places for rent all seemed the same as well, all except one. There was a new listing. It was in a really bad part of town, but he half expected that as he was looking to pay as little as possible. He was sure that even if the landlord had a "No Pets" rule that the apartment would have plenty of the six-legged kind. He looked at the contact information and noticed it was for an individual, not a company. Ricky closed his eyes for a moment and inhaled deeply before letting it out nice and slow. He knew this would probably be some slumlord, but what choice did he have? It was either find a cheap place or live on the streets.

His pay-as-you-go phone still had a few minutes left on it. He dialed the number. It rang twice then a voice said, "Hello."

Ricky paused, the tone of the voice throwing him off. It sounded unnatural as if he were speaking to a machine or something. It wasn't mechanical, but he felt it had no human feel behind it.

"Ummm, yes, I'm calling for Emmanuelle Quinz."

There was no response, but it didn't sound as if the connection had been lost. Ricky looked at the phone, not sure if he wanted to go through with the call. His stomach rumbled, reminding him he was making one package of Oriental noodles last him each week because he couldn't afford to buy food.

"Hello? Hello, are you still there? I'm calling about the apartment for rent you have listed in the paper."

"Yes," the distant voice replied. "The apartment is located at the end of Lake Dyer Road. It is apartment number three. The key is above the door. Feel free to view it." A few faint clicks followed.

"The ad said the rent was two fifty but didn't mention a deposit or anything else." Ricky waited, but he heard nothing. "Hello? Hello?"

A dial tone sounded. Perplexed, he hung up the phone. He thought to himself that the call had been the strangest conversation he had ever had with someone supposedly trying to market something. His stomach rumbled once more. He threw on his shoes and walked out of his place, locking the door behind him. He walked over to the next building and went up a flight of stairs where his friends, Kat and Brian, lived.

Brian was a nice guy who was into cars, hard rock music and drinking beer, a lot of the same interests as Ricky, basically. Unlike Ricky, who had a bit of a paunch and a couldn't press half his own weight even if his life depended on it, Brian had an athletic build, tanned muscles and made women turn their heads when he walked into a restaurant. Brian probably knew how good-looking he was, but he wasn't a player. He was totally in love with Kat, and judging by the things she said, what she wore and how she looked, he had no reason to be stepping out and looking for action on the side.

Kat was a bombshell. Ricky could picture her on the cover of any album or in any music video that required a gorgeous young babe. She had a smile that could melt a guy's heart and a body that could take that melted piece of meat and stiffen it right back up. She said she had tried modeling once, but the majority of the girls were so cutthroat and bitchy that she left the so-called glamorous world and opted for bartending. She made twice the tips as a bartender wearing Daisy Dukes and low cut tops in a cool rock joint as she did as a waitress. She said she once considered stripping but there were no classy joints in town.

Between what she made and what Brian made doing construction, they did okay for themselves, living in the modest apartment complex and saving up for a house. Then they'd get married and move away. The most Ricky could really hope for is maybe mowing their lawn or cleaning out their septic tank. Not that there was anything wrong with those jobs, but with his lack of skills and talents, that would be about the only way he could stay close to them if they ever moved away. The thought just depressed him and made him hate his situation even more.

He knocked on the blue-gray door, the paint peeling along the trim and crumbling to bits of hard flakes around the edges of the welcome mat. A flash of shadow covered the peephole then Ricky heard the slide of the chain lock and the click of the deadbolt as Kat opened the door, wearing a tight pink tank top and black spandex shorts that formed to every luscious curve.

"Ricky, what's happening, baby?" Her voice was bubbly and she bounced a little on the tips of her toes as she stepped forward and gave him a hug.

I could stay here like that all day and forget about the rest of the world, he thought to himself. He snapped out of it, not wanting to make the situation awkward, but damn if he didn't want her arms wrapped around him and welcoming him like that for a little while longer. It almost made him feel human.

"Hey, Kat, I was wondering if you or Brian had some time to take me to an apartment complex over near the lake?"

"Whoa, aren't we moving up in the world?" Brian said, coming down the hallway and entering the room. "Getting a place on the lake?" he asked in a joking manner.

"It's nothing like that," Ricky, replied, sheepish and ashamed. "It's at the end of Lake Dyer Road."

Kat wrinkled her nose. "Isn't that the side of the lake where the crappy trailers and pop-up campers are located?"

Ricky sighed and nodded his head. When Kat felt sorry for him he knew that his world sucked. He also knew there was no way he'd ever have a girl as wonderful or beautiful as Kat. Maybe if they just stole a cinder block and tied it around his neck they could drive over Lake Dyer Bridge and shove his ass off into the water, problem solved.

"Dude, you don't want to live over there. They had a murder in that area just last week," Brian said, shaking Ricky's hand and pulling him inside the apartment. He walked off into the kitchen and returned with a couple of cold beers. He handed one to Ricky as he took a swig of his own beer then passed it off to Kat, who took her own swig.

"Murders can happen anywhere…here, Lake Dyer Road, or even the fanciest part of town. I don't want to live there, but a job just ain't happening and money's getting really tight."

"I know things are tight, and I know murders happen everywhere. But they happen over in that area more than anywhere in the entire fucking county. That's like the third murder in less than four months. Not to mention all the people that go missing over there."

"Brian, maybe people go missing over there because they can't afford to live anymore and they 'disappear' on purpose to get away from the creditors and shit. At least over there I can make what money I have left last me a little bit and I can always cast a line and try to catch some fish or a turtle for a meal."

"Or an alligator, if he doesn't eat you first."

"Besides," Kat said, jumping back into the conversation, "without a vehicle it'll be even more difficult to get a job living way out there. How would you get to town for work? I mean, we don't mind giving you a lift now and then, but you know we can't make it over there every day with Brian's long hours and my night schedule. I normally don't get in until close to four and I don't get up until noon."

"Guys, I appreciate it, and I have thought about some of what you're saying, I really have. But the situation is getting desperate. I mean, if I could handle a hammer or wasn't scared of heights I would take Brian's boss up on that job offer, but I'm about as mechanically inclined as a snail in an ice storm."

Brian laughed as he finished downing his beer. He slapped Ricky on the shoulder as he stated, "Dude, I don't know what the hell you meant, but we'll take you out there. Let me get on a shirt and grab my buck knife. It ain't a gun, but at least it's something."

Ricky simply nodded his head and stared at his feet, his hands deep within his pockets. He felt Kat's hand on the back of his head and her lips kissing his forehead. He hadn't been looking for sympathy and was partially embarrassed that he must seem like such a sad case, but her gesture gave him enough spark to want to take another breath and not die just yet.

***

The ride took them nearly thirty minutes to get through traffic lights and Sunday rubberneckers. Brian was off but Kat had to go in and work in a few hours. She had tried to get Ricky a job at the bar, helping with anything from loading bands in and out to janitorial duties, but his prior DUIs and sketchy work history gave her boss cause to deny him a position. She had tried batting her eyes and pleading, but even that didn't work. Ricky truly believed in the old saying, "If it weren't for bad luck I'd have no luck at all."

They talked about other things during the drive, such as what new movies were coming out and what cool bands were hitting town, but Kat could see that talking about things that Ricky couldn't afford to do just depressed him more. She decided to go back to the subject of the apartment.

"So how much are they asking for this place?"

"Two fifty per month according to the ad," Ricky replied. "I was going to ask them about the deposit and if it came with anything, like a stove or fridge, but they just hung up. As a matter of fact, the voice was so strange and inhuman, I'm not even sure if I was speaking to a man or a woman. Get this, the *person* tells me the key for the place is above the door."

"Wow, talk about safety," Kat said. "Probably some vagrants have already moved in and the guy doesn't even know it."

"What was the dude's name again?" Brian asked.

"Emmanuelle Quinz."

"Maybe he couldn't speak much English. We've got day laborers on our crews that speak no English. We just point and do some miming with our hands to get our point across if there's no one on the crew that day that can translate. Hell, most of the times one of the foremen just drives by the parking lot over by the old shopping center, hold his hand up and shows a number of fingers and that many guys fight for who gets into the back of the truck."

"Yeah, it's pretty bad when I speak the language and come from this country and I'm getting outdone by a bunch of illegals."

"That's not what Brian meant, Ricky. He's just saying that with this being located over here and the person on the phone being a bit strange, maybe they just can't communicate really well and are used to dealing with immigrants. Maybe you asking questions in English threw the guy off."

"Or maybe it was one of those computerized prompters," Brian added. "You know, like it waits for you to say a keyword then it goes to a related message? Sort of like when you call the phone company and spend thirty minutes trying to get a real person instead of a machine and then they send you to some dipshit in another country where English is their third language and they say their name is Bob. Then you realize you were better off talking to the damn machine."

Ricky turned and stared out the window from the back seat. Who would've thought that living by a lake could be discouraging? Ricky noticed trash littered the road, children with saggy diapers and muddy faces—at least he hoped it was mud—played out in yards that could just as easily been the city dump, mangy dogs scrounged in plastic bags and dilapidated boxes searching for food. The cinder block came back to mind.

He heard Brian repeatedly calling his name and realized he must've been daydreaming. He answered, "What?"

"Dude, I think we're here."

Ricky looked in front of the car and saw nothing but the tops of bamboo and some scraggly trees. He couldn't even see the road. "Where?"

Brian pointed and Ricky scooted forward. He realized the car was parked at the top of a steep incline and that a gravel driveway plagued with potholes and garbage led to some ugly structure peeking out through the bamboo and unmowed grass.

"Now I know how people can disappear around here," Kat said in an uneasy voice.

"No shit," Brian said, checking to make sure the knife was still in its scabbard and attached to his belt. "Are you sure you even want to get out?"

Ricky nervously laughed before joking with the couple, "Unless you want to adopt me as a stray pet, I've got to do whatever I can, even if it means living in a shit hole like this."

"Maybe looks are deceiving and the inside, once we get past the bamboo and the trail of scattered garbage, will be sort of nice and pleasant." Ricky and Brian both looked at Kat like she was smoking some illegal substance. She meekly smiled. She was generally a positive person and even she had a difficult time believing the lie she just told.

Brian and Kat got out and began walking down the path, Kat gripping her boyfriend's hand as her eyes darted back and forth, keeping an eye out for anything dangerous. Ricky could see that Brian actually had the buck knife out, the handle upside down in the palm of his hand and the blade pointing upwards, hidden by his forearm from anyone that may be staring out from behind battered blinds in the apartment building. Ricky shook his head and took another deep breath then crawled out from the back seat of the Camaro. He closed the door and hadn't gotten more than a single stride when he heard Brian yell out to him to make sure the car doors were locked. Ricky looked back, tried the handle and ensured that they were locked. Although he figured in this neighborhood it didn't matter. If someone wanted the car or its contents badly enough they'd simply break a window or just shoot the three of them and take the keys.

He made his way to the overgrown bamboo entrance. He saw Brian and Kat standing with their heads inside the door to the apartment. They were backing out as he approached.

"Holy shit, Ricky. Tell me you got a match and some lighter fluid and I'll make this place look better in a heartbeat," Brian said in all seriousness.

Kat was holding her nose as she said, "Whoever decorated the place must've been colorblind. I'm going to go check out the lake view while you decide whether to run or to hurl."

Brian followed Kat; hand-in-hand again as they made their way down the sidewalk, sidestepping a plethora of broken toys and what appeared to be ruined doll parts strewn about. They turned a corner that appeared to take them around to the back of the garishly painted building. At least the paint was chipping and fading. If it all peeled away and blew off in a storm it would be an improvement.

Ricky sighed once again as he pushed open the creaky door. The stench was overpowering. Something had definitely died in here. *Or maybe*, Ricky thought with as much optimism as he could muster, *someone had a wet dog that rolled around in something dead and then they let it back into the house where it lay on the puke green carpet until mold set in.* That thought was about as positive as he could imagine with the scene which stood before him.

The walls did not compliment the carpet in any shape or manner, painted fuchsia and dotted with specks of brown nicotine stains that ran in rivulets here and there before sinking into the edges of the rotting carpet. Ricky covered his mouth and nose and went in, desperation knowing no bounds.

The living room had a small fireplace that no one had cleaned. It looked as if there was more than just wood on the grate—possibly trash and some more of the doll parts. He stepped on a dirty scarf and felt something hard beneath it. He used his foot to kick the scarf away, revealing a male mannequin hand. Ricky bent over and picked it up to examine it closer. The ring finger was broken off and there were deep gouges from the missing wrist joint all the way across the top to the middle of the remaining fingers. They appeared to have been made by fingernails. The center of the hand had a smudge of red, almost the same shade as the lipstick Kat loved to wear.

Still holding the hand, Ricky moved closer to the fireplace and studied the contents. "Strange, it all seems to be clothing and bits of mannequins. Maybe some demented fashion designer wannabe lived here."

He tossed the hand on the heap only to watch it roll out onto the floor. A rustle of something taking flight sounded down the chimney along with a fresh coating of soot.

Ricky moved along, checking out a pile of old fashion magazines and newspaper ads stacked in the corner of the room. He noticed some of them were dated over twenty years ago. He also noticed they were addressed to Emmanuelle and they were infested with silverfish.

"Lovely, this just keeps getting better. I can't wait to see the kitchen and bathroom."

Ricky proceeded to the kitchen, his expectations met. The stove was an old gas stove that looked as if it may have been in one of those houses they used at bombing test sites. It sat upon grimy tile, but the tile didn't appear to be stained with grease. There was a mixture of colors smeared across the floor, especially leading to a chute on the back wall that had to be for garbage disposal. Between the stove and the chute was an icebox.

"Damn, not even a refrigerator. This is like visiting my great-grandparents when I was little. I wonder if a milkman drops by every morning and leaves a bottle of Mad Dog on the doorstep?"

Ricky pulled on the door handle of the icebox, expecting to find Jimmy Hoffa. To his surprise, it looked brand new on the inside, clean as a whistle. He decided to try the oven door. Once again, spic and span on the inside, as if neither of them had ever been used.

He heard something skittering and looked over to see three large roaches shooting out of the sink drain and scurrying to crevices between the walls and faded Formica. A wolf spider crawled out of the drain, protecting its territory. Ricky let the spider be. Maybe it would eat the roaches.

He opened a cabinet then quickly wished he hadn't. A slew of magazines poured out onto his head and chest, smashing him in the face and bloodying his nose and lips.

"Damn, this sonuvabitch better give me the first month free if I have to clean this place myself before moving in," he angrily yelled. He tenderly put his fingers to his face to assess the damage. Blood covered his hands, but at least it wasn't gushing. He searched for paper towels and saw none.

He exited the kitchen and turned down a narrow hallway, made even more so by more stacks of magazines and ad slicks lining both sides of the hall. A small bathroom was the first door he came to. He looked for toilet paper or, being optimistic once again, a clean-ish towel. He found nothing. He looked at his face as best he could in the grimy mirror above the sink. Dirty, bloody finger and handprints marked the glass and the porcelain sink. Ricky didn't pay much attention to the prints or another cockroach the size of his thumb that was running away and heading behind the toilet. He turned the faucet on as he stared at his swollen nose and lips. Beneath his eyes, the skin was already turning color.

"Shit, I bet it's broken." He gingerly pinched the bridge with thumb and index finger. He winced and his world went a little wonky as he tried not to slip into unconsciousness from the pain shooting through his head. Never being that tough of a guy to begin with, and currently being a bit malnourished since he was broke, Ricky's constitution and pain tolerance was in dire shape.

He looked down at the water, which had been running for at least a good ten seconds, or so he thought. The water was still a dingy brown as if it were being piped straight from the lake. It reminded him of a nasty hotel he stayed in one time in northeast Jersey, an area of the country he liked to call the armpit of North America. He gave the water a few more seconds but there was still no change. He shut off the hot water and switched to the cold. Again, the water maintained its muddy sewer-like coloration.

He then tried the bathtub, hoping maybe it was just rusty pipes to the sink and the bath would be in better shape. He turned the handles. A small spider on a strand of silk floated halfway down between the faucet and the drain, but no water came out. Blood dripped from his face and splattered on the bottom of the yellow-stained tub.

"Fuck it," Ricky said, only it came out *fock it* with the damage done to his nose and mouth. He used his shirtsleeve and patted away the fresh blood. He tried to remove some of the clotted blood but it hurt too much. He would just wait until he got home.

Then, he would just see what stuff he could live without and sell it or just leave it. His necessities he would pack up as best he could into an overnight bag and sleep on park benches. At least there he would have semi-fresh air and no magazines bashing him in the face. Maybe a pigeon squatting and shitting on his head but that beat the hell out of this dump.

As he came out of his reverie, determined to leave and not even check out the rest of this little slice of pigsty heaven, he heard a rhythmic motion on the other side of the wall. He could also hear a faint squeak of springs. He stepped quietly, making his way out of the bathroom and down the cluttered hallway. An open door to the left revealed a room piled floor to ceiling with more ephemera. The rotting spines of some magazines were more than fifty years old. Silverfish and cockroaches scattered, the multitude of paper appearing to come alive. The hairs on the back of Ricky's neck and along his arms stood up as a shiver trickled like ice-cold water down his spine.

But he remained quiet, regaining his nerve and turning to the door behind him—the door where the repetitious sound was emanating. It wasn't completely shut, cracked open just a hair but not enough that Ricky could discern anything. He listened and could still hear the slow, rhythmic sound accompanied by the rustling of material.

Surely, Ricky thought, *if some vagabond couple was using this as a flophouse they would've heard the magazines crashing down, or my yelling, or the water turning on.*

He pushed lightly on the door with his bloodied fingers, hoping it wouldn't creak. It made a slight noise, but nothing as loud as the front door. He opened the door enough to look to his right in the dimly lit room where a bed was positioned alongside the adjoining wall to the bathroom. Beneath a disgusting quilt were three young male figures staring across the room at something behind the door and hidden from his view. All three were slowly masturbating in rhythm, transfixed on whatever was on the other side of the room.

Ricky realized that beyond this bizarre scene that something else was wrong. He took his eyes away from the motion of the quilt and looked closer at the boys. Their faces were all flat, with barely any reflection of what little light there was and the skin tone all the same with no characteristics or flaws such as freckles, scars and such. Their hair didn't move. Their eyes didn't blink.

"What the…? Mannequins? What the hell is going on? Why would some sick bastard rig these to a motor and make it look like they were jerking off," he asked himself as he pushed the door open.

To his left was the object of their perverted desire. A female mannequin wearing sexy lingerie was handcuffed from behind as a male mannequin with no head fumbled with her corset, attempting to remove it.

"This is just getting more fucking surreal by the minute. Maybe he can't get her clothing off without a head and eyes." He looked back at the boy mannequins and saw that they were ignoring him, their eyes still watching the woman being clumsily undressed.

He searched the top corners of the room as he flicked on a light switch. No light came on, leaving him to search in a room lit by the faint sunlight filtering through dirty windows and a stand of bamboo.

"Okay, where's the camera? Is somebody screwing with me? Fine, you got me. Ha, ha! Very funny. I hope when I sign the waiver to be on TV it comes with some pay."

No one answered—nothing revealed. He saw the boys still waxing their plastic boners, assuming they actually were endowed with something. Whomever the sick fuck was that came up with this crack-induced fetish probably gave them all plastic dildoes and glued them to their Ken-doll groins.

Ricky looked back and saw that the corset was about to pop off, leaving the mannequin in a black bullet bra and lacy black panties along with garters attached and black silk stockings. He had to admit that she was a well-made mannequin and dressed very sexy. Her hair was black and obviously a wig placed on top instead of being a part of the plastic mold. She had brilliant blue eyes. She reminded him of that famous pin-up model that his dad and grandfather had liked. What was her name? Bettie, Bettie Page.

Ricky heard a *click* and saw the cuffs drop to the carpet. The Bettie mannequin's head turned as her bra also fell to the floor, revealing pert breasts that had areolas realistically painted upon them. Her lips pursed and she tilted her head slightly to the right. Her right index finger bent and gave Ricky a *come-hither* signal, motioning for him to approach.

Ricky wasn't into blow-up dolls and what he considered weird fetish shit, but something enticing eschewed from those lips and eyes. He heard the rhythm of the boys stroking increase but he didn't turn to look. His eyes were now transfixed on the garters snapping free, the male mannequin was bent down behind her. His face would've been right at her ass if he had had a head. He thought once more of the Ken-doll situation and wondered if she could give him head to begin with since he was obviously missing one and probably both.

He watched the silk stockings being slowly rolled down and could feel his cock throbbing and getting stiff. He felt like an eleven-year-old sneaking peeks in the bathroom of the lingerie section in the Sears catalog, hoping that some bush or a nipple could be seen through the garments the models wore. As screwed up as he knew this entire situation was, he found himself taking a step forward into the room, his eyes locked on the fake Bettie. He was fighting the urge, but part of him wanted to see how realistic she looked once those lacy panties shimmied down her smooth legs and landed on the floor.

The male mannequin's hands pinched the elastic at the top of the underwear and began to peel them down her curvy hips. Ricky took another step towards Bettie as he imagined he would be removing those panties with his teeth, assuming his head was positioned at her ass like the mannequin's missing head should be.

The panties dropped, revealing a trim, black bush of hair. Ricky could swear that he could smell the sex emanating from her, wafting through the air. He could feel his own dick pulsate. In the back of his mind, he was wondering if he had walked through the doorway of some alternate universe. Could he actually have a hot time with this doll?

She lifted a foot and escaped the underwear. She pointed at Ricky then pointed down at the underwear. He knew what she wanted, to untangle her other foot and set her free. He decided he would get down on his knees in front of her instead of just bending over. That would easily position him to get a glimpse to see if she was real or fake down below; to discover if he was actually catching her scent; to see if there was any moisture in the realistic-looking pubic hair.

The boys' rhythm increased once more. The male mannequin, still on his knees behind her, was doffing his sports coat. Having no head, the tie he simply lifted up as it was more or less draped into position.

Ricky took one last step forward, the powerful and alluring scent washing over him in another wave. He could feel the wetness in his own pants, certain a dewdrop of pre-cum seeped from the tip of his cock. He knelt down in front of her, taking his time but not caring if it was obvious he was staring at her crotch. It was obvious she was toying with him so why ignore it? He raised a hand and softly stroked her pubes, using a little pressure to get past the curls. He could feel the soft flesh of her labia.

Bettie's hand smartly slapped his hand away. He looked up, his mouth at her pussy as he tilted his head back and stared at her beautiful face between the soft looking breasts. Were those real?

She pointed once more at the panties tangled around her toes, the expression on her face and the look in her eyes telling him to do it. He attempted to find the silk material without looking down, maintaining a pleasant smile as he looked up at her, the scent embracing his mind even more, or at least some part of his anatomy was being taken over.

He had no luck groping for the panties. They should have easily been within reach. He gave in, tearing his eyes away from her figure and looking down at her foot, the underwear wrapped around her toes. He tried to untangle them with one hand, but they were snagged on something. He used both hands, lifting her foot, feeling the slight curve of her calf. He didn't realize they made mannequins so realistic.

She wiggled her toes and he bent over more, the panties clutched in one hand against his cheek while her foot was still held by his other hand. He could smell Bettie on the material. Ricky kissed her calf and made his way down to the tip of her toes. The rhythm increased and the bed springs got louder.

A quick *swish*, followed by a *chop* and a *thunk* was all Ricky's mind could take in as he saw the floor and Bettie's foot make a circular motion and seemingly move away from him in a disturbing manner. Then he saw his body crumple and fall over, blood spurting from the top of his torso. His head and neck were no longer attached to his body.

Another mannequin carrying a broadax moved towards his head, blood dripping from the sharp blade. The mannequin was wearing all black, including a full hood covering its face. It looked like the executioners Ricky had seen in so many movies. The executioner's hand reached down and he could feel his head being lifted up and taken over to the male mannequin who was missing his head. He was still on his knees, right behind Bettie's shapely ass, which was beginning to blur and grow dim. Ricky could no longer hear or see. His senses were failing. His brain was finally dying.

***

Brian and Kat had somewhat enjoyed viewing the lake. Looking off into the distance it wasn't bad, cirrus clouds floating way up high in a brilliant, blue sky, a gentle breeze pushing sailboats along, people skiing and swimming, and a variety of birds were about.

In the immediate vicinity, it was a different story. There were a couple of gators sunning themselves, and a water moccasin was swimming along the shore, weaving in and out of pieces of Styrofoam coolers, empty beer cans and soggy baby diapers half out of the water. Another gator, his huge body covered by the water up to his eyes, stared intently at the couple, waiting for them to take another couple of steps his direction.

Disgusted with what she saw, Kat said, "If the people on the far side of the lake came over to this side, they wouldn't be in this water. How can people be so lazy? There's a trash dumpster right over there?"

"Because man thinks he's the Chosen One on this planet and that gives him the right to do whatever he wants to it and the other creatures. It's amazing we ever made it beyond sticks and termites." Brian put his arm on her shoulder and turned her back to the apartments. "Let's go see what Ricky is up to."

"I don't know what he's going to do, but we can't let him move in here."

"Kat, I hope you're not thinking what I think you're thinking."

She shrugged her shoulders, a look of guilt upon her face.

"I like Ricky and I even trust him. I don't believe he'd steal from us. But I don't think he'd ever be able to pay us back and we don't have enough room."

"What if we went ahead and found a house, Brian? We could get something big enough that either has an extra room for him or has a building out back? Or we could build a small room for him out back?"

"Kat, no. When we get our own place it will be for our family and us. Our plans are to get married, get a house and get settled, then start a family of our own. We can't have 'Uncle Ricky' living in a shed out back."

Kat had her arms crossed. Brian could tell by the way her brow was pulled down and tight that she was still trying to come up with a solution as they approached the closed door.

"Huh, why would he close it? To keep the smell and the flies in?"

"That's not funny, Brian," Kat said, slapping him gently on the arm. "He's in a bind and if this is the best he can do then we need to figure something out. I wouldn't let a stray dog with rabies live in this rat trap."

Brian ran his fingers through his hair while looking at Kat. "Okay, we'll figure something out but it's not going to be what you were thinking back there a minute ago."

He opened the door and they heard something banging and rumbling against metal. Then the sound of a door slamming shut.

"Hey, Ricky, you okay, man?" Brian waited for a response but none came. They stepped into the middle of the living room, looking around at the detritus. "Ricky, did you fall over a heap of garbage or something back there? Where are you?"

The executioner, shuffled as quietly as he could to the broom closet, hiding before the humans found him. He had been busy in the kitchen dumping the remains of Ricky's body, letting them slide down the chute and into the brackish pool of water that sat a mere yard from the lake, hidden by a wall of bamboo and weeds. The gators had dug the area out to bury their eggs at some point in time. Since then the pit had filled with water and become a buffet and the reptiles knew it. They simply had to bide their time and wait for lunch to come to them, then they could rip a body apart and have a meal or stash it underwater in a log for eating later.

"Ricky," Kat called out in with a more plaintive cry. "Let's go. This place isn't for you."

There was still no answer, but they heard a door swing shut somewhere in the house.

"Wait here by the front door. And leave it open. I'll go find him." Brian gave her a loving kiss then moved towards the hallway.

"Fuck that," Kat said aloud as she followed him. Brian turned and looked at her in a way that she knew he meant was serious and that she was supposed to listen, but she was the independent sort and that didn't fly with her. Brian knew it didn't but he thought it was worth a shot. He wasn't trying to be a jerk. He just wanted her to be safe and, in case Ricky had fallen and wasn't answering because he was injured, Brian wanted to make certain that it wasn't something that would freak Kat out.

She grabbed Brian by the crook of his elbow and walked behind him, the hallway being almost too cramped for one person to walk through, much less two side-by-side. Brian looked in the bathroom but Ricky wasn't in there. They noticed as they walked in the unlit hallway the carpet made a bit of a squishy noise. When they peeked through the bedroom door on the left, the room filled to the top with magazines, Kat looked down, but it was too dark to see.

They turned to the closed door across the hall and opened it. The last hint of sunlight filtered through the room. A nasty, unmade bed was the first thing they saw. In the far corner nearest the bed were three naked boy mannequins clustered together, facing one another as if conversing.

"Creepy," Kat said. "I think you were right about a match and lighter fluid."

Brian nodded his head in agreement as he opened the door the remainder of the way. A female mannequin wearing a dress from the 1950s stood motionless on a dark rug with a straw broom and a metal dustpan in her hands. A closet door stood partially open but their view was blocked.

"I don't think he's in here but I'll check the closet just to make sure," Brian said, trying to keep his composure. Kat could hear a tinge of fear in his voice, but she wasn't about to make fun of him. This place was really starting to get to her.

"Ricky, quit playing games, dude. Where the fuck you at? I swear if you're hiding and jump out to scare us, your ass is walking all the way home." Brian waited but still there was no answer. He looked on the other side of the bed, next to the trio of nude mannequins. A baseball bat was nearby. He picked it up and used it to lift the bed skirt. He bent over and peered beneath the bed but only found more magazines and newspapers. He threw the bat down on the bed.

"I swear, if this place did go up in flames the fire department would just think it was from all the shit piled up in here. I didn't even see or hear any other people around this dump. There's nothing but disgusting piles of rotting garbage. I doubt if anyone would even get hurt."

"I know, sweetie, but you can't talk that way. That's arson."

"Kat, in this case, it would be a boon to society."

She didn't agree out loud, but she figured he was right. She was looking down at her shoes, a bit ashamed for thinking that way. She noticed they were covered in something wet. She reached down and felt the sticky blood on her fingers. She screamed as she looked up and watched Brian open the closet door all the way. She saw a pair of mannequin hands come out and grasp Brian's throat. At first, she thought maybe it was crammed in there and was simply falling forward, but then she saw the hands tighten around Brian's throat as he tried to scream. He struggled with the mannequin as it forced him backwards. Exiting the closet, the terror they beheld was extraordinary, Ricky's head and neck sat atop the artificial being, mouth wide open as if surprised, the eyes wide with fear. Brian was forced to use both hands on the monster, attempting to break free, unable to reach for his knife.

The three boys had split apart, one held the bat. All three were sporting hard-ons, complete with testicles. Kat couldn't believe what she was seeing because they appeared to be real, but then again, so did Ricky's head. She saw the one with the bat draw back and prepare to swing, aiming for Brian's kidneys as he was still being forced backwards. She dove over the bed, bouncing on it and planning to bowl the boys over. The batter ignored her, but the other two turned to block her, a smile growing on their faces as they saw the attractive girl in a tank top and shorts coming their way. Kat wasn't a large girl, but her momentum was enough to knock the creatures over, saving Brian from being blind-sided with a bat as he fought for his life against the thing with Ricky's head.

She attempted to get up, but the downed boys held her fast, their dicks throbbing to the tempo of echoing heartbeats beneath their plastic chests. She screamed. They laughed and gripped her tighter. She could feel one of them close up against her, his penis sliding under the cuff of her shorts just below her left butt cheek.

The bedroom door slammed shut but bounced back open. The executioner filled the space, hiding any chance for escape. The Bettie turned, dropping the broom and raising the dustpan. The executioner moved behind Brian and grasped his arms so he could not break free. The Ricky monster fell to his knees and grasped Brian's legs from the side, holding him tight. The Bettie drew back the dustpan before shoving the razor-sharp edge through his Adam's apple until it smacked against his spinal column, not quite severing his head. Blood quickly filled the dustpan as it spurted from Brian's jugular veins. His body went limp and the mannequins dropped him to the floor.

Kat's screaming had turned to madness as she saw her boyfriend murdered. Being molested was no longer on her mind although her top had been ripped free and she could now feel two hard, fleshy dicks, one coming from each side of her shorts from behind, fighting for dominance over her ass. The third boy was trying to rip down her shorts with one hand, his groin rubbing fiercely up and down her leg, as he fondled her breasts with his other hand. Kat was in shock, not totally aware of what was happening to her own body.

She saw the Ricky monster drop his pants. He too had a stiff penis. He smiled and crawled upright on his knees to her nearly naked body. She thrashed and screamed even more. She didn't hear the hissing sound—and neither did the mannequins.

From beneath the bed, the scaly snout shot out, snatching the two boys on the floor trying to take the girl from behind. The gator's twelve-foot body extended under the bed and out into the hall, thrashing as it quickly moved forward and clamped down on Kat's head. Another muffled scream then she was dead, her body still twitching. The third boy was just pulling her shorts down to reveal her pink panties, oblivious to the gator.

The adult mannequins attempted to beat the gator back, but the gator was in a foul mood. He ripped the arms from the executioner, snapped the erect penis off of the Ricky mannequin, and clamped down on the leg of the Bettie, yanking her to the floor and proceeding to land on her, crushing her torso. The gator's tail smacked the other downed mannequins, pummeling them to rubbish. All that was left was the one boy trying to get the panties off the dead girl. He had them to her knees. The gator swallowed half of him down in a single bite, splintering him to bits before returning to his fresh kill. The panties came off as he tore a leg free of the hip socket, rending the meat and tendons loose while taking his time to enjoy his tender, young meal.

Two if by SCREEE!
Steve Wands

The road came to an abrupt end. Beyond the bug-splattered windshield was a heavy metal album cover from the bygone era of longhaired headbangers. The road didn't just end; it was gone—replaced by fire and monsters. Winged creatures carried still screaming victims into the gash of smoldering ruin just beyond the windshield.

"Go back," Tabitha said.

"Go back where?" Vivian asked, her eyes welling with tears.

"I don't know. Anywhere! Just go," Tabitha said, as she began to cry.

Vivian put the car into reverse and slammed on the accelerator. They sped backward in her grandfather's old cutlass as Vivian turned the wheel, spinning them around. She slammed down on the accelerator again, going back in the direction from which they just came. A bug looking thing the size of a hawk splattered into the windshield, causing both girls to shriek in response.

"Damn that was a big one. What are these things?!" Tabitha said.

Vivian's lip quivered in a lunatic sneer, "I don't know."

"That one kind of looked like a mosquito," Tabitha said, playing with the stretched out collar of her black t-shirt.

Last night they were sitting at a dive bar, drinking Jack and watching their friends' new doom metal band—Green Inferno—play. And now today they were living through the lyrics, but there wasn't a drop of whiskey in sight.

Thwack! Another winged thing broke upon the windshield. This time its exoskeleton chipped the windshield, leaving a tiny river of a crack barely seen among the magenta mush of bug pulp.

"Shit," said Tabitha, "that thing left a crack."

"We need to get off the road. The crack isn't our only problem. We're running low on gas, too."

They locked eyes for a moment, sharing a thought the way lovers do, before Vivian had to swerve out of the way of some creature plodding along down the road. It looked like some perversion of an animal with its innards outside its body.

"Oh, that was gross," said Vivian, ready to heave.

"Think goddammit, where can we go?"

Vivian didn't know. Her mind was beyond occupied just driving and trying to stay sane while the world around her went completely bananas.

"How about Headden's Farm? Maybe we can hold out in the barn or something?"

"We never should've left home."

"Too late to play that game," Tabitha said, knowing the bridge between here and there was replaced by a gulf of fire and there wasn't a thing either of them could do to cross it.

"The farm it is," said Vivian as a winged creature latched onto the roof, its claws piercing the top of the vehicle like a can opener.

The creature pulled, trying to lift them into the sky as they screamed in unison. It screamed back, loud enough to smother out their sounds and cause the car to vibrate. The creature wasn't strong enough to pull them up beyond a few inches but when it dropped them down it tested the shocks of the car like they had never been tested before. Sparks flew as the bumper touched asphalt and the car shimmied left and right as Vivian fought to straighten out and keep the car from flipping over.

The car kept going forward, Vivian pushed the accelerator all the way down, going far faster than she usually cared to. The car sounded as if it were towing soup cans now. The lovers looked up, trying to spy their winged attacker, but neither could see it till its claws punctured the roof once more. They could hear its wings begin to flap. Instead of screaming again, Tabitha opened the glove box and produced a large black flashlight.

"Better than nothing," she said, pleased with the weight of it in her hand.

She began smashing at the talons poking through the roof and a after a few blows was delighted when one cracked off and fell into her lap. The beast howled, and the car fell back to the road. Purple blood dribbled from the broken talon like pen ink and it smelled putrid.

"Keep hitting that thing," Vivian encouraged, and Tabitha did.

Tabitha kept hitting the beast till another talon broke off. Blood dribbled down once more and it retracted its claws and flew away.

"We need to get off the road. Now!" Tabitha said.

"We're not to the farm yet."

"That thing is going to come back, and maybe next time it brings a friend. If that's the case, up into the air we go and I don't want to think of how that plays out," Tabitha said, figuring it would end one of two ways; one being dropped back down from a higher elevation to go splat; and two being carried off to whatever hell these things were bringing people.

"Fine," Vivian said, cutting across the road, dodging an abandoned car, and pulling off to a small stretch of trees.

They looked out the window, trying to spot their attacker, but overhead in the hazy smoke covered sunshine it was hard to determine what was bird or beast, or even insect. A loud roar vibrated the windows. Neither of them could tell if it was from above, or below. It was so loud it seemed to fill the air.

Vivian turned on the radio, she searched the AM and FM bands for a broadcast, but only got few strands of noise, like the static pop and hum of plugging in an electric guitar to an amplifier. It wasn't enough sound to qualify as white noise. "Nothing," Vivian said, shutting the radio off again.

"Sounds about right," Tabitha said, "Of course the apocalypse wouldn't have a soundtrack."

For a while it was quiet and the lovers kept it that way. They clasped hands and held each other's gaze.

Last night, after their friends finished their set and they hung out for a bit the lovers headed home. Vivian had an apartment just a few blocks from her grandparents. It was a two family duplex divvied up into apartments and it had been her first home away from home for the last year or so. Tabitha had been dating her almost as long and somewhere along the line staying over had become a regular thing and Vivian's apartment had become their apartment.

Neither had gone to college. Both opted to work and while the desire for higher education was there, neither knew what they wanted out of life other than each other. They loved music, and drinking and getting high, and being together, but those things weren't careers. After too many drinks Vivian rolled a joint and they smoked it on the couch while listening to records. The night blurred till they found their way to bed, holding each other in the wake of orgasm.

Sometime after the sun came up and the coffee was poured did they find out that all hell had broken loose across the known world. They ran to Vivian's grandparents' house witnessing all sorts of insect abominations along the way. Neighbors were fighting them in the street, running in fear, and the smart ones were watching from behind drawn curtains.

They survived the chaos on the streets and made it to Vivian's grandparents' as creatures with wings descended and perched on nearby rooftops and telephone poles. They were the work of some concept designer gone mad; necrotic Pterodactyl's with horns and partial humanoid forms, barbed genitalia dangling like gasoline hoses. Her grandparents burst through the front door, fighting something that resembled a spider. Vivian and Tabitha ran to help them, only to lock eyes as the spider thing skewered them both through the chest with its spindly limbs and bounced away on wings that erupted out of its back like a burst pustule.

Tabitha held Vivian for a moment on the sidewalk, watching in terror as the winged beasts went after the spider thing. Her grandparents were torn apart in seconds, innards rained down and all manner of things with wings in varying sizes came to get what they could. They ran inside and then quickly back out with the keys to grandpa's Cutlass.

Now they sat in the momentary silence, certain it

would be their last moment of such, before they too suffered a violent death in the maw of some nightmare creature.

Finally, Tabitha spoke, "How much gas do we have?"

"Less than a quarter tank," Vivian said.

"Should we try to make it to the farm, or just sit here?"

Vivian didn't want to move. She didn't want to talk or to hear anything. She just wanted to go back to the unmoving silence. To exist in that moment with her lover, because she feared, the next moment of peace would be at the end of their, undoubtedly painful, end.

"I guess," Vivian said, putting the car back into drive, slowly moving back onto the road.

"Don't go too fast," Tabitha said, "maybe it came after us before 'cause we were going too fast?"

Vivian didn't reply. She thought that was nonsense. Tabitha was just fooling herself and trying to rationalize the irrational. Whether they were moving fast or slow the winged creatures would spot them and attack them again. Vivian considered what would go first? The windshield? Or maybe the roof? A flat tire? Or would they simply run out of gas? Despite her unpleasant thoughts, and to her surprise, she drove—without further incident—to the farm.

Headden's Farm was little more than a roadside market. Depending on the season, they had apples, corn, tomatoes, blueberries, pumpkins, honey and the like. They didn't have much in the way of livestock, just a few animals, barely enough to string together a petting zoo. Come Halloween they had a corn maze and a small pumpkin patch that did pretty well. The reason Tabitha thought of going to the farm, was the big red barn. If it was strong enough to keep animals in, she figured, then it had to be strong enough to keep some of the monsters out.

The field before them rose and fell. Between them and the barn was a field of corn and steep terrain.

"I don't think the car can make it to the barn," Vivian said.

"Shouldn't we try? You don't want to walk there, do you?" Tabitha asked.

"No, I don't want to walk there, but what if we need to get out of here and we end up getting the car stuck? Then we're royally screwed."

"You got a point there."

"So we'll walk?"

"I don't see any other way to get there. Should we keep the keys in the car?"

"Probably. I don't see anybody who might want to steal it."

"I wish we'd see somebody," Tabitha said, realizing the last person she saw was being carried over the fiery gash in the road by some kind of devil dinosaur.

Vivian left the keys in the ignition and stepped out of the car. Tabitha joined her, holding hands as they walked away from the car into the downgrade before the cornfield. They stopped just before the rows, Vivian turned to her lover, squeezing her hand tightly.

"You know I love you, right?"

Tabitha had always been the one to express her love and adoration freely. Though she knew Vivian felt the same way, she was guarded in how she expressed it. She rarely said the "L" word, avoiding it the way some parents avoided cursing around their kids. As if it would change them somehow.

"You don't say it much, but I know," she said, her voice barely louder than the wind.

Vivian stepped to her, caressing her cheek before she kissed her, "I just want you to know. To really know. It scares me how much I love you. We haven't been together long enough to justify it. In my mind at least."

"You make it sound like love takes time, but I knew right away."

Something not of this world screeched from above. The land thudded all around them.

"Run," Vivian said, squeezing her hand.

They ran as fast as they could, stalks of corn crunching underfoot and slapping them in the face. Then they slowed, keeping low and looking through the stalks in all directions.

"I don't see anything," Tabitha said.

"No," Vivian said, turning, "but I hear the corn moving—"

"And the ground, something big is coming. Go, go, go!"

They took off in a wild sprint in the direction of the barn as something chased after them in the cornfield. They followed the rows out to a clearing. A small dirt path between the tight fields. A shadow flew overhead, faster and larger than any bird either had seen.

"This must be what it's like to be a field mouse," Tabitha said.

"Must be," Vivian agreed, pulling Tabitha by the wrist and beating feet once again.

Something tumbled out of the cornfield behind them. They turned to see one of the winged creatures. It was the clearest view either had seen of them so far. Its head boasted curved horns; a thin muscular body pulsed like burning embers. It's hands and feet looked like prehistoric claws. There were no eyes either could see, only a long beak with way too many teeth. They didn't have to tell each other to run, the second it screeched at them they sprinted with all they had to the barn. They could smell it behind them. The smell of burnt meat and sewage in the summer heat.

Before the barn was stacks of hay bales and prominently sticking out of one was a pitchfork. Vivian hurdled over the hay and pulled out the pitchfork, turning to face the beast that was practically on top of them.

Tabitha, feeling the heat from the creature behind her, dove across the bales into a clumsy roll and slamming her back against the barn. If the creature saw the pitchfork it was unimpressed and undeterred. Vivian held out her weapon and charged forward, meeting the creature mid-step over the bails. She drove the pitchfork into the center of its burning ember chest causing purple blood to spurt out. The blood burned her on impact; it felt like hot oil from a stovetop splashing onto her arms. The creature swatted her away, easily knocking her several feet away, and slashing her in the process.

Tabitha ran to her as Vivian tried to push herself up, winded and dazed from the blow. Tabitha hoisted her up, throwing an arm over her should and walking her to the big double doors of the barn. The creature fell to its knees, trying awkwardly to pull the pitchfork from its chest. Vivian stood on her own, putting a hand to her bleeding side as Tabitha pulled the door to the barn open. Once inside the two lovers closed the heavy doors and locked it.

"I'm not impressed with that lock," said Vivian.

"I was hoping for something different myself, but after giving it a moment to think, why would it have a lock on the inside anyway? I always thought barns had the wood braces like you see in the movies. You know?"

Vivian shook her head, "Hopefully out of sight is out of mind for those things."

"You're bleeding," Tabitha said, lifting up her torn shirt to reveal a large gash just below her ribcage. "Oh, man, that looks painful and it's bleeding a lot."

"I hadn't noticed," Vivian said, with only a faint trace of a smile. "But maybe we should make sure we're alone in here before we worry about my boo-boo."

Tabitha nodded. She was so focused on getting inside the barn and away from those things that she hadn't thought of what could be lying in wait for them. Hand in hand they walked along the dirt floor. Most of it looked to be space dedicated to carpentry work and vehicle storage. Content they were alone, they sat at a workbench where a set of shutters had been left in mid construction. Vivian found a small work light and switched it on.

"Maybe that's not such a good idea?" Tabitha asked.

"There're no windows. I don't think it matters."

"Okay. Well, let's see if there's anything we can do about that wound."

The barn didn't have any needles and thread to attempt stitching it up so Tabitha cut off the torn section of Vivian's shirt, leaving her with just enough shirt to cover her breasts. She then cut the shirt into a few sections big enough to cover the wound. With Vivian lying on her side Tabitha duct taped the sections of her shirt snugly to her body. She then had her stand up and she wrapped a few lengths of tape around her completely.

"There, that should hold you together for a while."

"Looks great," Vivian said, patting the duct tape across her abdomen. "Now what?"

"I hadn't thought that far ahead," she admitted.

As it turned out, neither had Vivian. They sat for a while, listening to the screeching creatures outside. One or two took perch on the roof of the barn, and something shook the ground the way wild horses might if they were racing around.

"Let's just see if we can wait here till the morning," Vivian said, having no better idea.

Tabitha nodded, looking at her duct tape medical marvel and wondering if they shouldn't try to find some help sooner. She didn't object, as she didn't think they were likely to find any help anyway. After some time, they made a bed of hay near the light, holding each other while talking about anything other than what they might do come morning. Eventually they found a few hours of sleep.

"Rise and shine," said Vivian, nudging her lover

awake.

"I had the craziest dream," Tabitha said, then she looked around the barn before continuing, "Well, I guess it wasn't a dream after all."

"Coffee's on," Vivian said, looking pale.

"I wish," Tabitha said, sitting up, pulling random bits of hay from her hair.

"We can't stay here," Vivian said, "I'm bleeding again."

"Then let's go," Tabitha said.

At the worktable they found some hammers and a few utility knives, which they pocketed. Tabitha found a shovel hanging from a nearby wall, which she grabbed, sticking the hammer through her belt loop.

"Let's just take it one step at a time," Vivian said, "if we can make it to the car we'll figure out what to do next."

"Whatever's out there doesn't matter. As long as you're by my side I don't care."

"We can do this. We can do this together," Vivian said, as she opened the door, took her lover's hand, and prepared to face whatever hell awaited them together.

Lonely Bones
Joe Palumbo

Randolph Corry had skeletons in his basement, seven to be exact. This was not unusual considering the nature of his business. Randolph Corry owned the small, but successful, medical supply warehouse, Med-House and distributed all varieties of medical equipment to clinics, hospitals, and universities in and around the town of Black Hollow, Oklahoma. Even the fact that these were human skeletons was not strange. Until recently, it was common for medical schools, and even art classes, to have a human skeleton suspended from a metal stand in the corner. However, as time passed real skeletons were replaced with plaster or even plastic replicas. This left no home for the displaced skeletons and many of them were placed in permanent storage, much like Randolph's seven skeletons. So, despite how it may sound, having these seven humans stripped of their flesh and suspended on metal racks with wheels was not strange at all. That is until one of them decided to speak to Harpo Mott.

"Hey you," a woman's voice said from the dark. "What's your name?"

Harpo had been digging through crates and boxes in a search for a case of the large bulbs, that were used in the suspended lights in the warehouse above him, that he was certain were stored in the basement. Being preoccupied with his own thoughts, he did not hear the soft voice at first. He used his considerable strength to move a wooden crate filled with beakers and set it gently to the side. Puffs of dust drifted and swirled through the circle of light cast by the one naked bulb above him making him wish he had brought a flashlight. It was almost too dark to see in some corners of the basement, and it could be pretty spooky down there in the dark. He had never been able to remember everything though and continued to search in the dark.

"You're not ignoring me, are you?" The voice asked with a playful tone.

"Huh," Harpo turned and scratched at his thick beard.

"What's your name?" Asked the voice.

The voice was soft and sweet. It was a woman's voice but it didn't sound like the many young women that Harpo had seen running around the lakes in their swimsuits with their boyfriends that wear those visors. The same women that later would be getting felt up in the back of Jeeps and trucks. This voice sounded matured, not really in age but in attitude. Harpo couldn't describe the voice any better than that.

He pulled his battered ballcap off by the frayed bill and said, "Who's there?"

"I'm Elizabeth, the voice from the shadows said. "What's your name? It's only fair that you tell me your name, now that you know mine."

Harpo stepped from his own dark corner and squinted

to make out the source of the voice across the room. Could David had been playing one of his practical jokes? Harpo was an easy target, and it wouldn't have been the first time.

"I'm Harpo. Harpo Mott. Where are you?"

"I'm over here, to your right, behind these big crates."

"Well, why don't you come out? I won't hurt you."

"Oh, I know you won't, Harpo," she said with a voice that sounded like morning birds. "I've heard you talking to people and you are a very sweet man. However, I am a little stuck. I'm what you could call disabled, I suppose. I can't really move under my own power."

"Like in a wheelchair or something?" he asked.

"Something like that," she replied.

"Then how did you get down here?"

"That's a very good question. I hear Randolph call you an idiot, but I know that is not true. That question could tell anyone that."

"Hear? How?"

"This is an old building," she explained, "and his voice travels very well."

"So," he urged.

"So what?" There was genuine confusion in her voice. She then said, "Oh, yes. That really wasn't an answer to your question. I was put down here a long time ago." There was silence; when she spoke again there was a quiet sadness to her voice. "I guess I was no longer needed or wanted."

It was then he noticed a sound that was just under the surface of her words. It was a low ticking noise, like the sound of hollow sticks tapping together.

"Well everyone is needed," he said. "That's what my dad always said."

"Said? Why are you using the past tense?" Her voice had taken on a soft tone.

"He died. My mom did too. It's been," he looked up

and did some math, "shit, ten years now. Car accident." He then realized he swore and looked down at his shoes. "Pardon my French."

"I don't have virgin years or a virgin voice. So. How about helping me out of this corner?"

Harpo shifted nervously from foot to foot filled with indecision. It was true that Randolph had called him an idiot and a moron several times during his employ as the warehouse's janitor and maintenance man. He didn't need Elizabeth to tell him that he was not an idiot. He lived by himself in the house he inherited, owned his own car, even though he did not like to drive, and took care of his own life with no help. Yes, it was true that he was not as fast as others, and that he could be easily tricked, but he was not disabled either. He once heard David tell Randolph that he was only a single card short of a deck, instead of the actual saying of a few cards short. He still knew enough to question situations that seemed strange, like this one.

"I don't know," he said.

"Why?" Elizabeth asked

"Because this is all too weird, and I don't want to be tricked. If this a trick."

"I promise you this is not a trick."

"Why don't I get Mr. Corry," he said turning to leave.

"I don't want his help. He wouldn't even give me any help if I wanted it. I hear how he treats you and others. Besides, who do you think put me down here in the first place?"

"He did I guess," Harpo admitted. "He decides what goes where. I just clean, fix things, or whatever else he needs to be done."

During his five years of working for Randolph Corry, he had seen him do and say much more mean things than nice things. He nodded his head in a final decision and placed his cap back on.

"Okay," he said in a firm tone. "I'll help you out of

there."

"Oh, thank you, Harpo. You are indeed the sweet man I believed you to be."

A broad smile illuminated his face. He did love to help, and the excitement in Elizabeth's voice made this time even more pleasurable. He grabbed the first of the large crates and as he dragged it out of the corner, his muscles flexed and stretched the fabric of his blue work shirt and he worked. The weight and the size of the crates made him wonder what could be possibly stored in them.

Could they be holding coffins?

The thought made him shiver a little despite the sweat running down his back and arms. He pulled the last crate away with a groan and stepped back waiting for Elizabeth to emerge from the darkness and thank him. Maybe she would hug him; maybe she was pretty, she sure sounded pretty.

"Give me your hand please, and pull. Please be easy though."

He had another fleeting moment of doubt and even a touch of fear. The one bulb above them was dim and he would be sticking his hand in complete darkness. He took a deep breath and shot his hand in the shadow.

"Grab my hand if you can," he said.

"Okay," she said. "Now I don't want you to be startled when you see me. I don't look as nice as I once did."

He then felt her fingers wrap around his hand, and they were cold and thin. She must have been wearing a glove, or maybe some sort of brace because her fingers felt hard. He pulled on the hand, taking great care to be gentle. As he pulled, he could hear a faint squeaking. It was not the sound of a mouse or any animal for that matter. The sound was more like the wheels on his supply cart that he could never remember to oil.

"Thank you for this."

He pulled her fully into the light and what he saw filled

him with a paralyzing fear. Hanging from a metal rack, attached to a base with four rusted wheels, was a skeleton. The light gleamed off the bleached bones with a dull shine. Thick cobwebs clung to the skull and dangled from the jaw. A furry black spider crawled from under the jaw and then scurried into the left eye socket. A tangle of spiderwebs weaved throughout the ribcage, complete with the long-abandoned killing fields of spider's before.

His entire body shook with a terror that he had never felt in his forty years on the Earth. Cold sweat ran down his forehead and back in long streams producing a shine on his skin. His brain desperately tried to command his body to turn and run, but fear has an amazing ability to scramble communications between body and mind. The only part of his body he still had any control over was his eyes. He looked down and saw to his horror that he was still clutching the skeleton's hand. He pulled away with a violent jerk, stumbled back, tripped over his own feet, and fell hard on his backside.

The force of him pulling his hand out of the skeleton's grip caused it to swing back and forth on the metal cable attached to the top of the skull by an eyebolt that creaked as shadows danced over the skeleton. The skeleton raised its hands to its forever smile and started to laugh. Her laughter was sweet and light with a musical cadence and was in vivid contrast to the waking nightmare hanging from the rack.

"Oh, ho-ho. I am sorry for laughing at you," Elizabeth said. "I did tell you I don't look as good as I once did." She then placed her hands on her hips and said, "But, I am slimmer than I ever have been."

Watching the jaws work as she spoke, he realized with some disgust, that it was the teeth tapping together to create the odd noise he noticed earlier. He spun on the ground and got on all fours before getting to his feet. He slid on the layer of dust coating the floor and almost fell again when he tried to run for the stairs. He caught himself on the handrail but stopped with one foot on the lowest step when he heard that sweet voice again.

"Wait, please don't go. I've been down here for a very long time, and I'm so lonely. Don't you know how it feels to be lonely?"

He did know what it was like to be lonely. Harpo lived alone, he had no girlfriend, and the only person who he could even think of as a friend of any kind was David, but he was not a real friend. It was true that he helped Harpo when he needed it and never said or did anything mean. Even the jokes David played on him never contained any malice. He knew that even if he didn't like them very much. He turned and when he looked at the skeleton, he no longer saw anything scary. He saw a woman that was lonely like him, sure she didn't have any flesh or organs, but he could see someone who needed a friend.

"Yeah," he said stepping closer, "I do know what it is like to be lonely. There is a lot of people in this town, and I'm still alone."

"So, you know why I don't want you to leave," she replied.

Harpo frowned as he thought. He then felt a great pity for this woman, and following the pity, guilt snaked its way into his heart when he thought about how he reacted when he first saw her. No one could blame him for being scared though. How often do you encounter a talking medical skeleton? That was something that just didn't happen outside of a Boris Karloff movie or the pages of a horror comic.

He then brightened and announced, "I should get someone. Maybe David or—"

"No," she said sharply holding her hands out, "don't do that, Harpo."

"But why?"

"Because no one would believe you. They would think

you were crazy and try to lock you away like me. Even if you could get someone to believe you and took them to me, they would want to take me to some lab somewhere and try to find out how I am even able to talk and move. I would rather be with one real friend than to be surrounded by dozens of people who only want to study me."

"Hey Harp," a voice came from the top of the stairs.

He spun around and saw David Powell coming down the steps. He turned back and saw Elizabeth had gone limp. Her arms dangled by her sides and she swayed slightly in the breeze caused by the air conditioning.

"I'm here," he answered.

"What the hell are you doing down here?"

"I was just, well..." He looked back at the skeleton and couldn't think of anything to say.

David came down and looked around the basement. David was a thin man but rivaled Harpo in height. He had hair that was pulled back into a long braid and was as flat and black as a still pond at midnight. The light shined off the top of his head with a blue glow.

"Gross," David said when he noticed the skeleton. "Man, I tell you, those things creep me out. Corry should just get rid of them."

"Is he going to?"

"Probably not, unless he can make a quick buck off of them. Hell, he's probably forgotten about them by now."

"Yeah," he agreed.

David walked up to the skeleton and with a single finger, he tapped the skull on its forehead. The spider ran from its hiding spot in the eye socket and disappeared around the back of the jaw. He then kicked the bottom of the rack with his work boot sending the skeleton rolling back. It came to a rest just outside of the circle of light. Harpo could still make out the basic shape of her by the dim diffusion of light.

David headed towards the stairs. As he passed Harpo,

he placed an arm around his shoulders and said, "Come on man. Corry will have a shit if he finds you screwing around down here."

"I wasn't, I was just..." his voice faded as they headed up the stairs together.

He had lost his train of thought when he looked over his shoulder at Elizabeth. He could see her bring a single finger up to where her lips would be in a gesture that reminded him of his mother.

Shhhh.

The hand then extended into the light, and the fingers wiggled in a playful goodbye gesture that also reminded him of his mother. He was able to stifle the laugh that swelled inside of him, but he had less luck with the grin and touched his lips. He still wore the grin when they emerged on the ground floor, but it soon faded when he saw Randolph waiting for them.

"Just what in the almighty fuck were you two doing down there?" Randolph bellowed the question at them.

"I was looking for lightbulbs, Mr. Corry," Harpo said looking down at the planks in the floor.

Could Elizabeth be listening right now just under their feet? He thought that was likely. He kicked a small pile of dirt down between the floor planks.

"Why were you looking for them down there?" Randolph's round face was contorted with barely controlled rage. His lip quivered upwards, exposing the gap in his teeth where a right incisor would be.

"We keep them in the supply closet, Harpo," David said.

"He knows that," Randolph said directing his anger at David now. "Jesus weeping on his cross, I have told him that I don't know how many times. If you weren't such a damn retard."

"Why don't you just cool it, Randolph," David yelled and stepped in front of Harpo.

Harpo and Randolph both looked up shocked. Randolph's shock coming from the disbelief that anyone, especially an employee, would speak back to him in such a way, and Harpo's from the disbelief that someone, especially David, would stick up for him. He had never done that before.

"He may not be the fastest gun in the west," David continued, "and yes, he is forgetful, but that doesn't mean you can treat him like this."

"I should fire both of you dumbasses," Randolph growled.

"But you won't," countered David, "Because there is no one else who would do the same work he does and put up with your horse shit. You won't fire me, because you know I won't give a shit, so there will be no satisfaction in it for you."

"I should get those bulbs," Harpo said quietly.

"No, you won't," David said checking his watch. "It's quitting time. Let's go."

Outside David stood by his car and fished in his lunchbox for his car keys when he heard Harpo say from across the small parking lot, "David, can I ask you something?"

He leaned on the hood of the car and watched him come down the metal steps from the service entrance, then asked, "What is it?"

"Why did you do that?"

"Do what?"

"Stick up for me."

David tapped the hood of his car, looked up at the summer sky, and said, "Because everyone gets punched in the nose by life on occasion." He looked back down and dragged a finger around in the dust on his car. "I've known Randolph for a long time, and I can tell you, that man," he pointed towards the squat brick building behind Harpo, "has managed to avoid those punches or not feel them. That could be why he is the way he is. Hell, even when his wife walked out on him, he didn't really care. So, I decided to give him a verbal bitch slap. Maybe he would feel that." He then opened his car door.

"Are we friends?" Harpo asked.

David thought for a moment, then climbed in the car; the car started and when all four windows rolled down, he heard David's voice through the passenger window say, "Sure we are."

"Do you want to do something," he asked through the window.

"Can't tonight," David said, "it's a girl thing if you know what I mean?"

David shot him a sly wink before Harpo backed from the car and watched him drive off. He then unchained his bicycle from the cyclone fencing that flanked the parking lot and peddled home.

Harpo began spending all of his breaks and lunches in the basement of the warehouse. He would wait until David was gone or distracted with his own business before sneaking through the door and down the steps. He discovered it was extremely easy to keep his visits secret from Randolph. Since the confrontation with David, Randolph had spent his days secluded in his office. The only time David or Harpo had seen him was when he was needed to sign for a delivery, or when he decided to bark an order at one or both of them. Later in the week, Harpo told Elizabeth how David had defended him while he sat on the floor and ate his sandwich.

"Well, David has always sounded like a good man," she said.

He swallowed the last of his sandwich and washed the remains down with a swig of Dr. Pepper. He then removed a twin pack of Twinkies from his lunch box. He stopped and stared at them with a sudden sadness.

"What's the matter?" Elizabeth asked. "Don't you like

those?"

"They're my favorite."

"Then why do you look so sad?"

He looked up at the skeleton. He stared into the vacant sockets that stared back at him, then looked back at the snack cakes. He wanted nothing more than to share them with her.

"I've eaten a lot of lunches here and never thought about how you might feel about it."

"I love having you down here and talking to me," she said happily.

"I mean that you can't eat with me," he said with shame.

"Oh," she said with laughter, "I have not eaten in so long that I don't even miss it."

"Don't you get hungry?"

"No stomach to make me hungry," she said and gestured where a stomach would be.

He nodded and ate the cakes slowly. They were sweet, but the want he felt to do something nice for her, but unable to think of anything, left a bitter taste in his mouth.

The next morning, he could not help but arrive at work early. Randolph had not even arrived and this pleased him. He was too excited and did not think he could wait until his lunch break to see Elizabeth. He had finally thought of something he could do for her; a gift he could give her. She had always said that simply him spending time with her was enough but he wanted to do more. His mother had always told him that one of the greatest feelings in the world is the one a person gets when they do something nice for someone, and the feeling is even greater when it is someone you care about.

He flicked the switch by the door and the single bulb came to life. Harpo came down the steps and quickly crossed the room. He then pulled Elizabeth by the hand and rolled her to the center of the light.

"What's going on, Harpo? Why are you so early?"

He removed the bag from his shoulder and let it fall to the ground before saying, "I have a gift for you. I thought of it last night."

He knelt down and unzipped the bag. He then stood back up and he had a large horsehair paintbrush in his right hand, and a black rag in his left hand. Before she could say anything, he used the brush to sweep away the dust and webs from her bones. He started at the top of her skull and did not stop until he finished at the tips of her toes. As he worked, she laughed and held her hands up as if being tickled. He then used the rag to clean out each of the sockets, disturbing the black spider that skittered. Harpo flicked it off with the corner of the rag. They both began to laugh as he used the rag like a toothbrush and started cleaning her teeth. Then from behind a voice came—ending the laughter they both shared.

"What the fuck is going on here?"

Harpo turned around and, to his complete horror, he saw Randolph Corry standing at the edge of the light. He turned and looked at Elizabeth who had gone limp. He then spun back around still holding the brush and rag.

"Mr. Corry, I—"

"What sick shit have you been doing down here?" His voice maintained a composure that was unsettling.

"I wasn't doing anything."

"Really? So, you've been doing nothing down here all week? Did you think I didn't know you were going down here? I just didn't care."

"I..." His voice trailed off when he couldn't think of anything else to say.

"Do you have any idea in that small brain of yours what I am going to do to you? Firing you will only be the start, but first I'm going to get rid of that fucking thing," he pointed over Harpo's shoulder at the skeleton, "then I'm going to—"

"You are going to do nothing!"

Harpo spun around and looked at Elizabeth who had her hands on her hip bones. Harpo backed away and looked over at Randolph who was frozen to the ground by fear much like the fear Harpo experienced the first time he saw her.

Randolph swallowed and his throat made an audible click before he said in a rough whisper, "Elizabeth."

"That's right, Randy," she said sharply.

"But how?"

"Does it really matter?"

"I don't understand," Randolph shook his head as if frantically refusing what he was seeing.

"It really is simple. You killed me when you found out I was leaving, and to add insult to injury, you hung me up here like an old coat and pushed me in the corner. Why? Were you trying to hide me in plain sight? No, I don't think so. That would require a level of intelligence that you always lacked. I think it was some sort of sick gloating."

Randolph shook his head again and turned on his heels. He moved, as fast as his bulk would allow, towards the stares.

"Harpo!" Elizabeth yelled. "He's going to get rid of me again!"

Harpo did not think, he simply moved. With three large steps, he made it to the base of the stairs and had Randolph by the back of his collar. He spun around with Randolph and shoved him away from the stairs. He stumbled through the circle of light like a drunk actor who was late for his cue on stage and was stopped by Elizabeth's boney hands around his thick neck.

Randolph gagged and gasped as her finger sank deep in his thick flesh closing off his airway. Harpo stood stunned. He had no idea she possessed any strength, let alone the amount to strangle a grown man. He stepped closer and Elizabeth looked over Randolph's head at him.

"He killed me, Harpo, and then he was going to destroy me. He was going to grind me up and toss me in a lake. He will kill you too." She then looked down at Randolph's face, that was now turning blue, and said, "You are not going to hurt another soul, and you will never hurt Harpo again. He is a good man, hell, he is a man. That is more than I can say for you." She then looked up at Harpo again and said, "Would you be a dear and unhook the bolt."

He was not scared for his own safety, but for what he may see if he complied with her request. Her words clanged around in his mind and he knew she was right about everything. She was always right. What fear was on his face quickly melted away and was replaced with a cold determination. He walked up behind Randolph and, with one large hand, pulled the pin holding the cable to the top of the rack.

He expected her to fall in a pile of loose bones, but she landed on her feet. Randolph reached up and tried to pull the finger bones from the flesh around his neck but couldn't. She looked down at him and the light gleamed off of her freshly cleaned skull. She then walked backward, dragging the helpless Randolph into the darkness.

When Harpo was a boy, he loved helping his father cook. One of the meals that Harpo always enjoyed helping prepare, not to mention eating, was barbecued chicken. His father would buy a whole chicken before cutting it into its individual parts. One summer, while preparing the raw bird, his father had twisted the chicken's leg before ripping it from its body. The sound it made caused Harpo to wince and look away. Mixed in with Randolph's strangled screams, was that same tearing sound. Like when he was a child, Harpo winced again.

"Harpo," her voice came soft and sweet.

He turned and standing in the light was Elizabeth in the flesh. She stood naked and smiling at him, her hands and bare feet were stained with bright blood. She raised her hands and pushed her long black hair back from her face, revealing the most beautiful green eyes he had ever seen.

"Elizabeth?"

"Yes," she said smiling, "are we still friends?"

He nodded.

"Good," she said, "I hope we can be more than friends too."

David arrived for work and rolled his eyes at seeing Randolph's mustang. "Why the fuck is he early?"

David entered the darkened warehouse through the service entrance. Behind him, the door slammed shut making him jump. He shook his head and wished the small warehouse had more than just him and Harpo. The old building gave him the creeps from time to time, especially when the lights were out. He stopped at the time clock, mounted near the door to the basement when he saw Randolph's office door swing open, and to his shock he saw Harpo and Randolph walk out together, and they were talking. David's mouth dropped open as Randolph laughed and patted Harpo on the back. They both noticed the dumbstruck David.

"David," Randolph said, "I'm shutting down for the day. You can go home. Take an early weekend, and I will see you on Monday."

David could only nod and watch as the two men walked away and headed towards the service door. When they exited, David entered Randolph's office and peered out of the window down to where Randolph's Mustang was parked. Nearby, Harpo had chained his bike to the fence and David watched him unlock it from the fence before loading it the best he can in the trunk. Harpo then climbed in the passenger side and the car pulled from its spot in the lot. As he turned, David became confused because through the windshield, he thought he saw a woman with long black hair driving, and not Randolph Corry .

He stepped out of the office and gently stroked the stubble on his chin while looking at the floor in deep thought. He noticed a small piece of gravel on the ground, most likely a hitchhiker from the treads of someone's boot. He kicked the small rock and watched it roll and bounce across the wooden floor before falling through a gap.

Below David, the stone came through the ceiling. It fell and tumbled through the dark and dusty air. It made a hollow tock noise as it bounced off of one of the seven medical skeletons that were suspended from their metal racks; the one missing the right incisor tooth.

One Particular Night on Highway 365

Jeremy Billingsley

Listless like he's stuck in a fog, perhaps because it feels like years since he was home and perhaps it's because he's been driving so long that the terrain always appears the same, Dillon steers his car onto Arkansas State Highway 365. Above him the pines sway, illuminated by the gibbous moon as wisps of clouds drift slowly across the firmament. He wipes condensation off the windshield and his palm comes back frigid and wet, and from the dash the vents cough out the heat asthmatically, but this is nothing new.

***

And then he sees her. And the fog lifts.

***

Dillon's headlights illuminated her back as he crested a hill. Her head down, her thin sundress blew in the wind though her arms were pinned to her sides to try and control it. He braked, a loud squeak indicating disuse and he couldn't recall the last time his car had rested; she spun in the light, raising a hand to shield her eyes.

Stepping out of the car Dillon did his best to smile. "Can I offer you a lift?"

She wasn't dressed for the night. Her auburn hair whipped in the wind. She was pale but a pretty kind of pale, like she was studious or a homebody. She looked at him with a raised eyebrow and a focused gaze practiced out of distrust of strange men picking her up on the highway. "I'm fine. I don't have much further."

"Okay. But it's no trouble."

She glanced around again, still hugging her waist. Gooseflesh on her purple-pale arms, her deep-sunk eyes darted around as she hugged herself. Finally, she walked to the car.

The windows fogged then thawed, the outside cold battling the vented heat. She felt the leather, her seat preternaturally cold, the chaffs of rough leather picking at the back of her thighs. She adjusted herself and squeaked, made sure to press herself against the door and hoping that the door would hold. He looked at her a few times and smiled. She returned the look timidly.

"So how far are you?" he asked.

"About twenty miles." She stared out the window, biting her nails. The land was relatively flat with only minor curves and hills to break the monotony of the drive. The full moon and star-filled firmament did little to penetrate the thick shadows of the pine forest. She turned and offered him a small grin while her eyes remained downcast, blushing. "I guess a little too far to walk."

"I'm Dillon."

"Ashley. Nice car, what is it?"

" '70 'Cuda—my pride."

"Why are you out so late?"

"Going home too," he said. "Feels like forever since I've been home."

"You don't look old enough for it to have been forever," she said.

"And you?"

"My car broke down a ways back so I'm hoofing it."

He frowned but kept his eyes forward. He recalled no car a ways back anywhere, on either side of the road. But he had been driving for so long. He was tired and cold. He might have missed some things.

She shivered. Dillon turned up the heat. He reached for her hands but she jerked away.

"Nice night," he said, returning both hands to the wheel.

"Mmmh. Cold."

She was pretty but quiet. He'd hoped in picking her up that she'd provide a bit of company. The few words he'd said felt raspy; his whole voice felt dry and unused. He coughed to shake out the cobwebs before asking her how far.

"It's ten miles passed the diner." She still focused out the window.

"I haven't seen a diner," he said.

The car topped a steep hill, rounded a bend to a flattened stretch of road, where a diner sat a quarter of a mile away on the right. "Oh," he said.

"You want to pull in? I could buy you a drink or something, repay your kindness."

Dillon parked next to the only other vehicle, a semi-truck with no trailer attached. He shut the car off and looked down to the keys in his hand. It felt wrong. The keys should be in the ignition and he should be driving. Her door creaked open as though that were an unnatural position. He felt her eyes on him and her hand on his shoulder. He looked up to find her halfway in the car, leaning in with one knee on the leather seat. She smiled at him, but he saw also a look of concern on her face. Like maybe she thought he was going to leave her here.

"You okay?"

He nodded and fondled the keys.

"You looked like…"

"Like I was lost?"

"No," she shook her head. "Like you weren't where you were supposed to be."

He climbed out of the car and jammed the keys into jeans pocket. The wind forced a wish that he had something with a little more insulation than the lining-less shell of his black leather jacket.

The door opened to an explosion of glass. Behind the bar an overweight, balding man yelled. A young girl with stringy blonde hair—her nametag read MARIE—stood over a tray of dishes. She stared at Dillon. At the bar sat the trucker. All Dillon could see of him was the back of a jean jacket and a scraggily mess of brownish gray hair ruffling out between the collar and his black trucker's cap. His arm raised and lowered a coffee cup to his obscured face. He never turned around.

The lighting was sparse, the darkly trimmed room all the darker. The air reeked of cigarettes and stale beer. Dillon led Ashley to a corner booth and ordered a couple of sodas. The waitress stammered a yes and walked away even as the bartender asked what she was doing.

"Filling our customers' orders," she said.

The bartender looked at the trucker, then to where the waitress stood, then to them. He blinked at them for a moment, said nothing, and waited to holler at her until she had rounded the corner of the bar, something Dillon couldn't hear. He leaned over to Ashley.

"Well this is an interesting place," he whispered.

"To say the least," she whispered back. She giggled

and that brought out a smile in him. "I can't believe this place was reopened," she said.

"What do you mean?" he asked. He leaned in, elbows on the table, eager to engage in gossip and eager more to get her to speak. He was fascinated by her.

She sipped her drink and looked at the table and shook her head. "No, no." Conspiratorially she leaned in and flashed her green eyes and smiled and whispered, "I'll tell you when we leave."

He sipped at his soda until it was brown ice and his straw made slurping sounds and he smiled and was delighted to see her gaze warm and her smile seemed genuine. Whatever fear she exhibited toward him now seemed to dissipate.

"Now I've got this," she said.

"I'm a quick-draw with my wallet," he said, grinning.

"You such a chauvinist you can't let a girl pick up a bill?"

"You use a lot of big words."

"For a girl?"

"For anyone."

The waitress walked up to their booth and laid the bill face down. She offered them a smile but still seemed shifty. Over her shoulder, the bartender shot their booth the stink eye.

"What if we want another soda?" Dillon asked.

"Or what if we want something to eat?" Ashley asked.

"Just, we're about to close," the waitress said. "It's on me."

Dillon turned the bill over and saw no charge, as in his periphery the bartender began yelling at the waitress and pointing to them. They climbed back in the car and headed on down Highway 365.

"The diner did close once," Ashley said. "They say once it was run by an old man and his very young wife. He thought she was cheating on him. He beat her often.

Most said he was jealous, but as it turns out he was right, though he himself never saw the proof. Her boyfriend, a long-range trucker she only saw twice a year, came calling."

"What happened?"

"He drove his truck through the diner when he heard that the girl had gone missing. Everyone knew the old codger had killed her and stashed the body, but no one could prove it. So the trucker sought justice his own way. The impact killed them both."

"You're suggesting we just visited a haunted diner and saw three ghosts!" he said.

She laughed, a wild raucous thing where she tossed her hair around, and it wasn't till she caught sight of the terrain outside that she settled herself and spoke. "Right, here please."

Dillon did not see a street or a house; he slowed then stopped the car on the shoulder. Through the darkness her hand crept and found his. "Do you believe in ghosts?" she asked.

"I don't know."

"I have a dream all the time that I'm searching for my family and can't ever find them."

"I never saw nothing that suggested we go on."

"So you think this is it? That once we die, we just cease to exist? That all we experienced, all we saw, is just gone."

He could remember spending his life working on cars and teaching himself the guitar. He'd led a perfectly mediocre life, so that all he could see was him driving the Barracuda once it was ready and playing a few songs—Don McClean and the Animals and even some Jim Croce. Talk of the afterlife was reserved for church and ghosts were saved for Halloween.

"I guess not," he said finally but not convinced.

"I mean, if that's what you believe, that's fine, I

suppose. It just seems sad and depressing to me, a bit fatalistic, and could lead to a cynical world view. No accountability, if this is all there is."

"I suppose you think we get our just desserts when we die. Good people go to heaven and bad folks go to hell."

"It makes more sense to me," she said after a moment of introspection to consider his position.

Dillon just shook his head. "No ma'am, not me. Too much coincidence. But that seems to be the only two choices, doesn't it? Either we die and are judged or we die and nothing."

"You have a third option?"

"What if we die and just keep doing what we're doing, what we know and what we're used to and what we love."

"There'd be an awful lot of ghosts roaming around," she acquiesced. "They'd probably run into each other."

"Not necessarily," he said, really studying his position. "You don't do what I do, so if I'm just doing what I do when I die, then I wouldn't necessarily meet you. Maybe grandma likes watching her shows on the tube. Maybe the old teacher likes to read books in the library. Maybe the housewife from England in the Middle Ages likes to churn butter. If they're all just going on, experiencing their reality, there's no guarantee they'll run into any other soul."

"I like it," she said, matter-of-factly. "We all just go on, doing what we're doing."

"What do you want for?"

She looked longingly up the hill. "To finally make it home. You?"

He gripped the steering wheel and stared at the speedometer, and thought about how much he liked driving it, but said, "Me too," like he were admitting a deep, dark secret.

He put the car in park, but left it running. "I don't see anything nearby."

"I'll be okay. It really isn't far now." And then, almost to herself, "I really miss them."

"You want my jacket?"

"If you want. I'm just over the hill. Give me your address and I'll send it back to you."

"I'd like to see you again," he said. Corny, he hung his head and shut his eyes and laughed at himself. "What I mean is…" he looked up. His passenger seat was empty.

The car door never opened—he never heard it. He looked around for her. He got out. She must have left the car. Walking into the headlights, he searched the darkness, searched for a sign, a rustling of underbrush, the sound of footsteps, laughter, something. All was quiet, a still late-autumn night in the middle of nowhere; he was freezing and his jacket was gone.

He drove slowly on up the hill, searching for her, calling her name, and passed a lonely cemetery and then he saw a lone house on the ridge. He pulled into the drive and raced up to the porch. He banged on the door till it opened and a middle-aged man walked outside.

"Who's there?" he called.

"Sorry for the lateness sir, but I was just driving…"

"Who's there?!"

From inside a woman: "Who was it?"

"My name is Dillon." He stood right in front of the man who looked through him and all around.

"No one."

The woman appeared at the door.

Dillon said, "Ma'am, I think your daughter…"

"It's cold, Tom," the woman said. "Come back in."

"I heard a car," the man—Tom—said, and looked in the direction of Dillon's Barracuda but looked right through it. "I thought it might be another boy."

She hugged her arms. Dillon looked from one to the other, long since tired of trying to communicate. "It's about time for another one, sure enough. They seem to describe Ashley right. You think…?"

Tom scoffed, gave another glance around, then led his wife back inside, slamming the door closed. Dillon leaned against it and found he could hear their conversation still.

"Bunch of assholes all them boys are," Tom was saying.

"But…"

"She's been dead thirty years. Someday, maybe after we're dead and gone, maybe then they'll let it go."

Dillon's mouth hung open. He leaned on the door, clawed at it. She had been in his car and she had spoken to him and she had sat with him…and they both acted like he wasn't even there. And they said she'd been dead thirty years, and she'd sat with him…

The 'Cuda's tires spit gravel as he pulled back out onto the highway, and Dillon raced to the one other place he thought he could get answers.

The waitress stood in the middle of the floor, flanked by the trucker and the greasy bartender. Beads of sweat dotted her brow and her hair was soggy and drooping, her eyeliner smeared. Dillon thought he'd feel better getting answers here, but upon entering the diner he felt queasy and stumbled back against the wall.

"Don't you remember," the girl was saying. "He was first. His muscle car wrecked on this highway back in the early seventies. They say he died instantly, but you can still see his car, trying to get home. And she…she's always hitchhiking. People always talk about picking her up and then she vanishes right before they reach her destination. It isn't her home but the cemetery. They found each other this time. Somehow this time they found each other. They were here. I got scared and dropped the tray. That's who I was waiting on."

Dillon shook his head as he backed away through the door. It was all he could do. He could not comprehend what he was hearing, but merely stared at his hands then to the unopened door, his mouth agape, his eyes wide, as he now stood outside looking at the diner. He'd passed through the door without even opening it. He returned to his car and revved the engine, tried to scream over the noise of the Barracuda. The tires threw gravel as he peeled from the drive to the paved road, and soon he was back on 365, headed into the night, almost home, still shaking. He just had to make it home.

***

Listless like he's stuck in a fog, perhaps because it feels like years since he was home and perhaps it's because he's been driving so long that the terrain always appears the same, Dillon steers his car onto Arkansas State Highway 365. Above him the pines sway, illuminated by the gibbous moon as wisps of clouds drift slowly across the firmament. He wipes condensation off the windshield and his palm comes back frigid and wet, and from the dash the vents cough out the heat asthmatically, but this is nothing new…

Stop Me from Falling
James Pyles

"It's not a good idea for you to call me, Jonny. There's someone else. If he finds out about you, he'll kill you or worse." Her lightly accented voice made him think of her sensuous lips, crimson thickly dripping down her chin.

"Then why did you give me your number?" The thirty-two-year-old software developer gazed out of the third-story window of his San Francisco apartment, night and dense haze forming a solemn shroud over the Little Sisters of the Poor convent across Lake Street. The fog horns moaning near the Bay were the mourner's wail, a harbinger of what was to come.

"It was a mistake." She hesitated as if she couldn't quite believe her own words. "I shouldn't have done that. You need to hang up now." Where was she? What was she doing, and who was she with?

"I can't. Ever since that night, I can't stop thinking

about you."

"You have to stop. It was a one-night stand, nothing more. You should stay with Lucy."

"How do you know about…?"

"She's good for you. Leave me alone. You don't know where a relationship with me will lead, but I promise, it's no place you want to go." She broke the connection with a fatal click before he could say anything else.

"Jonny, what are you doing?" Lucy's voice, full with sleep, drifted like a dream down the hall from their bedroom. He glanced at his phone, his lost link to her, a sentinel to forbidden heartbreak. It testified "2:56" against him.

"I just got up to get a drink of water. Be back in a minute." He quietly strode like a cat around the sofa to the kitchen, putting his phone on the counter to shoot tap water into a dirty glass. It made him feel like he wasn't such a liar. Jonny took a drink, then closed his green eyes, listening, finally hearing her breathing slow, becoming regular.

Gazing across the kitchen counter back out the window, he saw himself asking Lucy to marry him. That was three months ago, a man in love, dark brown hair ruffled by the breeze, archaically on one knee in Golden Gate Park near the Japanese Tea Gardens. A verdant, early spring day suited her. She cried when she said yes. She was everything he'd always dreamed of, beautiful, honey-colored hair resting on almond-tinged shoulders, intelligent, funny, amorous in bed. She even liked his cat Smokey, and more importantly, Smokey liked her. He'd left the gray Maltese curled next to her on top of the quilt they'd bought together last year at some Berkeley street fair.

"How did I get into this mess? Oh, yeah. It's all Bobby's fault." Suddenly noticing the glass in his hand, he put it down on the counter.

A few weeks back, his "wingman" Bobby asked to meet him at some bar he'd never heard of called "Delirium." It was hard to find, down a back street he didn't even know existed somewhere South of Market. Jonathan had grown up in San Francisco so he thought he knew everything the City had to offer. This one was something new, though it looked very old.

He'd lied to Lucy, and not for the first time. This was either a bachelor party Bobby had cooked up for him or some other prank. In either case, his girlfriend—fiancée rather—wouldn't appreciate it. She'd never liked Bobby anyway.

It was nearly nine when he entered the darkened alley, its brick walls strangely blank. No windows, so no spectators to intrude on clandestine sojourners, out-of-place cobblestones wet but odorless, no trash or trashcans, no homeless, no human waste, no spent hypodermic needles. It was an anachronism for his city in the 21st century. He pulled his gray "racer's jacket" tighter around his shoulders, shivering with cold and apprehension.

There was only one doorway, dark, solid wood, set at basement level to his left. The wooden sign bolted over it pointing down into the cellar saloon said "Delirium, est. 1897." Later, Jon looked the place up on the web and found nothing, no hint such an establishment existed or had ever existed. So how could it have been here for over a hundred years?

Running shoes tapped wetly down five cement steps ending in a soft splash. No window in the door either, just a tarnished brass handle that felt like ice when he gripped it.

"What the…?"

The door creaked open, yawning before him like the grave, but inside the light was golden and tinged with smoke.

"Bobby didn't say anything about cosplay."

The bar in the back was of the same wood as the door, but polished and new. It curved to either side, gas lanterns suspended onto the top of the ornately carved cabinetry behind the bartenders, rows of glistening bottles of liquor displaying unfamiliar labels rapidly jostled as drinks flowed and spirits were made superficially merry.

Rows of tables and chairs dotted the landscape between him and where he saw Bobby at the bar smiling and waving to him. The patrons were a strange mixture of people he could have walked past on the street every day, and characters from a 19th century play with a touch of steampunk. Men wearing top hats or bowlers, ascots or foppish bowties at their throats, golden chains of pocket watches shining amber at their waistcoats.

Some of the women were dressed in full skirts draped to the floor, corsets of satin laced with whale bone or ivory, tight bodices suspending ample, rounded breasts, revealing generous amounts of cleavage.

Compounding one historical folly upon another, this scene from Victorian England included men and women from any place at all, not just Europeans, but Africans, Middle Eastern faces, Asian accents, as if a supernatural agency had opened apertures from past ages into his modern realm.

"Over here, Jonny," Bobby yelled above the din of voices. "I've got some people I want you to meet."

Making his way forward, he was jostled by the crowd, though no one seemed to mind. He shivered again, but was it because the saloon was too cold, or because he could feel bodies as frigid as ice surrounding him?

Breaking through the masses, he finally got a clear view of his best friend, still grinning like the literary Cheshire Cat, and at each side of him, a woman, one of his arms resting around their waists. Typical of his tall, cavalier, athletic friend's style, they were both gorgeous, and like the natives of "Delirium," each of them had stepped out of another time and place.

"Hey, buddy." He let go of the one on his right and grasped Jonny's hand, squeezing it too hard as always. "Glad you could make it." His arm resumed its former position. "I wanted to introduce you to some special ladies. On my right is Verona and on my left is Dolengen."

The two women regarded Jonny hungrily, greedily, as if he were a canary to their cats, but only Dolengen spoke. "Call me Dol."

They were both strangely beautiful, but with a whiff of the macabre. The instant he made eye contact with Dol, he couldn't stop looking at her, as if he'd fallen and was drowning in her clear, blue eyes. She had dark, nearly jet black hair, much darker than his, but her skin was so pale, like water in a shallow tidal pool, contrasting with vivid ruby red lips. Her dress was the color of Egyptian cotton, hemline to the floor, lacy, long sleeves, and very sheer. Her twin globular breasts rested in a bodice of alabaster.

"Dol." He said her name as if he were already drunk. Her gaze was hypnotic, narcotic.

"Want a drink?" She touched his shoulder with her left hand. Her nails were long and sharp, painted the same shade as her lips, red as blood. He felt her frozen touch right through his jacket and shuddered.

It was enough to bring him back to his senses. Turning to Bobby, he hissed in his ear, "Are you nuts? You know I'm engaged. I don't do this anymore."

"Oh c'mon, Jonny." He was talking too loudly. Did Dol know she was being used for a quick hook up? "Just for old time's sake. You've got to admit Dol's smoking hot."

Jonny looked back to Dol without meaning to, and yes, she was a portrait of loveliness, and yet also of terror, as if lovemaking for her wasn't about passion, or even raw sex, but feeding.

"Bobby…" Jonathan was pleading with his friend but all the while still staring at Dol.

"Look, Verona and I are going to step out for a bit. Why don't you let Dol entertain you?"

His head jerked left, but Bobby and Verona had already gone, vanishing like air. He couldn't even remember what the other woman looked like.

"What are you having, Jonny? I'll buy."

"Huh, what?" He wondered if he should order anything at all. Everything around him had become more unreal. Only Dol seemed substantial, material, and yet her presence still gave off something uncanny. "Margarita's fine."

He looked back at the packed room. There were the same men and women he saw earlier, but not as many. Some must have left like Bobby, but others became couples or threesomes. About half of them looked dazed or disoriented. Sure, this was a bar, but it didn't seem like they were buzzed. More like…he couldn't find the right word…enthralled?

"Here you go."

Jon turned back to Dol as she handed him his drink. For a second, he had the crazy thought that it might be dosed with one of those "rape drugs," but why the hell would a woman to that to a man?

He took a sip. "Pretty good." He nodded slightly, but looking, he couldn't find the bartender. "Aren't you having anything?" He noticed she didn't have a glass in front of her. In fact, scanning the room again, a lot of the people around him weren't drinking.

"I'll have something soon, Jonny." She looked into his eyes, her expression like a child who was pinning a live butterfly to corkboard. He felt as if she had undressed him and were appraising him the way he and Bobby used to size up women, like meat, something to use, enjoy, and then discard. He felt like the time he was thirteen and his sixteen-year-old sister Emily walked in on him in the bathroom while he was masturbating. He felt humiliated and ashamed, and yet, aroused.

"Want another?"

He looked at the glass in his hand and it was empty. Jonny felt ridiculous, out of place, and he knew better than to do this to Lucy. "Probably not. I should be getting home."

"Oh, you can stay a little while longer." Dol put a hand gently on his. Her flesh felt cold and dead. "I'm sure Bobby and Verona will be back soon." Taking the empty drink from his hand, she replaced it with a full one. He hadn't heard her order and still hadn't seen who was serving behind the bar. Jonny accepted it automatically, draining half the glass in a single gulp.

"Careful, handsome. You don't want too much of that in your blood all at once."

"My blood?" He thought if he tried to walk now, he'd fall, but it wasn't just because of the booze.

Time had passed but he couldn't tell how much. Dol was nuzzled up against him, peering through him like a pane of glass. He was walking after all, her arm around his, guiding him around the bar, to a doorway in the back. He remembered seeing others go through it before.

Her skirts were rustling and her footsteps were graceful taps on the hardwood floorboards. She smelled like wilted rose petals, silken hair whisking his shoulder.

"Where are we going?" He watched her hand push the door aside. The colors were surreally shifted and the air felt too thick to breathe.

"Someplace we can be alone for a while, Jonny. You want to be alone with me, don't you?" She had an elegant and dangerous smile.

He could feel himself getting an erection as he looked down at her cleavage. Her nipples were hard and he could see the slightly darker areola of each breast through her top. He felt he was a trapped animal; a sparrow under Smokey's claws, writhing and bloody, struggling to survive but already doomed. They walked further down the silent hall, passing closed doors on either side, an occasional oil lamp on the wall illuminating fierce darkness. One door opened to his left and a tall, bearded man led a young Asian woman out. She was still buttoning her blouse, unmindful of exposing small, brown nipples. Her neck was smeared with something red. A faint but insistent voice inside his mind told him to run, but his legs felt like blocks of wood.

"In here, lover." She opened the door at the end of the hall to the right. It was dark inside with just a few candles on a nightstand to keep the shadows at bay. She gently pushed him toward the four-poster bed and then he heard the door close.

"Now we can be alone." She was still behind him and he felt frosty hands reach around to unzip his jacket and then pull it off. His shirt became unbuttoned while he stood like a lifeless mannequin, and then it vanished.

He was in bed. They were both nude. He was on his back, under an eldritch spell, his thoughts and will molded like clay between her fingers. None of this was real, and she was a faint, ghostly seductress. The thatch of hair between her legs was as dark as her mane. She was a supple porcelain doll sparsely painted in onyx and scarlet, crimson lips glowing in the darkness, a fire almost lost in the abyss.

Dol sat on top of his erection and her cool moistness like thick honey invited him to eagerly enter her.

There was so much passion, arctic and yet on fire. He shoved his hips up rhythmically to meet hers. She cried out with each thrust and he could hear his own feral growls. They were moving faster. He could feel himself close to coming. She lay prone on top, pressing her crotch against him, rubbing herself faster and faster toward an orgasm.

They both cried out, and as he felt himself letting go, ejaculating hotly inside of her, there was something sharp, a pain, his neck. Her face was buried in his throat and the wonderful horror of her tenderly tearing his flesh, blood spilling on the bed, on her face, thrilled him as a man is dominated by the sight of his own death. He felt himself spasm to another climax, sure that she was also a slave to the same ecstasy.

The room was getting darker or was he dying? Either way, he collapsed into her embrace, a balloon with all the air rushing outward, deflating, expiring. There was no one else in existence he wanted to be nearer to than his delicate, dazzling Dolengen.

He sighed and it was over. She was gone.

***

"Where the fuck have you been?"

Jonny staggered through the door of his apartment sometime after two in the morning, but he didn't remember driving home or even leaving the bedroom at Delirium. Lucy was standing in the middle of their darkened bedroom, the blue terrycloth robe her grandmother had given her for her last birthday tightly wrapped around her slender dancer's body.

He teetered backward, closing the door behind him by falling against it. "I'm not sure."

"Oh my God, what happened to you?" She rushed toward the doorway, flipping on the hall light switch.

He cringed against the brightness, throwing an arm over his eyes. "Please don't."

She was already next to him, her voice reduced to a tender whisper, thin, warm arms guiding him into their bedroom. "What's wrong? Why is your neck bandaged?

Did you have an accident?"

"I don't know." He tried to remember. The night was a jumble, flashes of light and darkness. "I was supposed to meet Bobby somewhere."

"Oh, that asshole?" She spoke with parental disapproval. There was the click of another light switch and he pressed his eyes shut. "Let's get that coat off so I can see…"

A ball of hissing rage rose from the bathroom sink, fangs warning back a threat.

"Smokey?" Jonny was astonished as his cat scratched his hand, drawing fresh blood, and then shot out of the room, a charcoal blur.

"Never mind Smokey. He'll keep." Lucy guided his jacket off his arms and he heard it hit the floor. "What did you do to yourself?" He felt the pressure of her fingers against gauze on his neck and pulled away.

"Don't do that."

"Jonny, you're scaring me. You don't come home, don't answer my texts, and when you do show up, your neck is bandaged and bleeding."

"Bleeding?" He remembered blood.

"I'll be gentle, but let me see."

He opened his eyes but everything was still too bright. Tape separated from his skin and when she opened the square cotton pad, he saw twin, flaming red welts oozing blood, half-crusted with scabs.

"I don't know. I must have gotten lost. Taken a wrong turn."

"Where's Bobby?"

"I can't remember. He disappeared, or I never found him. I ended up like this."

"You were mugged?" Fresh panic filled her voice.

"I don't know."

"We've got to call the police."

He reached up and grabbed her wrist harder than he

meant to. "No. No police. I don't know what happened." Letting go, he slumped forward against the counter. "Just need some sleep."

"How much did you have to drink?"

"Drink?" He recalled the Margaritas. "Too much in the blood."

"What?"

Jonny used his reflection to guide his hand, pressing the bandage back in place, tape loose but holding. "Just need some sleep, that's all."

"You need to go to a hospital."

"Take me to bed." He faced Lucy and trembling arms gathered her to his chest. "God, you feel so warm. I missed you."

"I missed you, too." She sounded doubtful, wondering. "If you don't feel better in the morning, I'm taking you to the emergency room, then calling the cops."

"I'll be okay. I need to rest. I need you."

"I need you, Jonny."

His feet were moving again and she was pulling him toward bed. For an instant, he stiffened with fear. She'd taken him to bed, made love, and then…and then…

"What's wrong."

"No, nothing." The memory and the horror faded. "Nothing."

His clothes came off again, and he descended onto the mattress and into oblivion, only faintly worried that he still smelled of her sex.

His sleep was dreamless, except near dawn when he had visions of Dol, nude, delightful, inviting. Then she opened her mouth and he watched warm, red blood, his blood, gush out in robust, burgundy streams, contrasting against her gleaming white fangs.

***

Jonny listened to the unanswered ringing in his ear for the fourth time that morning but there was nothing else, not even voice mail. Sitting in the recliner in front of the television's unseeing eye, warm in a pullover and sweatpants, he turned the business card he'd found in his wallet over in his fingers.

"Dolengen." It was just that on the plain, white cardstock and a phone number, the area code wasn't local. He put the cell and card on the small end table to his right, then caressed long soft fur sitting in his lap. "At least you love me again."

His phone beeped, a text from Lucy: "How are you feeling?"

Smokey twisted his body is annoyance at the repeated intrusions. "Fine. Glad I called in sick. Hangover."

"Bad boy," she texted back. "Mommy will spank you later. Bye."

He smiled at the thought of his little "good girl" doing anything kinky, then his frown reappeared as he lightly touched his fading wounds. They were violet and swollen but no longer bleeding. Closing his eyes, he could see her again, and when he opened them, he felt both trepidation and lust.

Jonny had tried tearing the card up half a dozen times since he'd gotten out of bed, but he couldn't. He lifted it and pressed it between his fingers. "I should let you go. I don't know why I can't."

***

He managed to wait a whole week before giving into temptation again. After last time when she told him not to call her and told him about the other man, he knew she was right, but he couldn't help himself. She was a drug, an addiction, and the withdrawals were killing him. He'd do anything for another fix, even though he knew she was just as deadly.

Smokey was regarding him from the top of the kitchen cabinets near the stove as he sat again in his chair. He felt thankful or at least relieved that Lucy was out with her sister Nina. They spent two or three nights a month going shopping, hitting the latest "chick flick," and catching up with each other. It was a good time for Jon to be alone and watch videos that Lucy would hate, or games with lots of explosions and shooting, what her sister called "toxic masculinity." Tonight, television and gaming was irrelevant. He didn't need the card anymore. Her number was burned into his mind like a brand.

"Hello?"

"Dol. It's me, Jonny. I'm sorry about calling, but I need to talk to you. I can't get you out of my head. Please, just for a few minutes."

"I'm busy now. I'll call you in a couple of hours." She hung up without another word.

Walking over to the kitchen counter, he put the phone down and got a beer from the fridge. He turned on the TV and began watching a movie and then shut it off in disgust. Picking up a novel from the coffee table Lucy keep bugging him to read, he casually flipped through the pages, then tossed it back down. He paced, sat down, checked his text messages and email, started to surf some porn on his phone, paced again.

Jon was working on his third beer when his cell rang. Caller ID was blocked, but he had a pretty good idea who it was. Now if Lucy would just stay out for a little while longer.

"Hello?" He looked at the clock on the microwave. White numerals against black announced "11:32 p.m."

"It's me, Jonny."

"Dol." He put the bottle down on the counter, then gripped the edge to steady himself.

"I called to tell you I can't see you anymore and I don't want you call again."

"What? Then why did you leave me your card in the first place?"

"I didn't know you then. I didn't know about Lucy."

"You said that before. How do you know Lucy?"

"I found out from Bobby."

It suddenly occurred to him that he hadn't seen or heard from Bobby since that night.

"Bobby?"

"He told Verona. She likes to listen afterwards. She's odd that way."

"What are you talking…?"

"Listen, Jonny. It was fun. It was great. You are a wonderful lover and you taste…well, you taste very good. I enjoyed that part the best."

He reached up to the left side of his neck but her mark on his flesh was gone.

"I told you before, I'm with someone, someone dangerous. He doesn't mind my occasionally stepping out, in fact he expects it for reasons you wouldn't understand. Anyway, he won't let me see a man more than once…well, not and let him go. I like you Jonny, so I'm giving you this warning. Don't ever call again. Don't try to see me. If you do, your life will be destroyed. Don't let what happened to Bobby happen to you."

"What happened to Bobby? What did…?" He didn't finish the sentence because he was talking to dead air.

"Bobby." Jon called him from his contacts list. It went right to voice mail.

"Bobby, it's Jon. Hey, buddy. Long time, no see. Give me a call. Really, it's important. Day or night, call me. I need to talk to you." He heard Lucy's key hit the lock and turn. Jon broke the connection and then plugged his phone into the charger. His third beer was still sitting half-finished on the counter.

What had Dol meant about not letting what happened to Bobby happen to him?

Strolling down the hallway, Lucy shrugged her long coat off and draped it over her arm. "Enjoy your man time alone? Hope you didn't drink all the beer." She hadn't mentioned that night again, hadn't given Jonny even the suggestion that she suspected. Was she naïve or just forgiving? He buried his face in the open refrigerator to hide his guilty blushing, reaching for a bottle, moisture welcoming his fingertips like Dol's glacial breasts.

***

"I'm sorry, Mr. Renfeld no longer works here."

"Wait. When did that happen? Bobby would have told me if he'd…when did he quit?" Jonny was working without any clues, trying to find a man he'd known since high school who had, as far as he could tell, been swallowed up by the earth.

"Mr. Renfeld hasn't been employed with us for approximately three weeks."

"Did he say where he'd be working? It's really important that I reach him."

"I'm sorry, company policy prohibits me from disclosing any more. Is there any other way I can help you?" She might have been the model for every voicemail directory he had ever been tangled inside.

"No, no thanks."

"Have a good day, Sir." The connection went dead.

"Yeah. Burn in hell, you bitch." He put the phone down on the small table in a coffee shop he'd never visited before. Something told him to avoid his usual flight patterns right now. He was caught in a web of mystery which, in real life, wasn't at all adventurous or romantic. He'd been searching for any trace of Bobby for a week. Cell phone disconnected, his landlord said he simply stopped coming home and paying rent. He hadn't been at work for a month, none of their friends had seen or heard from him either. Bobby Renfeld had dropped completely off the grid, and the last person to see him was Dol's friend Verona.

"Oh no." He ran his fingers through unshorn hair, only vaguely aware of the barista approaching. He looked up at her and shook his head as she opened her mouth. Jonny figured it was the haunted look in his eyes he saw that morning while shaving that warned her off.

He thought about Dol, how he felt, that irresistible compulsion to be near her, even for a few moments, and then the ghastly realization of Bobby's fate settled into the pit of his stomach like a fist or a spider contemplating its victims.

"I've got to know." He picked up his phone again, tapping it against his empty cup, foamy remnants of his mocha latte squiggling on the bottom. "One more lie, just one more lie, Lucy."

***

Jonny stepped into the eclipsed obscurity of the alley, tendrils of fog stalking him like apparitions or vipers. His footsteps echoed louder than the last time and there was an unidentifiable something missing.

He was nauseous. Jonny couldn't remember the last time he had eaten. Guilt and fear clawed at his entrails, erasing his appetite. A month ago, Bobby and Verona had abandoned him to Dolengen's supple mercies, but tonight, it was as if he had betrayed Bobby, as he was once again betraying Lucy. "I should never have come."

He stopped. There was only the sound of his ragged breathing and the distant traffic noise somewhere behind him. Jonny stepped hesitantly forward. He quivered, imagining himself opening up that door again. This time, everyone would know who he was, what had happened. Did he really expect anyone to help him locate a man who was already lost?

Jon's feet rested an inch from the first step downward. The short stairs were still there and so was the door, but there wasn't even the slightest indication a sign had been mounted on the brick.

"Last month, this place was jumping." Footfalls padded one at a time downward, testing each step to make sure the concrete was really there. On the bottom, he gripped the handle. It was cold, wet, and locked. Jonny pressed an ear to the door and heard only the silence of the dead.

"I told you not to try to see me, Jonny."

He jumped and spun. She was at the top of the stairs, looming over him like a dark angel, her thin overcoat as black as a raven's wing. Her hair melded into the shadows on her shoulders. She stepped backward as he ascended. Her face was like paste and only her eyes and lips gave her color.

"I'd hoped it was over."

"I didn't come here for you, I…" It was another in an endless stream of lies. "I had to see you. Something won't let me end it. Why won't you let me go?"

"It makes no sense to be falling. You've got her, I've got him, you shouldn't even be calling."

"Who is he? What if we…I don't know…run away together?" He knew what madness felt like right then. It wasn't his voice, they weren't his thoughts. He loved Lucy, wanted to spend the rest of his life with her. He'd do anything for her love. He would leave her in an instant if Dolengen told him to, but it wasn't right. What happened to Bobby?

"No, Jonny. Lucy is good for you. She's a good woman. I know. I've seen her, talked with her."

"What?" His heart could have stopped as he

envisioned Dolengen and Lucy together.

"I had to be sure because I had to convince you to be sure she's the one, Jonny."

"To convince me or yourself?" For the first time, he thought he could see through her bright blue eyes into a fragment of her darkness.

"She is the one for you. I have a sense about people. I'll tell you the truth. I lifted her credit card from her purse when she was shopping with her sister, then pretended to find it and give it back. They invited me to have a coffee with them. We got to talking. She loves you very much, Jonny. You belong with each other in your world. You should stay away from mine."

Dol kept slowly walking backward while Jon felt rooted to the spot, a study in granite and tragedy.

"I live in a dark and dangerous realm. You have only seen the smallest portion of it and of me."

"I've seen everything about you. We made love."

"I used you, Jonny. I didn't drink with you that night at the bar, and while Lucy and Nina were having their coffees, I let mine grow cold in front of me. There's only one drink I crave, one food I long for, and for that one night, you shared with me what I needed. Now it's time for both of us to move on. You have Lucy and the sunlight, and I have only the night."

"But…"

"You don't want what happened to Bobby to happen to you, Jonny."

"What happened to Bobby?"

"He fell. He belongs to Verona now. Bobby's one of us. He wouldn't stay away from her and Verona…well, if you knew her, you'd understand. She likes to keep a few pets."

Jon held out his arms imploringly, his empty arms, and then dropped them seeing a shadow approaching Dol from behind, a man, tall, just a silhouette at first.

"It is time, my dear. Come."

He had a slight accent very close to hers, but Jon couldn't place it. He could see the man's arm embrace her shoulder. She looked at his hand and then up at him as he moved into the light. His face was as pale as hers, boasting thick dark hair lightly streaked with gray as was his luxurious beard. His jacket wasn't quite as long as Dolengen's but it was caped in the back. His eyes held the look of a predator who had no equal, who lived in a world of helpless victims.

"Go home, boy, before something bad happens to you." His voice was smooth and calm and yet laced with terrible menace.

They both opened their mouths and loudly hissed like untamed and rabid beasts, fangs gleaming, saber-sharp canines, the pain he'd felt in his neck that night, the wounds, the blood.

His blood. She fed on him and in spite of his dread, he couldn't look away from her, even now. For an instant, she turned to her dark lover and passion was replaced by an ancient repugnance. What was the look in her eyes when she returned her gaze toward Jonny?

Jonathan Harker swiveled and ran and ran and ran, the dark man's laughter echoing after him, fading with the distance. He staggered to the edge of the alleyway, fog making pedestrians and passing traffic into specters.

Glancing back, there was nothing but mist, not even their shadows, yet he could still hear her voice faintly, like a breath on the wind. "You have her and I have him, but if you don't need her anymore, really don't need her, I might call. It will be our little secret, lover."

Driven by lunacy, he raced up the sidewalk, shoving people aside, desperate to escape. He got to his car, frantically looked back to see if she were coming after him. Jonny fumbled with his keys, dropped them, picked them up, looked back again, managed to press the fob to unlock the door, and then rushed inside. He gunned the engine and roared away from the curb, almost hitting a bicyclist. He recklessly swerved, ran a red light and kept going.

Lucy would be waiting for him when he got home. He had to work late. Yes, that's what he'd told her. He had to work late. But that's all it was and that's all it would be ever again. It was the last lie. He had her and she had him and he would never phone her again.

But what would he do if she called him? Did he even know what love was anymore? Had he ever?

A Retching Story
Micah Castle

In the early morning, sitting at his desk placed in front of the only window in his one-bedroom apartment, Richard stared at the typewriter and the blank sheet of paper inside. His fingers rested on the black topped, steel keys.

Write something, he thought. *Write something, anything! It could be about a monster who comes to a small town and runs rampant; it could be about a kitten who finds itself lost in the alleyways and must venture forth to find a new, loving home; it could be about a dragon perched high upon a stone tower, awaiting the day a formidable foe will knock it off its perch.*

No matter what ideas came to him, Richard never finished them. They all seemed too lackluster, too boring, or the premise would be intriguing but once he began the story, it would deflate like an untied balloon, be ripped out from the machine, and thrown away in the trash bin nearby.

"Why can't I write anything?" Richard seethed, jumping up to his feet, knocking over the chair. "Just one book! Just one damn book and I'll be a bestseller, I know it!"

Maybe I need a break, it's been a few hours. Yes, perhaps a stroll downtown, visit the bookstore and I'll be right as rain.

Richard set the chair back on its feet, got his coat, and left his apartment. He went down a rickety flight of stairs, through the slightly crooked double doors, and came out onto the cobblestone street. There were not many people about, most were in church, and others seemed to still be sleeping. It was Sunday after all, and nearly everyone in Picaly considered it to be the Day of Rest.

He made it to the corner, took a left, and entered the business district. Small, wooden signs with flourish lettering hung from flaking, painted black metal beams jutting out above the entrances of each shop. Richard passed *Florane's Flowers*, *Larry's Leather Works*, *Coffee & Tea by Cathy and Ted*, and *Ink, Pens, Pencils & Other Items*. The doorway to *Forevermore Books* was open, and as he went to go inside, he glanced down the street to see another, new shop had opened. He pivoted and moved closer to read the sign hanging over its door.

"Vanessa's Potions & Herbs."

Perhaps I will find a potion that'll help me write a book, he thought, chuckling. "Likely not," he muttered.

Inside, the palpable air was thick with burning incenses, smelling of cinnamon spice and unnamable earthy scents, protruding from an urn in the far corner. In the opposite corner, a large potted plant with enormous, hanging leaves stood. The leaves blocked out a doorway, which Richard assumed was to the backroom. Tall shelves ran along each wall, brimming with relics, charms, bottles, tarot cards, books, and other things. A gold trimmed, royal purple oriental carpet covered the floor, and a bronze chandelier hung from the ceiling, softly illuminating the store.

He stood for a moment, taking in the place, then his vision snapped to the back doorway when a thin woman with black hair, emerald eyes, and a pale complexion strode through, leaning forward to avoid the plant.

"Greetings sir are you looking for something in particular?" she said, standing before him with her hand out. He shook her hand, cold despite the shop's warmth.

"Oh, nothing in particular. I saw this place was new and decided to see it for myself."

She nodded, smiling. "Ah, yes. New places are often attractive, are they not?"

What a queer woman, he thought, but nodded. "Yes, I suppose they are."

A brief silence fell over them.

"Well," she said, "if you require my assistance, please let me know. I will be in the back, just call for me. My name's Vanessa."

"I will, thank you."

She disappeared into the backroom as Richard walked over to the first bookshelf. Crescent moons, pentagrams, sigils, small crystals of amethyst, quartz and various other pendants danged from thin, black string from the top of the shelf. Pushing aside the necklaces, he glanced at the row of books. Some were bound in brown leather, others purple and yellow velvet, and a few were in dark red, or soft blue, or pine green paper. They appeared to deal with apothecary, fortune telling, rune deciphering, palm reading, and so on.

Richard moved to the second shelf on the adjacent side of the room. Behind small, granite runes and alchemic tools like a pastel and mortar, a small alembic, and a retort, were more books. He did not closely inspect their bindings until he came to one, tucked away behind a potted plant.

The Foundation of Achieving Your Dreams Through Magick by Jabari Dagher.

He took it from the shelf, flipped through the pages, laughing a little.

Am I seriously contemplating purchasing this? Have I come that far in my life that I require something like this to write a successful book?

He turned the book over to find the back cover blank.

Some writers pray, some have superstitions like only using a specific kind of ink, or paper, or typewriters, and there are even other, odder rituals—I would even go as far to say in all likelihood that they, too, would use this book if there was even an inch of a chance to further their work and chisel it into the foundation of literary history. Might as well give it a shot, if it does not work out, maybe Gunther from the bookstore would purchase it secondhand.

He went and set the book down on the counter. There was a small silver bell nearby and he patted it with his palm. Vanessa came out from the backroom, avoiding the plant again, and strode behind the desk.

"Did you find something worthwhile, sir?" she asked, taking the book, turning it in her hands.

"Yes, I suppose I did. It's interesting, to say the least."

"Yes, yes," she said, nodding, "magick is intriguing." She slid it in a brown bag, then handed it to him. "Five cents, please."

He handed her the amount.

"Thank you and have a good day. If that book helps you achieve your dreams, please let me know," she said, smiling.

"I will."

He left the shop, stepping into the fresh, crisp morning air.

II

He sat in the rickety chair near the window with Dagher's book. He riffled through the pages, stopping when he came to something that seemed promising.

CONCOCTION OF MASTERFUL LITERACY
CLASSIFICATION: POTION

TOOLS

CAULDRON — TO BOIL WATER AND OTHER
SUBSTANCES
ALEMBIC
GLASS BOTTLE — TO STORE SUBSTANCE

MATERIALS

1/2 CUP OF SAND
4 LEAVES TAKEN FROM THE MARIPOSA LILY
1 CUP OF FRESH MILK
3 CUPS OF SEA WATER
1/4 CUP OF BARK TAKEN FROM AN OAK TREE

Below were simple instructions, and an incantation he was to recite before consuming the potion. After everything was said and done, Richard would drink the concoction thereafter.

He glanced out the window.

Am I honestly doing this? Am I going to be spending what little money left of my inheritance on this?

He faced the empty sheet of paper sticking out of the typewriter. A cold sweat formed over his body, and something uncomfortable rested in his stomach.

"It's worth the effort to at least try," he said to the empty room.

***

The remainder of the day was exhausting. He gathered the more natural, earthy materials: sand, sea water, and bark, from the beach, sea, and the stretch of woods circling the town. Then, as the sky was turning fuchsia, he went to *Vanessa's Potions & Herbs* and purchased a 1 oz bottle and an alembic. Afterwards he briefly stopped at *Florane's Flowers* before she closed, bought a mariposa lily without a vase, then ran to the small grocery near his apartment and purchased a bottle of milk.

***

In his apartment, Richard took a rusted steel pot and placed it onto a Bunsen burner.

"So…" he murmured, standing in the kitchen, pot in front of him on the counter, and Dagher's open book to the side, following its instructions.

The ingredients were poured into the pot and stirred together, becoming a milky light brown color, then he switched on the burner. While he waited for it to boil, he set up the alembic. It took a few tries, but he finally lit the small burner below the bulbous section of the tool with a match. He uncorked the 1 oz bottle, placing it below the elongated end.

The substance in the pot came to a boil, and he quickly removed it from the burner and set it onto the counter.

When the liquid had cooled, Richard poured it into the alembic.

It came to a boil again almost an hour later. The potion bubbled and frothed and rose in the glass container, then trickled down the long end, dripping into the glass bottle.

***

His hands trembled so fiercely he nearly spilled the bottle when he picked it up and carried it to his bed, where he sat. Dagher's book was pinched in between his arm and body.

He limbs were cold yet sweat beaded his forehead. Anxiety and excitement intertwined, enveloping him. He was smiling when he lifted the bottle to his nose, smelling the ripe, overpowering odor of bark and mariposa, milk and water.

Before he allowed himself to doubt, he opened the book, recited the phlegmy, incoherent words of the incantation, then tossed the book aside and put the bottle to his lips, throwing his head back. The gritty taste of sand and salt mixed with the bitterness of flowers coated his mouth, his teeth, feeling like a ball of metal had entered his stomach.

He tossed the bottle across the room when it was empty. A sharp, hot pain exploded inside him, shooting up into his chest. He wrapped his arms around his abdomen, toppling back onto his bed. The pain stretched, reached every end of his body, like a fiery snake coursing through his veins. He breathed heavily through his mouth, sweat seeping from every pore, and his head began to throb. The room swam, darkened, the flames dancing in the lamps becoming nothing more than blurs of dull yellow, orange…black.

III

Sunlight fell onto his face, streaming through the window. The lights were still on. The smell of burnt bark and sour milk still lingered in the apartment. Richard rolled over, grumbling. Slowly he opened his eyes, realizing he was on the floor.

He joints cracked when he got to his feet. He felt a layer of grime coating his skin. Richard tried to blink away the burning in his eyes as he turned off the lights.

"I need to get this awful taste out of my mouth," he mumbled, his mouth dry, gritty.

He went into the kitchen, rifled through his cabinets until he found a small bottle of rum, then unscrewed the cap and emptied it. He coughed as his throat burned, and his stomach churned when the alcohol reached it.

He went to his bed and sunk into it. He held his head in his hands.

What happened last night?

Images of the boiling substance, the alembic, the strange words, the small bottle to his lips flashed through his mind.

Oh…yes, that.

He shuttered, remembering the smell, the taste. He rolled his stinging eyes towards the typewriter, but a dense fog shrouded his mind. Even with the help of the potion, he did not think he could even write a sentence.

Sleep…I need sleep…Tomorrow, I will write…

He forced himself to his feet, drew the curtains, then fell back into bed.

***

Richard was awoken that night by a sharp pain shooting up from his stomach into his lungs. He snapped forward, gripping his abdomen, toppling from the bed onto the floor. He squeezed his eyes closed as a cold, prickly sensation washed over him, and bile rose in his throat.

He turned over, his mouth facing away, before the vomit erupted from him. His body trembled as sweat covered him, the taste of grit and dairy coating his tongue. It felt like it had gone on forever, but when the retching finally stopped, he opened his eyes to find not vomit on the floor—but a layer of transparent liquid that hastily evaporated into the floorboards, leaving behind letters, words, punctuation marks…He could hardly believe his widening, bleary eyes…There were sentences scrawled in thick, black—what he believed to be—ink across the floor, as if he written them himself.

***

The coldness enveloping his body was immediately replaced by heat. He groaned as he got onto all fours, then to his feet, stumbling away from the words. He wiped the drool from his bottom lip.

Words, words on the floor!

He raced to the light tap, igniting the lamps. The words gleamed under the soft glow. They were in English, written in a flowery lettering. Curious, he drew closer, but another bout of pain exploded through him. He fell forward, caught himself on the bed with one hand, and puked onto the floor again, and again, and again…

When his stomach finally settled, he sat, shivering, his arms wrapped around his body. Mucus clogged his nose, so he forced himself to breathe through his mouth. His sweat-drenched dark hair stuck to his forehead.

More words were revealed when the transparent liquid disappeared…Run-ons, compounds, fragmented sentences…Statements, dialogue, action scenes…The prose was that of his favorite authors—*no*—*excelled* his favorite authors. The literature covered most of the floor, and partially the bottom of the far wall.

After some time, Richard felt strong enough to stand, and walked around the room, reading the text. He was cautious with each step, afraid that the ink would smear under his feet.

They need no editing, no revisions…They are perfect.

He went to his typewriter, ripped the blank sheet from it, then took a pen from his desk. Quickly he jotted down the story on the floor, ignoring the pain aching in his fingers.

"Rest," he murmured, finishing, tossing the pen and paper onto the desk, turning off the lights, moving to his bed. "Sleep, I need…"

He fell face-first onto the mattress, and within minutes, he was asleep.

IV

He felt wonderful the following morning and jumped out of bed and took to his washroom. In the mirror, as he dried himself from the bath, he found that he had grown pale. He pulled the purple bags down from under his eyes, stretched the flesh around his bluish tinged lips, inspected the flappy skin hanging from his arms…

Coming down with something? Possible…

Not enough sun? Maybe…

Not eating enough? I did retch up everything inside me…

He shook his head, lowering his arm and grabbing his clothes from the floor.

No matter now, I must write!

He sat his desk, staring at the work he transcribed from the floor. He could not believe for one moment something this good, something this *amazing* had come out of him. He tried to continue to story, but soon found that where he guided it did not work; then he trashed it, and began a prologue, adding backstory, but it only made the story feel flat, deflated.

He sighed, letting his pen roll away from him on the desk.

Now what am I to do? Can't do much with what I have and nothing I write improves it.

Perhaps it will come later—a lot of great writers work their best at night, some even stay up until the early hours of the morning just to write a few sentences.

To be renowned, one must mimic those who already are.

In that case...

He got up, put on his jacket and wandered into town. He only had a little money to spare, so he spent it on fried dough and honey black tea at the tea shop. As though the warm drink and food gave him confidence, he did not doubt a random idea that popped into his mind, but became anxious, excited, and did not have any hesitation when he left there and went into the potion shop.

It was vacant inside, and he assumed she was in the backroom, like before. He rang the bell on the counter and waited with his hands in his pockets. Vanessa came out from the backroom dressed in a black and royal purple dress, her wiry dark hair tied up in a bun, and she had too many copper and jeweled rings on her fingers to count.

"Hello again, did you have any luck with your book and ingredients?"

He nodded, wiped his forehead with the back of his hand. "Yes, some luck. I was curious..." He fell silent, glanced at the shelving, the chandelier, the carpet, anything but her emerald eyes, her thin lips.

"Curious of what, sir?"

"Curious..." He coughed into his hand. "Curious if you would join me this day for a stroll around town? If you are otherwise engaged I understand, and really," he looked at the floor, speaking lowly, "it was silly of me to ask anyway, and—"

"I will go with you," she said, "but only if tell me about what *luck* you have had with the potion."

He faced her, grinning stupidly. "Absolutely, absolutely I will."

She strode around the counter, took the shop keys from an unseen shelf, and went to Richard. "Well, shall we take our leave?"

***

They caught a carriage to the outskirts of town. There, they walked the winding dirt path through the woods. The morning air was crisp and cool. Birds chirped and flew from one treetop to the next, and furry vermin dashed across the path into the underbrush beyond. By afternoon they had reached the beach and removed their shoes, walking in the sand as they watched the tide wax and wane.

They sat near the water, reflecting the open blue sky, and let their feet soak. Vanessa inhaled the rich, salty air, then spoke about herself, her life. She did not believe in all of what she sold, only that there was a guiding force in life and people do not have entire control over their lives up to a certain point. She also briefly mentioned she had a brother in Maine and her parents lived in a place called Portsmouth.

He let her finish talking before he spoke, enjoying her soothing voice. When it came, he delved in.

She learned that he had been born and raised in Picaly as a single child. His father had left when his mother was young, and she succumbed to consumption later on his life, leaving him with a small inheritance that, he embarrassedly admitted, would soon run dry. He moved the conversation to his dream of writing a renowned book, whose story would last until the end of time. Of his beliefs, he simply stated, "I will live my life as I do now and see what comes when it comes."

The sun drifted towards the horizon, casting blades of fiery colors across the sky. They decided it was time to return, so they stood and brushed the sand off their clothes and walked back to the outskirts of town, where they caught another carriage. They were dropped off in front of Vanessa's shop.

They stood under one of the gaslit lamps lining the street. Vanessa's eyes glistened under the soft illumination.

"Thank you for accompanying me today, Miss. I hope you had an enjoyable time," he said.

"I did, I did," she said, smiling, "though I never learned of that luck you had."

He laughed. "Yes, well…We do not always receive what we want."

"True…"

A silence fell around them.

"Well, I must be off," Vanessa said. "The shop opens early tomorrow, and I require my beauty rest."

"No amount of beauty rest could make you even more beautiful than you are now." He caught his breath the moment he said it, as if he released a plague onto the world. He shut his mouth, gritting his teeth, and sweat rolled down the back of his neck.

God, why would I say such a stupid thing?

What sort of idiot am I?

She laughed a little, her cheeks reddening, and smiled. "Thank you, Richard, the last time I was spoken to like that I was a little girl."

A stifling silence followed.

He did not know what to say or do or think. He opened his mouth to speak but nothing came out. Awkwardly he leaned forward, kissed her cheek, mumbled, "goodnight," rushing away, back to his apartment.

***

He slammed the door, threw his jacket onto the floor, and went to the window, opening it. Closing his eyes, Richard let the cold air drift over him.

Why would I say such at a thing?

After all that?

Botched it all.

He turned and made his way to the washroom, removing his undershirt, when something like electricity shot through him from his stomach, forcing him onto all fours and vomiting onto the floor.

When the nausea gave a slight reprieve, he rolled onto his side, gripping his abdomen. Another wave of sharp, prickling pain ran through him. He retched again and again. Richard didn't understand how or why there was so much coming out of him. He hardly had eaten the whole day, had not consumed anything that could warrant what was expelling from him, yet it continued. With every bout, his joints racked with throbbing pain, his weakening muscles tightened until they were like bound rope about to snap; even when he could open his eyes, veiled in tears, the colors of the room appeared duller, washed out, and he tried to think of anything—*anything at all!*—other than retching but he could not, his thoughts heavy, listless, like a thick fog blanketing his mind.

Please!

He dug his nails into the floor, pulling towards the bed.

God! Let it stop!

Spit, mucus, and bile ran down his chin, his body. He grimaced as he reached out towards the bed.

My insides are on fire!

Richard got onto the bed, his knees pulled up to his chest, his sweat coating him like an extra layer of flesh. The nausea had passed, though he anticipated its return at any moment, terrified of more fiery pain. His apartment illuminated with moonlight coming through the window, and he blinked away the sweat and tears and saw the floor covered in flowery script and—

No, no, no…

Is that blood?

He gritted his teeth, shaking his head.

No, no, no—just a trick of the light. No blood at all, not a drop.

He winced as he swallowed the saliva collecting in his mouth and closed his eyes.

Inhale, exhale; inhale, exhale.

Slowly, gradually, the pain encompassing his body subsided and soon Richard drifted off into a dreamless sleep.

V

It was nearly noon when he came to, lying in a puddle of sweat and what must have been his own urine. His mouth tasted sour, gritty, chalky, and when he swallowed, it was like swallowing stones. Richard tried to sit up, to only have black spots appear in his vision then wash over him, forcing him back down and into unconsciousness.

***

He awoke a few hours later. Again, he tried to sit up and successfully did, though his stomach throbbed with dull racks and his back whined with pain.

Have to get up…

Cannot stay here in piss and sweat and—

If I stay here alone…

He shook his head, not wanting to think about it.

He uncoiled his fingers and gripped the edge of the mattress, pulling himself to it, then slowly placed his feet onto the floor. His joints were on fire, as if he had written through the night, and it took him longer than he expected for the numbness of his legs to dissipate.

He placed his hands flat onto the bed.

Inhale.

Richard pushed himself onto his feet, his legs trembled under his weight, and he stumbled forward, backwards, then forward again to crash against his desk. He gripped it for dear life.

He closed his eyes, exhaling. The vertigo passed after a while, and he opened his eyes to find the room still swimming before him.

"Once it stops spinning," he said aloud, as if hearing his own words would help. "I will wash up, then get dressed and go into town to find help. This…this sickness will be death of me, if I do not receive proper care."

***

Vanessa, wide-eyed, reached out and caught Richard before he collapsed onto the floor of her shop. His flesh was clammy and cold to the touch, and his red-rimmed, sunken eyes had dark splotches hanging underneath, contrasting harshly with his pale skin.

"What happened to you?" she asked, gently setting him down onto the floor, his back against the counter.

"Bout of illness," he gasped. "I have come…I have come to ask for a favor, Miss…" He gulped at the air and wiped his dangling hair—wet with sweat—from his brow.

"Of course, of course, what can I do?" She knelt before him.

"I need—I need someone to help me through this…illness…I need you."

"Me?" she said, putting her hand onto his, "but why? I am not a nurse, or a doctor—there are doctors in town, Richard—"

"I cannot afford them," he waved his hand in the air, and his arm slumped to the floor, "I only need—want *you*." He coughed into his shoulder, leaving a splotch of red. "I know, I know it is a lot to ask of someone you hardly know but—" A coughing fit seized him, forcing him to double over and hack into his lap. When he sat back up, Vanessa saw more blots of red.

"I will help you," she said, leaning forward, "though I cannot say how much I will truly be able to do."

He smiled, revealing pink tinged teeth. "Wonderful, wonderful…"

***

She had half-carried, half-walked him back to his apartment. As soon as Vanessa stepped into his sun-lit home she stopped immediately. She took in the black drawn words covering the floor, the walls, ends of letters reaching the ceiling, some even coiling under his desk and chair.

"Do not mind the literature." Richard coughed, stretching his arm to the bed. "For now, please just bring me to my bed."

His blankets were drenched in sweat, something yellow, and more black words. "You do not want to wash these?"

"No," he shook his head, "not until the sickness has passed at least."

Vanessa bent at the knees and gently let him slump into bed. He smiled, relieved.

"What would you like me to do now, Richard?" she asked, flattening her dress with her hands.

He raised his arm towards the kitchen. "There is some money in a pot in the far-left cabinet, in there. Use that and purchase food, medicine—whatever you believe will help—and if there's any left, coffee or tea, whichever you prefer."

She glanced at the soiled sheets once more. "Are you certain you do not want those washed? They are riddled with disease."

"I am certain, they are important…" he said, smiling, his breath heavy. "I lay upon my best work."

Your work? She thought but did not bother to ask. Vanessa went into the kitchen and retrieved the small amount of money from an old, dusty pot hidden away in the back of the cabinet.

At the door, she asked, "Anything else you believe you will need?"

"No," he called, "just be quick, please."

***

A wave of nausea rolled over Richard when Vanessa's footsteps could not be heard. He snapped over to the side of the mattress and puked. The words already etched across the floor rearranged, making room for the new additions, and the ones on the outstretches of the walls grew over the ceiling like vines. He wiped his mouth on the bedsheet and closed his eyes. It felt like only a minute had passed, but he was sure it had been longer, when Vanessa came back with two bags full of fruit and bread, coffee and tea, and medicine.

She set everything in the kitchen, quickly got him a glass of water and medicine, having him take it, no matter how foul it might have tasted.

Soon, night fell over Picaly.

As the crescent moon rose into the starless sky beyond the window, Richard's sickness strengthened. He knelt from the bed for hours, vomiting transparent liquids lined or filled with red. The veins in his temples and neck stood out like sinewy rope, and he was forced to remove most of his clothes due to the overwhelming amount of sweat and heat generated with each forceful, fiery retch.

All the while Vanessa was at his side, mopping his brow with a cold towel, rubbing his back, soothing him with words her mother once said to her when she was ill as a child. Although she had already seen the words across his apartment, Vanessa was still surprised when more fell from Richard's lip and wrote themselves onto the floor, the words moving to make more and more room.

By dawn, the nausea, it seemed, calmed and Richard fell unconscious.

She found a musty, clean blanket in the washroom closet and wrapped him it, then went back into the washroom and soaked a rag in soapy, warm water. With it, she scrubbed the floor around the bed, wiping up the blood, mucus, and saliva, but found the words impossible to remove, as though intertwined with the fibers of the wood themselves.

She stood when Richard moaned and before she could reach his side, he began puking once more.

***

This continued for days upon days. With every moment she believed he was getting better, he would vomit, and have cold sweats, and would not be able to get up from his bed to use the toilet. She worked feverishly, ensuring that he was kept as clean and as healthy as possible, even using her own money to purchase more medicine, until her wallet dwindled to nearly nothing.

When he laid in his bed, his eyes glossy and staring off into the ether, she sat by his side, and softly said, "I do not want to leave you—I know I sound selfish, but my shop has not been opened for a week, and if it remains like so, I am certain I will be penniless by the end of the month."

His body had grown so weak that he could not move his neck to face her. He looked at her from the corner of his eye. Her skin had grown pale, almost as his pale as his. She had lost weight, too, her cheeks no longer plump but shallow. He swallowed, licked his lips. "Go, please, it does not seem…" he coughed, sharp pains rattling through his chest. "It does not seem that I am getting any better. It is a waste for you to nurse me when it will not change. Just…just go, but may I ask another favor?"

She nodded.

"Please take care of yourself, first. Eat."

She laughed and wrapped her arms around him. "I will, I will also wash, too."

He coughed, then said, "You require that, if you do not mind me saying."

She gently slapped his shoulder, laughing. "Look at the one who is speaking."

Then, she moved the hair from his brow and placed her hand onto his sunken cheek, looking into his bleary, reddened eyes. "You will get better, Richard, I promise…I will think of you while I'm away, and I will close the shop early and come back."

"Thank you, Vanessa," he whispered, "now go before I keep you anymore."

She kissed his dried, crackling lips, got up and quickly left.

He wanted to touch his lips, as though he could feel her again, but his arms refused to move. After a while, he gave up and closed his eyes, allowing sleep to take hold of him.

VI

It was evening when Vanessa was able to lock up and return to Richard's apartment. The sky was a dark fuchsia and the horizon was ablaze with orange. She strode past the shops, up the street, and into the small stairwell to his home. She did not bother to knock, so she opened the door quietly, just in case he was sleeping.

"Richard?" she whispered, entering the dark home. The window was still open.

Vanessa turned the lights on as she crept to his bed. The soft glow illuminated the room.

Richard looked asleep, his eyes closed, his lower lip partially drooping with dried saliva down his chin, but when she sat next to him on the bed and placed her hand onto his cheek to stroke it, it was like touching a block of ice. She pulled her hand away and held her hands to her gaping mouth as tears began to veil her eyes and a shriek echoed from her lips.

"God, oh God no!"

The rest became a blur of crying and running. She was out the door, down the stairs, and sprinting as fast as her legs would allow to the nearest doctor's office past the business district. The doctor stumbled out from his small office with his bag of instruments and followed her back to Richard's apartment.

Vanessa paced the room as the doctor checked Richard's eyes, his pulse, and put his stethoscope to his bare, pale chest.

He nodded.

She stopped.

"What is it? What is it, doctor?" she muttered, her fingers running over her collar.

He shook his head, turning to her. "I believe his heart gave out."

Her legs went out from under her too quickly for the doctor to catch her. She laid upon the word-etched floor and sobbed into her arms. The room swam in a haze, as though she looked through the surface of a lake. She closed her eyes as her chest beat against the floor with every rack of tears.

"It will be okay, Miss, it will be okay," the doctor muttered, kneeling beside her. "I will take care of it."

***

It did not last long, but it felt like forever.

The door was closed behind the men from the coroner's office, taking Richard with them, leaving Vanessa alone in his apartment.

She looked from her gnarled, white-knuckled hands to the floor, then the walls, then the ceiling and the bottom of the desk and chair and finally her stinging reddened eyes rested on his writing supplies.

Her chest rattled when she sighed. Vanessa wiped her eyes as she got up and moved to the desk, snatching the pen and paper from it.

Vanessa was not certain where to begin, but she picked the far-right corner, near the kitchenette, and began writing the story surrounding her, the story Richard had created, the story that he left behind.

***

It took years to gather enough money to hire an editor to understand and untangle the flowery prose, but soon thereafter, she discovered *H & H Publishing* and they quickly accepted the book for publication.

They titled Richard's story, *The Path on the Edge of the Sea*, and placed Richard's name in large, white lettering at the bottom of the cover. It was released in the summer.

She wrote the publishers every month, wanting to know what the sales were, how many readers it had, and so forth. At first only a few copies were sold, then the following month there were dozens, then hundreds…She could not keep track of the numbers *H & H* sent her soon after.

The royalties gave her enough to close her shop and live in Richard's apartment, where she could still feel his presence in the walls, the floor, the ceiling, the desk and chair she sat upon.

The words Richard left in his home remained, and though she had read the story many, many times, she always found herself reading it again on a day when the sky is blue, and the air smelled of the sea.

The Madness of Two
Glen Damien Campbell

He did it again!

Tara Clemens clenched her teeth as she tightened her grip on the stem of her wine glass.

One more time, she promised herself, *if he sniggers at me one more time I'm going to toss this merlot onto his stubbly, smug face and storm right out of here, to hell with the scene it'll cause and to hell with dessert.*

His dismissive amusement at Tara's remark about the paucity of feminist literature on the shelves of the library where she worked assuredly meant that the man dining opposite her was a chauvinistic oaf, and, probably, long overdue for a humiliating put down by a woman.

"So you're a feminist?" he said, not even trying to hide the contumely in his voice.

Tara sat up straight in her chair, looked at him squarely and said, "Yes, I am. Aren't you?"

He sniggered.

That does it!

Tara picked up her glass, but, instead of being thrown onto her date's face, the wine went into her mouth.

One more time, she promised herself again as she absentmindedly emptied her glass.

"No, I'm not a feminist," he announced, "and, to be honest, I don't trust guys who go around calling themselves feminists."

"Why not?" Tara asked.

At this, as if she had asked a stupid question, once again, he sniggered.

"Because they're not feminists," he said, "no matter how loudly they declare themselves to be; guys are guys."

"And what does that mean?"

"It means that, deep-down, in our narcissistic, primal cores, what the average heterosexual guy wants and what you feminists want is completely antithetical." With his fork, Tara's date skewered one of the few remaining king prawns on his plate and popped it into his mouth.

"And, in your primal cores, what do you guys want?" Tara asked.

Her date, his brown eyes sunken deep in shadowed sockets, stared at her frankly.

"Guys want to dominate," he answered as he chomped on the crustacean's spicy pink flesh. "Plus, in my experience, guys who go around proclaiming themselves to be feminists are really just wolves putting on sheep's clothing."

"Maybe you're right," conceded Tara as she stared down at her wine glass, twirling its stem between her thumb and forefinger and wishing it wasn't empty.

She was thinking about Alec, her last boyfriend, a vegan-eco-anarcho-feminist, and, most definitely, as Tara found out towards the end of their relationship, a wolf in sheep's clothing.

"What's wrong?" her date asked.

Tara looked up from her wine glass and smiled. "Nothing's wrong," she said, "you just jogged my memory about someone, that's all."

"A feminist?" he asked, raising his eyebrows.

"A hypocrite," she answered.

He sniggered through his teeth again, though, this time it wasn't so annoying.

It had taken two courses for it to happen, a starter and a main, but her date, Curtis Tallant, the second black man she had ever dated, was finally beginning to make a favorable impression. He was a straight-talker, it seemed, no bullshit! Tara hadn't appreciated this at first. The brusque way he had said, "I think the bill for a first date should be split fifty-fifty, so, if this doesn't work out, nobody feels indebted or cheated," as they arrived at the restaurant, and other blunt comments since, had annoyed Tara. The accepted first date protocol of the man making every effort to impress the woman was being flagrantly disregarded and Tara had taken this as a slight upon her desirability. As a result of this, the getting-to-know-you *tête-à-tête* over the first course was embarrassingly stilted. Indeed, for a while, the date was going so awkwardly that, as they waited in uncomfortable silence for their main course to arrive, Tara, having determined that online dating was not for her, had resolved to promptly remove her name from erostrophy.com's database of lonely-hearts as soon as she got back home. Now, though, with her date proving to be not entirely devoid of charm, Tara was feeling more favorably disposed towards the dating site. Perhaps erostrophy.com's matching algorithms had got it right, pairing Tara with Curtis, and those two hours she had spent registering with the site, answering a succession of questions, like 'Out of all the attractive men you know, how many of them have you imagined having sex with?', and identifying ink blots, were not a waste of time.

From its position on the floor at her feet, Tara felt her handbag vibrate. Her phone was ringing. It was Chloe calling, Tara was sure of it. It was the third time her phone had rung since the date began. Chloe, who had recommended erostrophy.com to Tara on the back of using it to meet her latest beau, Ray, was clearly eager to get an update on how Tara's experience was progressing.

"Would you excuse me," Tara said, picking up her handbag, "I'm just popping to the ladies'."

***

"How's it going? What's he like? Is he handsome?"

"He's nice," Tara told Chloe as she checked her teeth in the sprawling mirror above the sinks. "How about I call you after the date, you know, when I have more information to go on?"

"Aw, I'm sorry," Chloe said, her tone completely unapologetic, "I don't mean to butt in, it's just that it's Saturday night, I'm home, I've just gotten back from the gym, and I'm a bit bored, I guess. Shaun's upstairs playing video games, like always, he's got to get out more, and I keep wondering about how your date's going. I'm excited for you. What is this, your first date in two years?"

Ignoring the question, Tara said, "Why don't you give Ray a call if you're bored?"

"Nah," Chloe replied, "I think that's run its course."

"Why?" Tara exclaimed, shocked. "You two seemed so good together, from what I saw anyway. And I thought you liked the idea of dating a doctor."

"I do. And we *are* good together," Chloe admitted, "it's just—" Her voice trailed off. "I lose myself a bit too much when I'm with him, if that makes sense." It didn't, but Tara didn't say anything. "Plus, Shaun doesn't like him."

In response to this, Tara wanted to bring up an article she had recently read in a magazine about teenage Oedipal complexes, which detailed how teenage boys of single mothers often want to replace their father themselves, and so rarely like their mother's boyfriends, but, remembering she had a date waiting for her, Tara instead just said, "Listen, I can't talk right now, Chloe. Call me tomorrow."

***

"So, you're not a feminist, you've made that clear," Tara said as she sat back down at their table, "but do you believe in anything?"

Curtis shrugged and, after a moment's thought, said, "I don't believe in Beatles, I just believe in me."

Knowing the reference, Tara smiled and added, "Yoko and me, that's reality."

He sniggered and, in almost an imitation of him, Tara sniggered too.

"John Lennon," he said, once the sniggers had settled; "now there was a hypocrite."

Tara laughed. "Absolutely," she agreed; "'imagine no possessions', well, how about first just imagining not having a temperature controlled closet for your fur coats, John!"

Her date laughed, not a snigger, but a proper open-mouthed guffaw, which Tara took as a personal triumph.

Curtis was still laughing when the Chinese waitress, wearing a red and gold dragon brocade cheongsam, sidled up to their table and began to clear away their empty plates.

"Would you like to see the dessert menu?" she asked, her strong South London drawl at odds with her Far Eastern get-up.

Curtis looked at Tara questioningly. She nodded in reply.

"Yes, we would, please," he answered.

The waitress bowed her head and then, with their dishes piled up in her hands, walked away.

"He may have been a hypocrite," resumed Curtis, "but he made up for it with some great music."

"You like the Beatles?" Tara asked, sounding surprised.

"Of course," Curtis answered, "we brothers aren't just about hip-hop and soul, you know."

"I didn't mean—"

"I know, I know," Curtis interjected. "I'm just teasing." He grinned. "And what about you, do you like the Beatles?"

"Of course," Tara said, "we white girls aren't just about ABBA and Stevie Nicks, you know."

He laughed; another hearty guffaw.

"So, who's your favorite Beatle?"

"Well, it has to be John, doesn't it," Tara said; "he was the walrus. The politics and hypocrisy only got bad after he met Yoko; he went a little crazy after meeting her."

"But wasn't he crazy before he met her?" Curtis challenged. "Perhaps being with Yoko just gave him the courage to be his full crazy self."

"Maybe," Tara yielded.

"I always admired how madly in love John and Yoko seemed," Curtis said; "the bed-ins, the love songs, the naked album covers; romantic, wouldn't you say?"

"I suppose, but I'm not sure I'd ever want to be in a relationship that made me crazy enough to pose naked for an album cover."

"But wasn't that what was so great about their relationship; they just didn't seem to care what other people thought. It's like they were living in their own secret world, where no one else mattered."

Tara chuckled.

"What?" Curtis asked.

"Déjà vu," she said.

"Pardon?"

"I said 'déjà vu'," Tara explained, "but, actually, I suppose it's not déjà vu, just more like a bizarre coincidence."

"What is?"

"What you just said to me," Tara said. "It's strange, but, today, when I was getting ready, I was daydreaming about what could happen on this date, you know, just fantasizing, and, in that daydream, we were having dinner, like we are now, only you were wearing a turtle-neck, not a suit. I guess I imagined you in a turtleneck because, I think, that's what you are wearing in the erostrophy.com profile picture I had seen of you." Curtis nodded his head. "Well, anyway, we were eating and then you said something exactly like what you said just now, you know, about lovers having a secret world."

"I guess you must be a little psychic," Curtis said.

Tara shrugged. "I don't know about that," she said, "my lottery numbers have never come up."

"Not yet," Curtis quipped. "So, was that it?"

"What do you mean?"

"In this daydream, did anything else happen?"

Tara flushed red, now regretting bringing up the daydream.

"Yeah," she admitted, surprising herself, "something else happened."

"What?"

"After saying something about living in a secret world, where no one else matters, you stood up, came over to me, stood me up, and lay me down onto the table. You then hiked up my skirt, pulled aside the crotch of my panties, pulled out your cock and started to make love to me, right in front of everyone."

"You fantasized about me doing that?" Curtis asked.

Tara nodded.

"That's crazy."

Tara nodded again. The confession had set her heart aflutter. It then began to race as she watched Curtis stand up.

What are you doing! she was about to say, but the words became stuck in her throat and so she said nothing.

Unchallenged, Curtis approached her, reached out, touched her elbow and then gently coaxed her to her feet.

Tara knew what was about to happen, and, as if she was an actress mechanically playing a part, she, following the script that she herself had outlined, lay back on the table.

Spreading her legs, she allowed Curtis to step into the space in between them.

The eyes of all the other diners where on them now, Tara could feel them watching, feel their consternation, their shock. They were just voyeurs, though, too spellbound to interrupt proceedings, paralyzed by arousal and their curiosity to know, *'How far will they go?'*

As if to answer the rapt, salacious expectations of their audience, Curtis downed his fly. There where gasps as he pulled out his engorged member. He and Tara were criminals now. Lewd conduct, anti-social behavior, public indecency, Curtis's veiny seven inches of erect muscle had broken some law.

At the sight of his hard penis, Tara tightened her legs against Curtis's hips, giving him the encouragement he needed to proceed.

With a colossal thrust, he entered her.

***

The next morning, Tara woke up earlier than she would have liked. Sunday was traditionally a day of rest and Tara usually liked to uphold that tradition. Today in particular was a day where to be in bed, asleep, unconscious, dreaming, in a state where she wouldn't keep thinking about what she did last night, was all she wanted to do. Cruelly, though, her body and mind were betraying her; sleep just wouldn't come.

In her bed clothes, pajama bottoms and a t-shirt, with her long brown hair a mass of tangles, Tara shuffled from her bedroom to the living-room and collapsed onto the sofa. There, for the umpteenth time since it happened, she began to think back to the end of her date.

"You tramp," she said, burying her face into the palms of her hands.

The metallic rattle of a key entering a lock brought Tara's thoughts back to the present. The door to her flat opened and, Kyle, her neighbor, who had been entrusted with Tara's spare key only for emergencies, entered.

"Oh, hey, girl," he said upon seeing Tara, who was staring at him only half-reprovingly. "I thought you'd still be asleep," he explained. "You don't mind if I pinch some milk and some instant coffee, do you?"

Tara didn't answer. There was no point. By the time he had finished speaking, Kyle had already entered Tara's tiny kitchenette and taken a bottle of semi-skimmed from her refrigerator.

Dressed in a red Hugh Hefner style smoking jacket, black silk boxer shorts and slippers, Kyle had entered the flat carrying one of his many Dr. Who mugs, this particular one having Sylvester McCoy, the Doctor's seventh incarnation, decorating its side, (Tara hated that, due to her friendship with Kyle, a Dr. Who fanatic, she had involuntarily acquired an impressive amount of knowledge about that sci-fi show she barely liked).

At the kitchen counter, Kyle put down his mug and the milk, unscrewed the lid of a jar of Nescafe and flicked the switch on Tara's kettle. Water began to boil.

From the sofa, in a state of internal conflict, Tara watched Kyle filch her coffee. She was in two minds about whether or not to tell her affable neighbor about last night's disturbing sexual transgression. She wanted to talk to someone about it, get an outside perspective on why she had behaved in such a deviant way, but, at the same time, she was being swayed by the argument that it might be best if she kept the incident to herself, have it be her dirty little secret, the less people who knew about it the better, treat the incident like a secret treaty between herself, Curtis and the shocked diners and staff of the Eastern Queen on Farrow Lane, a restaurant and street she would now spend the rest of her life avoiding.

Unable to make up her mind, Tara decided that she would let Kyle make the decision for her. If he were to ask about her date, she wouldn't lie, she'd tell him exactly what happened, but, on the other hand, if he were to just make his coffee and leave, no questions asked, Tara would take it as a sign that the dirty little secret approach was the way to go.

After a moment or two, as she, deep down, really expected, Tara's uncharacteristic silence attracted Kyle's attention. He looked up at her and studied her posture and expression carefully.

"What's wrong with you?" he asked. "You look like a woman who's done something nasty and thinks she should be feeling guilty about it."

Through a hangdog expression, Tara seemed to confess that that was exactly her problem.

Sensing gossip, Kyle's eyes lit up and he smirked.

"Oh yeah," he cooed; "you had a date last night, didn't you? How did it go?"

Tara sighed.

"I did something, something—" her voice trailed off as she rummaged through her internal lexicon for a suitable adjective, "crazy," she said, finally.

"Crazy!" Kyle repeated, a touch of cynicism in his tone; Tara was not someone he associated with 'crazy' stories.

Nevertheless, with the air of an indulgent confidant, he abandoned his appropriated coffee in the Dr. Who mug, walked over to Tara and joined her on the sofa.

"What happened?" he asked.

Tara opened her mouth as if to speak, but then quickly closed it again without saying anything.

How do I put it into words!

A look of impatience mixed with indulgence flashed across Kyle's face.

"Come on," he encouraged, "just spit it out, what happened on your date?"

"We fucked," she said.

With a scoff, Kyle rolled his eyes, clearly disappointed.

"Screwing a guy on a first date is not *crazy*, Tara," he said, throwing up his hands to make quotation marks out of his fingers for the word *crazy*, "if it was, believe me, I would have been carted off in a straightjacket years ago."

"We did it in the restaurant," Tara added.

"In the restaurant," Kyle repeated, sounding a little impressed, "where, in the toilets? I've done that."

Tara shook her head.

"We did it on the table we were seated at," she said, "we went at it right in front of everyone."

"You made out with him on your table," Kyle said, "in front of everyone?"

Again, she shook her head.

"We didn't make out, Kyle," she corrected. "We *fucked*."

There was a pause.

Then, unexpectedly, Kyle rose to his feet and began to applaud.

"Oh, bravo, girl," he said. "Now that's an anecdote. I knew there was a libertine in you just screaming to get out. That's amazing. Oh, how I would have loved to have been there, to have been one of the diners watching you guys go at it. I would have called to one of the waiters;

'I'll have what she's having.'" Laughing boisterously, Kyle sat back down next to Tara. "So what happened after?"

"What do you mean?"

"I mean, after the sex, what happened did you sit back down and order coffee, or did you get busted?"

"We ran," Tara said, "we didn't even pay the bill. And the date was pretty much over after that. We parted at a bus stop. It was a little awkward."

"Did you like him?"

Tara nodded. "I didn't at first, but, eventually, he won me over. The longer we were together the more in sync we became. I liked it."

"And you met this guy through an online dating site, right?"

"Yes."

"Sounds like you've might have used *folie-à-deux-dot-com*," Kyle said.

"*Folie-à*-what?" Tara asked.

"*Folie-à-deux*-dot-com," Kyle began, adopting a pedagogic manner, "you've never heard of it?"

"It's new to me," Tara admitted.

"Well it was to me, too, before last year," Kyle said, "but it's quite an urban legend, apparently." He glanced up at the clock on the wall, 9:40 a.m. "Too bad it's too early for a glass of wine, this story should really be told with a drink."

"Just tell me," Tara ordered, trying to reclaim her bibulous neighbor's attention. Coffee gone from his thoughts, Kyle's eyes were scanning Tara's flat in search of something stronger.

"Okay, remember last year," Kyle said, giving up the search for alcohol, "when I went through my brief Grindr phase."

"Yeah, I remember," Tara said, although she wouldn't have described it as a brief phase, and was just about to tell Kyle as much before thinking better of it.

"Well, one of the dates I went on was with this software engineer, I think that's what he was, it was something geeky, for sure, but he didn't look like a geek, believe me, this guy was chiseled and toned, he had an ass that could crack a chestnut. Well, anyway, we're on our date, and it's going well, we're getting on like Laverne and Shirley, in fact, we're getting on too well; we're drinking too much and becoming a little too rambunctious. Then, after we got kicked out of a bar, he says, 'I don't normally behave this way, it's like we've met through *folie-à-deux*-dot-com not Grindr.' I ask him, 'What's that?' He tells me that *folie-à-deux* is French and it means the 'madness of two' and that *folie-à-deux* -dot-com is the name given to a website, a dating website that's constantly changing its URL, and then he tells me that what this dating site does is it brings people together who shouldn't be together, and the reason they shouldn't be together is because they're too compatible, so compatible they make each other crazy. And then he tells me a story, which he says he heard from someone who knew one of the men involved, but they all say that, don't they? Anyway, the story was about two men who met through the site, a tattoo artist and a bookkeeper. The bookkeeper, though, was married, he had a wife and two kids; he was just using the dating site for a bit of naughty fooling around. But now, the unexpected has happened; he's crazy in love with this tattoo artist, who's also a BDSM and body modification enthusiast, who, like a kinky inked-up white rabbit, leads this repressed bookkeeper into a Wonderland of flesh mortification. Disturbingly, their fevered infatuation for each other spurs them on to increasingly bizarre extremes of algogania; from body piercing to scarification to suspension, you name it. They indulge themselves in anything that will satisfy their mutual perversion for pain. They were two masochists in love. But the tattoo artist was jealous of the bookkeeper's family, and the bookkeeper didn't want to leave his kids. So they came up with an idea which would unite them all."

Kyle paused, trying to build suspense.

"What did they do?" Tara asked, captivated, it was an engrossing story, but Kyle was right, it would have been better told over a glass of wine.

"One night, the bookkeeper and tattoo artist drug the wife and two kids, load them into the back of a car, and drive to a slaughterhouse out in the country. They break into it, switch on the large meat grinder and, there, along with the wife and two kids, throw themselves into it."

"That's horrible," Tara said.

"That's the madness of two," Kyle retorted.

"Well, I don't think I've used that follow-a-Jew-dot-com or whatever it's called," Tara said.

"Probably not, but you never know," Kyle teased; "fucking a guy on a table in a restaurant in front of all the diners is pretty unusual behavior. When you've finished eating, you're supposed to ask for a doggy bag not doggy style."

Never shy about being his own biggest fan, Kyle cackled raucously at his quip. Tara just smirked.

"So what's the name of the site you used?" Kyle asked, after the laughter died.

"Erostrophy-dot-com," Tara said. "Chloe told me about it, she's met someone through it, a doctor."

"Show me it."

She reached for her smartphone on the coffee-table, grabbed it, lit up the screen and began to tap.

"Huh!" she said, after a moment, looking down at the screen of her phone.

"What?" Kyle asked.

"I can't get it."

Tara handed her phone over to Kyle, who, after taking it, looked down at the screen and read:

Unable to Connect:
Browser can't establish a connection to the server at erostrophy.com.

With a wide grin on his face suggestive of someone who had just been handed the punch-line to a great joke, Kyle looked up at Tara and began humming the opening bars of the *Twilight Zone*'s theme tune.

***

"Do you know what's happened to Chloe?" Phyllis asked.

Tara shrugged. "No, I don't know. I called her, but there was no answer."

Phyllis sighed.

"Well, it looks like, for whatever reason, she's going to be a no show today. Will you be alright manning the checkout desk by yourself?"

Tara made a show of looking around the library, there was, Barry, the bearded bike mechanic, browsing the sci-fi and fantasy section and a pregnant woman in the baby care section, besides these two and a smattering of students using the computers, the library was empty.

"I think I'll be able to manage," Tara said.

"Thank you, Tara," Phyllis said, seemingly oblivious to Tara's sarcasm.

Manning the checkout desk had long ago stopped being a two person operation, but Phyllis Watson, in denial about the fact that Bellingham Library, the place where she had worked for over thirty of her fifty-eight years, was a mockery of what it used to be, would never admit this.

After giving Tara a verbal itinerary of non-urgent tasks that needed to be carried out, Phyllis went off to reload the printers with toner, leaving Tara alone at the checkout desk. With her superior gone, Tara picked up her Jeanette Winterson paperback, opened it at the bookmark and resumed reading.

She read for about five minutes before putting the book down again. She couldn't concentrate. Chloe was on her mind. She hadn't spoken to her friend since their brief phone conversation in the ladies', and Tara was surprised, even a little upset, that she hadn't been in contact to get a more comprehensive report on her date since then.

I'll try calling her again tonight, Tara resolved.

Her thoughts then turned to Curtis, and she wondered if he would call.

***

Tara got home from work at about six p.m.; her usual time.

The first thing she did once she was through the door was notice the box of cornflakes on the kitchen counter; this had been in the cupboard when she left.

"Kyle!" she moaned, shaking her head angrily.

After placing the cornflakes back in the cupboard, alongside the porridge, muesli and all the other breakfast stuff she didn't have time to eat in the morning, Tara went to the bathroom and took her habitual post-work shower, during which she sang songs by Motley Crue, one of her guilty pleasure bands, and Jefferson Airplane. She also again wondered if Curtis would call.

When she was finished in the shower, she donned a white terrycloth robe and went to slouch on the sofa. It was while there that she remembered she needed to call Chloe and find out why she hadn't shown up for work.

She grabbed her phone and called.

No answer.

She tried the house phone, hoping Shaun might pick up.

Again, there was no answer.

For a while, Tara sat motionless on the sofa, staring off into the middle-distance, before finally deciding that, unless she wanted to be worrying about it all night, she would have to drive over to Chloe's house and find out exactly what was going on.

With an air of frustration, Tara put on a pair of jeans and a blouse, grabbed her bag and headed out the door.

When she pulled away in her green Skoda hatchback, almost simultaneously, a silver Ford sports car also pulled out from the row of cars lining the street outside Tara's small block of flats. Tara noticed the coupe as she adjusted her rearview mirror, but paid neither it nor its driver, obscured in shadows, any scrutiny and proceeded to drive, indifferent to the car trailing behind her.

***

When she parked her Skoda outside Chloe's impressive Edwardian house, Tara was relieved to see that the living-room light was on. This was almost enough to make her turn the car around and go back home. She wasn't in the mood to socialize, particularly as she was sure Chloe would ask about how her date ended and going over that episode again was the last thing Tara felt like doing. But, knowing that turning back would only end up being something she would regret tomorrow, if Chloe didn't show up for work again, Tara got out of the car and proceeded up the broad cobblestone walkway that led to the front porch of number fifty-four, Malmesbury road.

Tara pressed the doorbell. The monophonic peal of the Westminster Quarters broke the silence of the night.

After a moment, emanating from somewhere beyond the white paneled door, Tara heard movement.

Someone was coming.

The door opened, only slightly, three, maybe four, inches, just enough for Ray to peek out and see who was standing on the doorstep.

Didn't Chloe say she was going to dump this guy?

"Tara," he said, squinting as if he was struggling to recognize her, which was understandable, Tara supposed; they had only met twice before.

"Hey, Ray, is Chloe home?"

At this straightforward question, Ray's eyes looked past Tara and began to frantically dart about, seemingly trying to find an answer to Tara's unintended brainteaser somewhere out in the moonlit world behind her. Tara resisted the urge to look over her shoulder, to see if there were indeed any answers there. Instinct told her that there would be nothing to see.

"Yeah, she's home," Ray said, finally, his eyes refocusing on his visitor. He opened the door wider, an invitation to enter. "Come on in," he said.

Tara took half a step back.

"No, that's okay," she said, "I'm not stopping. I just wanted to make sure she was okay—"

"She's fine!" Ray interjected. "Why wouldn't she be?"

"She . . . she didn't come in to work today," Tara explained, almost stammering.

"Oh." Ray's attitude was now amiable again. "She's sick," he said.

In a voice that she hoped betrayed none of her interior doubts, Tara backed away another step from Ray and said, "Okay, well, give her my love and tell her to call me when she feels better."

"Who is it, Ray?"

Coming from deep within the house, the living-room, Tara guessed, the voice was unmistakably Chloe's.

"It's Tara," Ray shouted back into the house.

"Is she coming in?" Chloe asked.

Ray looked at Tara, his eyes throwing Chloe's question at her.

In response, Tara took a step forward, then another. With her third step, she entered the house.

Not squandering a second, once she was in, Ray closed the door behind her.

"Chloe's in the living-room," he said.

With Ray shadowing her, Tara traversed the dim hallway until she was standing within the doorway to the living-room. From there, staring into the stuffy room, she saw Chloe lying on a sofa, a patchwork blanket covering her from the chest down. She looked sweaty and pale. Tara noticed a bottle of codeine on the coffee table.

The room was warm and clammy, the work of body heat, not the cast iron radiators.

Tara didn't like how quiet the room was; no TV, no music. It was strange. What had they been doing before she came, Tara wondered; just talking? Maybe she had disturbed them mid-coitus. Perhaps, beneath her blanket, Chloe was naked from the waist down, Ray's semen running down her legs.

Tara braced herself with this oddly reassuring thought as she entered the living-room.

"I won't stay long," she said, sitting down in the armchair closest to Chloe, "I just wanted to make sure you were okay. It's not like you to not show up for work without calling."

"Oh, I'm sorry I worried you," Chloe said. "I should have called; I was just feeling so terrible this morning."

"What's wrong?"

Chloe looked to Ray, who, standing there like a bulwark, had taken up the position in the doorway that Tara had vacated.

"She's got the flu," he said, answering for Chloe. "She'll probably be off for the rest of the week."

Chloe definitely looked sick, she seemed drowsy, her eyes glazed, but flu didn't seem to fit the picture Tara was seeing. Where were the snotty tissues, runny nose and sniffles?

"Would you like something to drink, Tara?" Ray asked.

Tara didn't want a drink, but she did want to speak to Chloe without Ray being there.

"A cup of coffee would be great," she said.

"Anything for you, sweetie?"

Sweetie, Chloe, shook her head. "No, I'm alright, honey-bug," she said.

Ray traipsed off towards the kitchen, taking with him the air of repression that he seemed to cast over the living-room like an ominous shadow.

"So, I guess, you changed your mind about what you told me you were going to do on Saturday then?" Tara said as soon as she heard a rattle of mugs coming from the kitchen.

"What did I say I was going to do?"

"You know," Tara prompted, "about giving him," she pointed towards the kitchen, "the elbow."

"Oh, that," Chloe said, "that was silly of me; me and Ray are meant to be together. I think I was just scared of falling in love again. But Ray and I had a good, long talk yesterday and we sorted out all our problems. Actually, we had a real breakthrough; made some important decisions. He's going to move in here, with me; to take care of me."

"Chloe," Tara exclaimed, "you've only known him a month!"

"So?"

"So, don't you think you're rushing into this? He could still turn out to not be the person you think he is."

Chloe shook her head. "I know who he is," she argued, "and I need him, Tara. He completes me and I complete him."

"Is Shaun okay with this?"

Chloe looked at Tara sharply. "Shaun's none of your business!" she said, spitting her words at Tara so as to make each syllable an assault.

"Fine," Tara stood up; if that was going to be her attitude, let the silly cow rush into a mistake. "I'll tell Phyllis you'll be off for the rest of the week."

"You're not staying for coffee?"

Blocking Tara's exit, Ray was again standing in the doorway.

"No, I better be going," Tara said.

She headed for the door, but Ray refused to make way for her.

"I couldn't help but overhear that you think it's a bad idea I move in here with Chloe, but don't you think someone should be taking care of her?"

"Why can't she take care of herself?"

To Chloe, Ray said, "Show her!"

At this command, Chloe threw off the blanket covering her. The shrill gasp that followed from Tara was surely only a decibel or two away from being a scream.

"Oh, God, what have you done to her?"

Appalled, yet mesmerized, Tara couldn't take her eyes off the horrific sight her friend had almost gleefully presented to her. Where Chloe Southgate used to have legs, long, enviable, gym-sculpted legs, legs she used to love showing-off in high-heels and short skirts, she now only had stumps, stumps wrapped up in gauze dressing.

"I asked Ray to do it, Tara," Chloe explained, "so I'd never think about running away from him again."

"The madness of two," Tara muttered under her breath, remembering Kyle's story about the witchy dating website. Tara knew it was crazy to now believe that story was true, but then, wasn't the situation she was in now crazy? Why not use crazy to explain craziness?

Scream and run, these were the two things that Tara wanted to do more than anything else in the world. What stopped her, though, was the portentous feeling that screaming and running were exactly the two things that would most likely make her situation worse. No, for Tara to extricate herself from the presence of these two crazed lovers, she would have to be smarter, subtler than that. However, before she could conceive of that smarter, subtler approach, Ray's hand, holding a pungent cloth, clamped onto Tara's mouth.

The odor coming from the cloth was chloroform, Tara suspected. And she was right.

***

A clammy hand clasped tightly over her mouth, to stop her from speaking, no, to stop her from screaming, was the first thing Tara felt as she came to.

She opened her eyes, only for them to meet more darkness. Gradually, though, shapes began to form within the black pall that seemed to enclose her. One shape in particular stood out, a face staring down at her, a face belonging to the hand clasping her mouth no doubt, the whites of its eyes punctuating the night like stars.

The face spoke. "Tara," it said.

She recognized the voice. It was a man's voice, but it wasn't Ray. Who then?

Curtis!

She could see him clearly now. Curtis Tallant, the man she had fucked on a table in the middle of a crowded restaurant, was standing over her, one hand clasped over her mouth, the other, perched on her midriff.

Tara tried to move, to pull away from him. She couldn't. Her hands and feet were tied to the wrought iron frame of the bed she was lying on.

"Tara, relax," Curtis said as she squirmed in dissent against his fingers, "I'm going to get you out of here. Just promise me you won't scream if I take my hand off your mouth; they're downstairs."

With these few words, the situation quickly became more comprehensible to Tara; Curtis was not her capturer, he was here to be her rescuer.

The room she was in, with her eyes adjusted to the darkness, Tara recognized it now as Chloe's bedroom.

They, Ray and Chloe, were her antagonists.

Tara remembered Ray's hulking presence in the doorway, Chloe's truncated limbs and the smell of chloroform. She then nodded her head to indicate to Curtis that she was ready to comply with his request.

True to his word, he removed his hand from her mouth. Tara didn't scream.

"What are you doing here?" she said.

"I followed you," Curtis confessed, "I've been following you since our date. I've not been able to get you out of my head. I followed you here. I watched you come into this house and then I crept up to the window and spied. I saw that guy knock you out and then take you up here. I climbed the trellis and came in through the bathroom window."

"I was just hoping you'd call," Tara said, dryly, "but, I suppose, this has worked out okay." She smiled at him. He smiled back, but then Tara, remembering her predicament said, "Are you going to untie me or what?"

"Sure."

He reached for the stockings that were binding Tara's wrist, began to untie them, but then pulled his hands away at the sound of footfalls coming up the stairs.

"That's them!" he whispered.

"Well then untie me quickly," Tara insisted, convulsing with anger, panic and frustration.

Her hapless rescuer shook his head. "There's no time, but don't worry, I'll get you out of here."

Before she could protest, he scampered away from the bed and disappeared into the adjoining bathroom, leaving the door slightly ajar behind him.

Almost immediately after Curtis was out of sight, the door to the bedroom flung open and Ray walked in, carrying Chloe in his arms like she was his new bride and this was their honeymoon.

"You're awake," Ray said, looking at Tara, studying her carefully. "You're a good girl for not screaming. You like being tied up in a bed, do you?" He turned to Chloe. "Looks like she's up for this as much as we are?"

"I thought she would be," Chloe said, "she's overdue for a good fuck. Isn't that right, Tara?"

In a measured, firm tone, with no animosity, Tara said, "Chloe, would you please tell your boyfriend to untie me?"

"Damn it, Tara," Chloe said, "why don't you just relax and have some fun with me and Ray. You can be so uptight sometimes; like not dating anyone for two years because your last boyfriend hit you. You know, you're on your way to ending up a frigid old bitch like Phyllis."

Ray approached the bed. He then carefully deposited his cargo on top of Tara, positioning Chloe so that she was sitting on their captive in the cowgirl position, her bandaged stumps straddling Tara's waist. Pinned beneath her friend, Tara wriggled and noticed that her wrist fetters were looser than they had been. Before fleeing, Curtis had done some good; he had slackened her bonds

"Have you ever fantasized about a threesome, Tara?" Chloe asked as she began unbuttoning Tara's blouse. "I bet you have. I bet you've fantasized about it a lot." While Chloe talked, Ray was stripping off his clothes. "That's what's great about finally having someone like Ray in my life. We are not shy about sharing with each other our fantasies, no matter how weird they are. That's when you know it's love, when your partner accepts your peculiarities."

"Where's the lube, sweetie?" Ray asked. He was naked now and massaging his cock into life.

"It's in the bathroom cabinet, honey-bug."

Traipsing off to get his lube, Honey-bug entered the bathroom.

Tara tensed.

It took longer to happen than she expected, so long that, when the cry of distress did finally come from the bathroom, it surprised Tara and she flinched.

"Ray!" Chloe screeched in reaction to the clamor.

Ray didn't respond, but more noise, the sound of a scuffle, answered her.

With her warden distracted, staring off towards the bathroom, Tara began to unabashedly tug her wrists free from their tethers. Soon enough, one hand was free, the other then immediately followed.

In a heartbeat, Tara reached up, wrapped her fingers around Chloe's throat and began to squeeze.

Fighting for her life, Chloe struggled, but her resistance was pathetic. Unable to steady herself on her stumps, she couldn't gain the composure nor summon the strength to mount a defense. Instead of fighting back, Chloe's arms flailed about hopelessly.

Despite realizing her opponent was practically defenseless, Tara kept squeezing and, soon enough, the moment came when she knew the fight was over.

Tara tossed the body from off her, letting it tumble to the floor. She then sat up and untied her ankles.

A commotion was still coming from the bathroom. Arming herself with a nail file, taken from off the bedside cabinet, Tara, feeling liberated, rushed to render Curtis whatever assistance she could.

The two men were grappling on the floor when she reached them, and, although he was the slightly smaller man, Ray, naked and still evidently aroused, was winning the fight. He was on top of Curtis and trying to pull his wrists free of the black man's clutches, so he could start pummeling his face with punches.

With only a vague idea of what she was going to do, Tara approached Ray and tapped his shoulder. Instinctively, he turned to look at her. Then, as she soon as he saw his face, inspiration struck, and Tara plunged the point of the nail file into Ray's left eye.

He howled.

Pitilessly, Curtis, seeing the wounded animal, pounced. Taking a handful of Ray's hair, he forced the half-blind man's head, face first, into the shallow pool of water at the bottom of the toilet and held it there until the kicking and thrashing stopped.

For a while, except for panting, there was silence.

Finally, Curtis said, "How's this for a second date?"

Tara eyed him critically. It was a grim joke, but she smirked and re-joined, "I've had worse."

"Let's get out of here, shall we?"

At this suggestion, Tara nodded enthusiastically.

Together, they quickly left Chloe's bedroom. In the landing, though, Tara stalled.

"What?" Curtis asked.

"That's Shaun's room," she said, pointing to the door with the 'Do Not Enter: Gaming in Progress' novelty sign plastered on it.

"Who's Shaun?"

"Her son," she told him.

Recognizing his cue, Curtis walked into the room, but then soon came out.

"Is he in there?" Tara asked.

Curtis nodded. "He's in there, but you don't want to see him."

Tara understood.

*****

Leaving behind the privet hedges and pandemonium of Malmesbury Road, in her Skoda, Tara followed Curtis's coupe through the winding, lamp lit streets of London for over fifteen minutes before he eventually pulled it into a deserted car park at the rear of a supermarket. Tara spent most of that time contemplating veering off into a side street to try to give Curtis the slip. She needed to get away from him. She knew that the insanity that had consumed Chloe and Ray, the madness of two, was also acting upon her and Curtis, and although she was aware of its influence, she was subservient to it, which was why, as she strangled Chloe, the weaker her friend became, the harder she squeezed.

Tara pulled into the parking bay next to Curtis's sports car.

Curtis, already out of his car and resting his backside against its side wing, watched as she parked, then greeted her with a warm smile as she approached him.

"Whose car shall we take," he asked; "yours or mine?"

"What do you mean?"

It was a silly question to ask, Tara knew exactly what he meant. What did they call it in those old Bogie and Bacall *noir* movies? They were going on the lam!

Curtis sniggered. Oh, how she loved to hear him snigger!

"To keep travelling in two cars will be a little inconvenient, don't you think? Besides, I want to be close to you."

"We can't run away, Curtis."

"Why not, it's better than staying here and having to explain what we just did."

Tara agreed, but thought better of saying so.

"Where would we go?"

Curtis shrugged. "Does it matter? We can just keep driving until we find somewhere."

It sounded tempting, even a little romantic, but Tara shook her head, trying to shake away the temptation.

"We're bad for each other, Curtis."

"No," he seized her by the waist, clasping his hands together at the small of her back and hugging her body up against his. Tara could feel Curtis's erection trying to burst free from his pants. "We're good for each other," he continued. "Didn't you feel it in the restaurant, when we fucked on that table with everyone looking? It's like when I'm with you, I don't care. I don't care about anything except you. Don't you feel it?"

Tara nodded. "I feel it," she admitted, "but that feeling is dangerous, it's what they had back there at the house and it's what made them crazy. It's that damn dating site, it puts people together who shouldn't be together—"

"No!" Curtis objected, squeezing her closer. "We *should* be together. We're perfect together. You make me stronger and, in return, with me around, I'll always protect you, rescue you from peril, like I did today. Oh, and take a look at this."

He let go of her and scurried over to the trunk of his car. Tara followed.

When she joined him, the trunk was open. She looked down into it.

"I caught him snooping around your flat while you were at work," Curtis said. He and Tara were staring down at a dead man. "It looked like he was making himself very comfortable; he was making breakfast in your kitchen."

Recognition came to Tara gradually. The body in the trunk was disfigured, mangled practically, and covered in caked blood, but the silk boxer shorts put the pieces together for Tara.

This was no burglar or criminal she was looking at. Curtis had blundered, but, still, *what a majestic gesture it was!*

"You did this for me?" Tara asked as she gestured towards the mass of pummeled flesh that used to be her neighbor.

Curtis looked at her gravely. "I'd raze the world for you," he said, and Tara didn't doubt it.

She quivered. Her genitals moistened, an involuntary bodily response which told her this was love. Not the domestic love so common nowadays, the love of security, of compromise, of insouciance, of convenience. No, Curtis's love (or maybe passion was the more appropriate word) was uncompromising in its ferocity. To Tara, this was evident in the way he had savaged Kyle. Written in blood, here was his love letter to her.

Tara, overcome by this, threw her arms around Curtis and kissed him.

"Let's do it," she bellowed, it felt good to finally capitulate to her true urges, "let's run away together, let's fuck at every stop we make, and God help anyone who tries to tear us apart."

Under a Switchblade Moon
Tiffany Michelle Brown

Cat knew that she was breaking the rules, but she didn't care. Instead, she reveled in the fact that she was out in public despite strict orders to remain at home for the next 72 hours—under surveillance no less—albeit lazy surveillance since she'd managed to sneak out undetected. She grinned, recalling her great escape and imagining how pissed off her caretakers would be when they discovered she was gone.

A flash of white—a crisp, sterile memory—transformed her smile into a sneer. The white coats. Cat clenched her jaw and ignored the agitated pulse in her temple. What did they really know about her other than her list of medications and what her brain looked like after a scan? She was fine. The empty place in her chest no longer ached. Her wrists itched from time to time, but she could deal with that.

Cat drummed her blue fingernails on her paperback copy of *The Departed Don't Lie*, Robert Hoffstead's latest novel. He'd read an excerpt from the book earlier in the evening, his voice gruff and mangled—much like his characters. He was most definitely a smoker. Cat imagined him dipping his fingers into something harsher, too. Something like cocaine. She was convinced you'd need more than nicotine in your body to come up with all those imaginative ways to kill people.

Though she'd been tight-lipped and antisocial since arriving at the high school auditorium for the book signing, Cat felt a strange sort of kinship with the people seated around her. She imagined them all sweaty and twisted up in bed sheets, Robert Hoffstead's stories shattering their cycles of REM. They asked for it—just as Cat did—staying up late into the night, reading about the horrible things that happened when you weren't paying attention. When you weren't ready to defend yourself against the darkness.

The nightmares spawned by Robert Hoffstead's horror novels were the only things that made Cat feel alive anymore. She'd wake up in the night, her knuckles white from gripping her sheet, sweat making her forehead slick, a huge grin on her face. Fear was something she could understand. She craved it. Yearned for it. And the white coats simply couldn't understand that.

Looking around the packed auditorium, Cat knew she wasn't alone in her feelings. Yes, everyone at the book signing was just as fucked up as she. The only difference was Cat did something about it. She tapped into it and explored it, because she was brave in the face of fright.

A sudden clatter wiped the lazy smile from Cat's face and made her jump. She gritted her teeth, closed her eyes, and whispered, "You are in charge. Don't let them in." She clasped a hand over her racing heart. "You are in charge. Don't let them in."

After a deep inhale, Cat opened her eyes and sat up a little straighter in her scratchy, theater-style chair, anxiety draining from her midsection to her extremities. *Okay*, she admitted to herself, *the white coats are right about that mantra bullshit. I'll give them that.*

"What was that?" Male voice. British accent. To her left.

Cat sighed. She should've kept her mouth shut. She had to be better about remembering that mantras could be internal recitations.

Well, too late now. Cat had a choice. She could ignore the question…but she had to admit, she was a sucker for an accent. She wanted to get him talking.

"Something that helps," Cat said.

"Does it now?"

"Sometimes."

"What happens when it doesn't?"

Cat turned to take in her inquisitive counterpart. A shag of red hair, strong cheekbones, eyes like blue glass, and thin lips the color of salmon greeted her. She smirked, thinking that messing with this boy was going to be much too easy. "Bad things."

The stranger let out a low, throaty laugh. "Perhaps I should find another seat."

Cat shrugged. "I'm okay—for now."

The stranger smiled. It was a nice smile, one that caused bravado to bloom in Cat's belly. She reached into her purse and pulled out a small, white tablet. "Want some X?" she asked. At the startled look on the stranger's face, Cat snickered. "It's just a mint." She crunched the mint between her teeth and watched him smile.

"I would've dropped with you," he said.

"You would've, huh?"

"Yes."

"And why should I feel inclined to share with you?"

"Because you owe me. Your boot is on my knife."

Cat looked down and noticed something shiny in the crevice between the ball of her foot and the heel of her black boot. She bent at the waist and slid the knife out from beneath her. The metal was cold against her palm and a wave of adrenaline rushed from her waist to her toes

190

and then back up to her heart. She smiled, delighted. "You brought a knife to a book signing?"

"Yes," the pale stranger said.

Cat turned the knife in her hands and held it out to its owner, handle toward him. As the blade slid out of her grasp, goosebumps erupted on her bare shoulders. "You're unexpected," she said.

"How so?"

"I don't imagine ginger Brits who look like prep school boys carrying knives. I imagine you drinking tea and eating crumpets."

"You are so very mistaken."

Cat bit her lip and then turned her attention to the auditorium stage, to the line of people inching closer and closer to the greatness of Robert Hoffstead. A college-aged girl melted as the author shook her hand.

"What's your favorite book of his?" the man beside her asked.

"*Under a Switchblade Moon.*"

"Uncanny." The stranger held up an old paperback, the pages dog-eared and tired. It looked deliciously loved. "That's the book I brought for him to sign."

"You *are* a fan," Cat said approvingly.

The stranger leaned closer, and Cat waited to feel his skin against hers. She never did. Instead, she felt his breath on her ear. "More than you know."

Cat's heartbeat quickened as the stranger settled back in his seat. She could feel heat in the tips of her ears and struggled to breathe evenly. "Prove it," she challenged, smiling brazenly. "And lucky for you, you have some time to figure out how you will." The stranger frowned at Cat as she stood. "I'll be right back."

Cat hurried through the crowd to find the ladies room in the rear of the auditorium. In the bathroom, she went to the furthest stall, sat down, and studied the genius that is high school graffiti—*Pancho's meat makes my heart beat!*—until her thighs stopped throbbing.

She'd just wanted to fuck with this stranger, scare him a little bit—but Cat found herself losing control and swimming in the strangest of attractions. She'd usually write this guy off, what with his good-boy looks, but there was something about this Brit that inspired a dangerous instinct to take hold of Cat's insides. An instinct that wanted skin and sweat reflected in the blade of a knife.

She'd been under tight supervision for months. No one to flirt with, no one to tease, no one to fuel her fantasies.

This flirtation, it felt good. Dangerous. Dark. And the white coats would most definitely disapprove. Cat licked her lips and took a deep breath.

At the bathroom sink, she reapplied her dark lipstick and adjusted her corset. Happy with her reflection, she left the bathroom.

When Cat returned to her seat, the Brit was nowhere to be found. Her shoulders slumped as she scanned the room, hoping to catch a glimpse of red hair and a jagged cheekbone in the cheap, harsh lighting. She craned her neck and even stood on her seat cushion, but to no avail. He was gone.

Disappointed, Cat collapsed into her seat. She flexed and scratched her wrists, suddenly uncomfortable and unsure of whether she wanted to stay.

As she crossed her legs, Cat's boot made contact with something on the floor. Peering down, she spotted the stranger's copy of *Under a Switchblade Moon* and frowned. Why would he leave this behind?

She picked up the book. A yellow slip of paper stuck out of it about three-fourths of the way through the pages. Cat flipped through the novel to the bookmarked page. It was the first page of Chapter 14. On the yellow paper, lined and torn from a notepad, it read: *I predict you're a superb actress. And I like your mouth. Meet me on the south side of the building. Bring the book and read Chapter 14 before you meet me. You'll know what to do.*

There was no signature.

Pins and needles shot through Cat's wrists. She scratched at the sensation, relishing the dull pain from the pressure and friction, until it subsided. And then she looked down at the invitation nestled in her lap, her mouth stretching into a smile.

The offer was enticing. She knew what he was asking for, knew it because Cat had read this book at least five times. She knew the story, and Chapter 14, well.

This stranger was offering her an experience that would not be bound by a cover and sold on Amazon. It would be real. It would be dangerous.

Cat reread the note and rolled her shoulders back, letting excitement swirl in her chest. She stood and started walking, clutching the stranger's copy of *Under a Switchblade Moon* in her right hand and abandoning her copy of *The Departed Don't Lie* in the aisle. Someone called after her, tried to return the book, but Cat ignored the Good Samaritan and continued on her way.

Though the sun was sinking on the horizon, summer heat hit Cat like a hot iron as soon as she exited the building. She felt perspiration bubble on her forearms and dry air scratched her lungs. She walked past food trucks parked near the entrance of the auditorium and took a right when she hit the building's edge. She watched her shadow bob as she walked, and then it disappeared as she approached an area of the high school where lighting was sparse. Cat slowed her pace and pressed herself against brick. She opened the book to Chapter 14, brought it close to her face, squinting hard, and read it as quickly as she could.

When Cat reached the final page of the short chapter, she smirked, took a deep breath, and steadied herself. She was ready.

Cat pushed herself off the wall and stood up tall, elongating her neck. She rolled her shoulders back and pressed her chest forward. She slinked along the building, the book hanging by her side in her left hand, her right hand skimming warm brick.

She reached the next corner of the building and turned, both knowing and not knowing what she would find beyond it.

The stranger leaned against the wall a few feet away, smoking a cigarette. "I knew you'd come." Cat recognized the first line of Chapter 14.

"You knew nothing," Cat said in what she hoped was a sultry voice. She pressed her right hand to her hip.

The stranger took a drag, then turned to look at Cat. His face was shrouded in darkness, but his right cheekbone, smooth and sharp, protruded out of the shadow and into the burgeoning moonlight. She couldn't see his eyes, but Cat could feel them—blue electricity, sparking, calling, prickling.

"You're a beautiful woman," the stranger said.

Cat took three steps closer to him, just like Angela did in the book. "And you have a death wish." She looked him up and down.

"You think I want to die?"

"I know you do."

Cat took the cigarette from the stranger's lips and inhaled. She dropped the stranger's book at her feet. Neither of them flinched as it thudded to the pavement. Cat let the cigarette fall to the ground. She stepped on it with her boot and twisted her leg twice, savoring the scratch of her shoe against concrete.

Cat stared into the stranger's eyes for a few moments and then her hands floated to the top of her corset. She undid five hooks and let her hands float to her sides. "Your move," she whispered, no longer recognizing her own voice.

The stranger smiled, but Cat kept her stare steely and cold, the way it was supposed to be.

"You're perfect," the stranger said.

"I'm a better actor than you," she said. "That line's not in the book."

"No," the stranger said, "but the rest of this will be." And in that moment, something behind his eyes changed.

The stranger closed the gap between them. Cat could feel heat radiating from his body. His stomach against hers felt like stone, and Cat imagined him swimming laps in an Olympic-sized swimming pool or running soccer drills. He guided her hands behind his neck, and Cat laced her fingers there. His fingertips grazed her back, winding their way down her spine until bone turned into the soft flesh of her backside. The stranger cupped Cat's ass in both hands and gave a squeeze, which catapulted them both into a fury of passion.

Cat's mouth found the stranger's and opened hungrily. The taste of cigarettes rolled over her tongue, strong and smoky. Cat's pulse traveled to her abdomen and she imagined an ancient drum inside her, sounding the rhythm of a primal need. She dug her fingers into the stranger's neck and pulled him against her, moaning into his mouth. She loved the taste of him and the way he held her body like something that he wished to break and then put back together.

Cat almost got distracted. Almost.

When she broke the rhythm of the kiss, Cat was out of breath. Her hands found the stranger's chest, and she pushed him into the wall with a brute force she didn't know she possessed. She stepped closer and lifted her knee to the wall beside the stranger's left hip. It didn't take long for him to grab her leg, to squeeze it. And then the kissing began again.

One of the stranger's hands held Cat against him while the other traveled up her torso and into her corset to cup her breast. The skin of his palm was rough, weathered, and Cat pulled back from the kiss to cry out in pleasure. She pulled his face to hers, kissed him deeply, and bit his lower lip.

Cat pulled back from the embrace and when the stranger tried to pull her in again, she resisted. She took two measured steps backward. Keeping her eyes locked on his, Cat reached beneath her skirt and pulled her underwear down to her ankles. She stepped forward, out of them, and then delivered her line slowly, "It appears you've chosen your fate."

The stranger grabbed Cat's waist, pulled her forward, and spun her around so that her back was against the wall. With one hand on her belly, the other fumbled with his belt and zipper. He stepped closer to her, grabbed her left leg, hooked it on his hip, and slid into her.

Despite the speed and power of that first thrust, Cat didn't feel pain, the itch of her wrists, her broken past— only heat and electricity and connection. She stared into the stranger's eyes those first precious moments, dumbfounded and awed, then sank into another fevered kiss. Her hands pressed into his back, dissected the muscle there, then slinked down to his hips, pushing and guiding him into her in a desperate rhythm.

Suddenly, Cat remembered. She remembered the moon and the blade and the promise and the words. Despite feeling full and exhilarated, it was time.

As the stranger continued to move to his own ancient rhythm, Cat let her hand travel down his side to his pant pocket. Her fingers slipped in and she recognized the cold of metal. It was there, just as she knew it would be. But this knife was different than the one the stranger had dropped in the auditorium. It was lighter, sleeker, more sure of itself. Cat's breathing became labored and she closed her eyes, summoning Angela into her small but able hands.

With a soft, guttural cry, Cat activated the switchblade of the knife and plunged the blade into the stranger's side. She felt flesh give and then shock and stiffness overtake the stranger's body. The passionate kisses stopped, and the moment teetered on the precipice of a dark void. The stranger looked into Cat's eyes, shocked and saddened, before he crumpled to the ground, gasping and moaning.

That was when Cat expected to wake up—from either a dream or the medication the white coats administered when she was having one of her fits, the pills that knocked her out cold so she wouldn't endanger anyone.

But her entire body felt like lead, entirely present. Her body turned to ice as she watched the stranger fall to the ground. She stared at him, expecting him to vanish or seep into the ground, because surely this was a hallucination, a fantasy, a dream. He hit the pavement hard with a *thwack*.

Cat opened her mouth, but nothing came out. The man on the asphalt twitched and rolled, holding his side. Cat closed her eyes and tried to will the sickening vision away, but when she reopened them, the body was still there. The unmoving, cold, stiff body.

Cat swallowed heavily. "I thought it was what you wanted," she whispered to the heap on the ground. "I thought..."

The body rolled over.

"It *was* what I wanted," it whispered to her.

Cat backed into the wall and winced as her shoulder blades met brick. "I stabbed you."

"I wasn't sure you would," the stranger said.

"I did."

"Yes, you did. And you should see your face right now. It's so perfect, beautiful, terrified." The stranger smiled at her. He climbed to his feet, zipped up his pants, and bent to pick up the knife. When he stood, he locked eyes with Cat and shook his head. "You're truly spooked, aren't you?"

"I haven't killed anyone before."

"You still haven't."

Cat's eyes darted from the stranger's face to his chest to his side and back up to his face. He wasn't bleeding.

The stranger did a 360-degree turn to show that he was, in fact, completely alright. Then he took the knife from Cat's hand and jabbed it into his palm. The handle of the knife swallowed its blade.

"It's fake," Cat said.

"Yes." The stranger took a step toward Cat and took her face in his hands. "Look at me," he said. And she did. Her heart slowed and her breathing, too. Calm washed over her like seafoam.

The stranger smiled and somehow Cat could smile back at him, at the man she'd almost killed because a book had told her to. She placed her hands over his and laughed wildly. Her cackle echoed off buildings where children learned how to solve mathematical equations and analyze the works of Kate Chopin. The stranger joined her, laughing his throaty laugh, his fingers weaving through her hair.

When their laughter subsided, Cat ducked under the stranger's arms. She stooped and picked up his tattered edition of *Under a Switchblade Moon*. She removed the yellow strip of paper, her invitation, folded it up, and stuck it in her boot. She held out the book to the stranger, but he made no move to take it.

"Keep it," he said.

"Okay." She picked up her discarded underwear and also stuck that into her boot.

Cat stared at the stranger, the pavement sizzling in the Arizona heat between them. He gazed back at her, a smirk tugging at his lips. "I feel like I know you. We've just met, yes, but I know you," he said. "Go for a walk with me? Tell me your ghost stories?"

Cat admired the stranger's sharp features in the moonlight. She remembered his hands on her body. She imagined wading into the blue pools of his eyes, naked and brazen. She knew. She knew him.

"Only if you promise not to get scared," Cat quipped.

The stranger gave her a nod and held out his hand. The pair walked into the shadows of the building toward swing sets and faded hopscotch courts behind the school.

With the stranger's hand in hers, Cat didn't feel emptiness or aching or itching. She felt far, far away from the white coats. She felt safe and understood. She felt ignition as his fingers grazed her palms.

Cat smiled up at the stranger and relief enveloped her like a fleece blanket on a cold, bitter night.

She'd found it. She'd found him. Someone with whom to share her nightmares.

The Curious Case of Dr. Cherry Pauper

Candace Gleave

"Professor," Georgia called out as she stepped into the empty class room. "You in here?"

"Yes, yes, I'm in here," Dr. Cherry's muffled voice came from the storage room. "I'm just getting a few things, in this infernal godforsaken room."

Sounds of heavy items falling, followed by grunts and cuss words kept Georgia from stepping any closer.

"I'll just wait here," she said hesitantly.

"Good call," Dr. Cherry responded in a frustrated voice. "If this lousy university had proper storage rooms, all my troubles would be over. Well, that's not true." He prattled. "For I do have a lot of troubles," he finished in a dry laugh to himself.

Georgia absentmindedly scratched her elbow and looked around. Her eyes wandered to her usual place, next to Dr. Cherry's desk. Teacher's aid. Looking down at her fitted red shirt with a scooping neckline, she adjusted the plunging view, lower. Dr. Cherry was the most interesting mathematician and not to mention the most attractive. Too aloof to know his own gorgeous looks from a pig in the road, Dr. Cherry seemed to make all his female students swoon for numbers. Numbers are sexy.

"I swear one has to cross Dante's nine levels of hell to get to anything in that monstrosity of a closet," Dr. Cherry emerged from the storage room. Hands carrying a small cardboard box filled with all sorts of odd trinkets. He wiped his shiny forehead on his long sleeve shirt. "Thank you for coming," he smiled to Georgia as he approached her.

"Of course, any chance for extra credit," she paused. Truth be known, she would have come to clean his toilet. "Say, what are we doing anyway?" her eyebrows came together in trying to decipher all what Dr. Cherry was carrying.

"Oh, yes," Dr. Cherry said rather loud and abruptly. "We don't have much time. What does your watch read? I lost mine last night. Pamela took it."

"It's 9:00 p.m.," Georgia said with a grump. Jealous thoughts filled her mind. *Who the hell is Pamela? Whoever she is, I don't like her.*

"Blast, we don't have time to go to the hardware store," Dr. Cherry stamped his foot dramatically. His barely turning salt and pepper hair tossed about as he looked around. His frantic eyes traced all over the empty class room, in a desperate, unproductive search.

"Something you need, professor?" Georgia tried to follow his darting gaze.

"I think not," his eyes found Georgia's concerned face and smiled dryly. "Come, we must be off."

***

The university grounds backed into a disgusting looking forest. Neatly manicured lawns were stopped abruptly by scrub oak trees. Their scratchy limbs that grew in tangled madness kept everyone at bay to this unwelcoming wildwood. Marching with high knees, Dr. Cherry strode into the backwoods, pushing past the scrub oak with strained efforts. Pokey ends of the tangled trees clung and held on to one's clothes, making them tear and rip.

"For fuck sakes." His arms still carrying the box jerked his torso in great effort to free his shirt that had been caught. The well worn fabric stressed with tension. In one last grand tug the shirt gave up the ghost in a ripping noise.

"That was my last good shirt, you beastly, horrid forest." Dr. Cherry vented loudly, clutching the box tightly, he fought the urge to kick it into the air. "I'm gonna come back in daylight hours and take a machete to these godforsaken trees and make them twigs."

"I'm sorry, professor," Georgia sympathetically touched his shoulder.

He jumped slightly at her touch. Realizing it was Georgia, he relaxed again.

"The universe is against me, dear," Dr. Cherry shirked and maneuvered around endless piles of deer droppings and stepped into a large dog turd. Figures. "I hope you don't mind stepping on any deer excrement," he said over his shoulder to Georgia. "They are tiny pellets, but can be troublesome in piles of large quantities."

George suppressed a sigh, as she looked down to her open toed heels. "I'll be fine," and tip toed around the smeared dog turd, making sure to avoid it.

"We don't have much farther to go," Dr. Cherry directed. "Just until we find a clearing, any clearing will do."

"Okay," Georgia's eyes looked ahead to see if a clearing was drawing closer. She saw a couple of possible places, but kept her findings to herself. Unsure of what Dr. Cherry had in mind.

"Aww, yes, I see just the place," Dr. Cherry beamed happily and increased his strides. "Just over here, Georgia, right here."

***

Under a crescent moon, Dr. Cherry and a very confused Georgia had lit candles all arranged in a circle, with a diameter of 5 ft. Various birthday candles, small votive candles, and aroma therapy candles all burned brightly together in a hodge-podge of vanilla and paraffin wax. Dr. Cherry stood in the middle of the mismatched circle with his hands high above his head.

"*Ite et vos auferat canis rabidus*," his voice proclaimed loudly, with closed eyes.

Per instruction, Georgia was to throw glass marbles at Dr. Cherry. Holding a bag of large and small marbles she tossed the colorful glass orbs at him, one at a time. Little flinches of the professor's facial muscles held the tell that they were indeed hitting him.

"*Ite et vos auferat canis rabidus*," he repeated even louder. His tone of voice squeaked from the constant harassment of flying glass objects.

Chewing stale gum for the past hour, Georgia stopped mid chew and looked at the candles, Dr. Cherry, and threw a couple more marbles at him. Nothing happened.

Dr. Cherry opened up one eye, then the other and peered cautiously at Georgia.

"Was something supposed to happen?" Georgia puzzled, getting ready to throw more marbles at him.

"No, don't," He shielded his body with his hands. "Those little fuckers hurt."

"What do you want me to do?" she asked.

Dr. Cherry bit his bottom lip and reached in his trousers. Pulling out a small pink hand mirror, the professor held it up before his face.

"Did I miss something?" he asked the mirror. "I put the candles all around and had the girl throw marbles at me."

Georgia swallowed her spit wrong and began choking. Dr. Cherry ignored her and kept his gaze fixed in the mirror.

"Maybe I need an animal sacrifice?" he rubbed his chin, contemplating the idea. "You think that would work?"

"Who are you talking to?" Georgia questioned through broken coughs.

"An all white goat?" Dr. Cherry asked the mirror. "Okay, I'll give that a go."

"Dr. Cherry, who are you talking to?" Georgia waved her arms, trying to get his attention.

Dr. Cherry put the mirror back in his trouser pocket and finally acknowledged Georgia.

"I was talking to Pamela. Unfortunately, it didn't work. Damn," he said at last.

"What didn't work?" Georgia's vision of the insanely hot professor vanished and now could only see a deeply disturbed man. *He talks to a mirror, named Pamela. Why are the hot ones always the crazy ones?*

"The ritual," Dr. Cherry shook his head befuddled. "The candles should have been a dead give away. Kids these days. In any case, it didn't work."

"I gathered," Georgia pulled up her neckline in defeat.

"You free tomorrow night, dear?" Dr. Cherry bent down and began picking up the candles and marbles.

Georgia quickly lowered her neckline again and joined him, cleaning up.

"Why, yes. Yes, I am."

***

"Wasn't it supposed to be an all white goat?" Georgia questioned the needed animal for the ritual. In her hand, she held a leash to an all white poodle-golden retriever mix. A goldendoodle. The 12 year old dog, completely blind in the right eye, sat in the middle of the circle of candles and didn't move.

"I couldn't find an all white goat," Dr. Cherry knelt on the ground and began lighting the candles with his pocket lighter. "And, I'm pretty broke, so, I took 'ol Dakota Joe here from an old spinster that lives three houses away from me."

"You stole her dog?" Georgia looked at the poor animal with sadness. A patch of fur near its shoulder blade had been worn down to the skin. Revealing a very red and exposed rash. The beast looked as if it had suffered from an extreme itch.

"I didn't steal anything. I merely opened the gate of the yard and had bacon in my pocket."

"Unbelievable," she shook her head.

"I can justify anything in my mind," Dr. Cherry put down a purple aroma therapy candle that smelled of lilac and picked up a rose votive candle and lit it. "Isn't this pretty?" he gestured to the rose candle.

"It is," she said with a grin, not noticing the change in topics.

"I find this candle the most radiant," Dr. Cherry placed it down and picked up the next in line. "Though, it doesn't shine quite as bright as you, dear."

Georgia's fair complexion flushed, "Oh, professor."

"It's true," he said more so to himself. "Your blonde hair is like white gold. Pamela is terribly jealous."

Georgia's smiled faded into a pout in hearing Pamela's name.

"Who's Pamela?"

Dr. Cherry looked up alarmed, "What do you know about her?"

"What?" Georgia blinked confused.

"Oh, never mind," Dr. Cherry stood up and brushed his hands clean on his grey slacks. "We need to hurry."

Standing next to the languid Dakota Joe in the circle, Dr. Cherry pulled out a small leather journal from his slack's pocket. Thumbing through the pages he stopped on a passage with thick black pen marks and hectic scribbles. Georgia peered over to see what was written, but couldn't decipher the chaotic texts.

"*Ya eahirat al'ard aleazimat, 'aqbil hdha alkalb wadhahb*," Dr. Cherry yelled from the agonizing pit in his stomach to his foul, wretched wraith. "*Yumkinuk allaenat qubalatan, alkalbat.*"

Dr. Cherry threw the leather journal to Georgia with a cry, "Turn to page 10 and start reading the chant. Quickly, now."

Fumbling with the tiny journal, Georgia spied the barely legible numbers scribbled at the bottom of the book. Finding page 10, a two word chant in a language she didn't recognize was written over and over again, filling the page.

"*Vittu sinut,*" she said hesitantly.

"Yes, that's the phrase," Dr. Cherry raised his hands to the sky. "Say it loudly, we need this to work."

"*Vittu sinut, vittu sinut, vittu sinut,*" Georgia's thunderous voice rang out loud and strong. The weather that had been abnormally warm for late autumn suddenly became quite cold. This sudden chill made Georgia catch her breath through chattering teeth.

"Yes, it's working," Dr. Cherry beamed with freezing joy. "*Bamilana, ya muhbil qadhar, atrikni washani.*"

Dakota Joe began baying an unnatural, eerie howl. The shrill pitch of his distressing call irritated the ears, making hairs stand on end.

Standing over the anguished canine, Dr. Cherry reached into his pocket and pulled out the pink hand mirror.

"Oh, dear god," Dr. Cherry gasped in horror as he held the mirror up to his face. Hands trembling he fumbled the haunting mirror and in a great spasm it slipped from his hands. Georgia, standing just outside the circle, quickly bent forward and caught the falling pink pier glass.

"No," Dr. Cherry screamed. "Don't look into the mirror."

Holding the speculum before her, Georgia beheld her reflection and just behind her, as if she could reach out and touch the figure, the most disturbing dark entity her eyes had ever witnessed. Words failed her comprehension in staring at this hideous creature. Black oil oozed off the wraith, like madness free falling to hell. A woman's figure, noticeably, with willowy limbs and long, shaggy, tousled hair. This horrific, unkempt creature peeked back at Georgia. The ghastly face of the wraith, resembling a color of decaying death, bore her sharp, razor teeth at Georgia. This menacing grin was that of ultimate hate.

The wraith hissed. Its curved talon-like nails reached out to Georgia, trying to lacerate her face. Her horror transfixed reflection.

Breaking the bewitching power, Dr. Cherry took the pink mirror away from Georgia, and stuffed it quickly back into his trouser pocket.

Georgia stood perfectly still. Her eyes blinked dumbly at Dakota Joe and the well worn dress shoes of Dr. Cherry.

Dr. Cherry started pacing around the circle and every so often stopped, nodded his head and made a very unpleasant grunting noise.

"Dr. Cherry," Georgia finally shook off the last of the paralyzed delirium. "What was that?"

"Pardon?" Dr. Cherry unconsciously answered between his pontificating thoughts.

"Was that Pamela?" Georgia took a step closer to Dr. Cherry. "Was that for real?"

Dr. Cherry pulled out the pink mirror one last time from his trousers and looked into it.

"It almost worked," he said triumphantly into the mirror. "Perhaps, one last go?"

"Dr. Cherry, please," Georgia fought off tears and was unsuccessful. The salty frustrations rolled down her face. She wiped them away just as fast as they fell. "I need to know what I saw?"

"Dearest," Dr. Cherry looked up from the mirror and took in her distressed state. "Come here."

Georgia flung her arms around Dr. Cherry's torso and pulled at him tightly. He smelled of saddle wood and musk.

"I'm sorry to have dragged you into this," he started. "Truth is, I am terribly attracted to you. Your curves make any man want to ravish you. While your angel face with your two dimples holds such a delicate radiance. I wanted your help not just because I find you beautiful, but how smart you are. I have told no other soul about this ordeal. I have no one to help me."

Georgia's heart fluttered, "You really find me beautiful?"

"You are the most beautiful woman on campus," Dr. Cherry kissed the top of her head.

"Thank you," she blushed, bashfully. Unaccustomed to a man's praise and tender kisses.

"That thing in the mirror," Georgia said after a few seconds of silence. "You need to banish it, right?"

"Oh, yes, that," Dr. Cherry forced a laugh. "Pamela, she is my deceased wife."

"Dear god," Georgia backed away from Dr. Cherry.

"She died in a tragic accident," His voice broke, followed by a dry cough.

"What kind of accident?" Georgia inquired.

"The bridge on I-90," Dr. Cherry looked down to the ground, reliving the memory. "It was winter and the whole road was ice. She slid off the road, into the river."

Georgia blinked, "I remember the news story. That was her?"

Dr. Cherry nodded, "Sadly,"

"I'm so sorry," Georgia stepped closer to him and wrapped her arms around him once more.

"She has been haunting me ever since," Dr. Cherry stated flatly. "Her visitations have become more and more terrible and maddening. I need to get rid of her, so she can finally rest."

Georgia nodded, empathetically. She hadn't said anything, but had observed Dr. Cherry's complexion had taken a drastic turn for the worse. Dark purplish circles hung under his blood shot eyes, hazel eyes. His thinning frame looked as if a few years of life had been sucked from his body.

"How can I help you?"

"Good question," Dr. Cherry still holding the mirror looked into it and made sure to avoid the direct line of sight with Georgia. "No, really? A virgin? That's preposterous. I don't care what you demand, Pamela. The answer is no."

"What?" Georgia's heart raced with panic. "What does she want?"

"She needs to have a virgin ceremony be preformed." Dr. Cherry shook his head. "This university isn't a very good one….and I'm very doubtful that virgins would attend this shabby place. Now if she wanted a coke whore addict, I'd ask Debbie. . .but a virgin?"

"Um, professor," Georgia said timidly.

"Yes, sweetheart?"

"I'm a virgin."

***

Hardly the right circumstances to lose one's virginity, Georgia sat awkwardly on a scratch wool blanket. Dr. Cherry, like the two previous nights, had set up the candles in a circle, lit them, and sat with his long crossed legs on the blanket next to Georgia. A tree root had found its way right into Georgia's butt. With every adjustment and shift the gnarled root only dug into her further. Ouch.

"How is the ceremony supposed to be preformed?" Georgia bashfully brushed her blonde hair behind her ear, a few strands still stuck out.

"Well," Dr. Cherry gently reached up and tucked the last of the golden strands behind her ear. "For this type of ceremony to be effective, the female needs to be pleasured."

Georgia's fair faced began to crimson.

"You've never been with a man before?"

"No."

"I shall try and not disappoint you," Dr. Cherry gently reached for Georgia's legs. They were so smooth and welcoming to the touch. She was wearing a tight, short summer dress that made him hard just seeing her. He could take her right then and there but fought the urge.

"I've had a crush on you since two semesters ago," she said sheepishly.

"Is that so?" his hand slid further up her firm thighs, giving them a squeeze.

"That's why I signed up to be your teacher aid," she caught her breath due to his advancing touch.

"You ever think naughty thoughts about me?" Dr. Cherry only half interested in her response as his other brain started to take over. His fingers had found their way up to her honey pot. Smooth kitty. Pushing aside her panties, a wet pussy beckoned him.

"Very naughty," she nodded and looked into his brown eyes. Without another word or question, Dr. Cherry leaned in to taste her lips.

Her responsive mouth kissed him hungrily. He stuck his middle finger deeper into her starved, reactive body. Oh god, how wet and delicious she was.

He guided her down onto the blanket. Leaving her mouth with his kisses, he traveled down her neck. Kiss, bite, kiss, the seasoned mouth globally covered her collar bone and further down found her perfect breasts. An overgrown cat sneaking back to its mother couldn't have had a more maddening effect. Dr. Cherry pulled down her neckline, black bra, and with parted lips attacked her taunt nipple. He groaned with desire as he smacked, licked and devoured her.

Georgia's hand came to the back of Dr. Cherry's head and held him into her. Her chest breathed heavily up and down as she watched him move back and forth between her bosoms.

In leaving his breast work, Dr. Cherry lifted her dress that had already been hiked up to her waist and reached for her black thong and pulled it down her obedient legs. Removing her panties completely, Dr. Cherry gently widened her legs and lowered his head to her pink folds.

"Oh, god," Georgia exclaimed as she felt his tongue and mouth kiss and torture her pussy in the most glorious and fantastic of ways.

"You enjoy this?" he asked between oral pleasings.

"It's amazing," she purred and moaned, wanting more.

"You have such an exquisite pussy," he lapped up her wetness as it flowed freely.

Georgia wiggled and arched her back, giving in to her body's nirvana. Her legs trembled as Dr. Cherry relentlessly teased her. Looking up into her eyes, Dr. Cherry gave a wry smile and got to his hands and began to unfasten his pants. His cock had been hard and ready for the last ten minutes and couldn't prolong anymore.

"Take off your dress," he instructed.

Taking off his own clothes, Georgia watched Dr. Cherry lean over her with his lean, but, strong physic. Completely naked, he pressed his weight onto her. With parted legs he reached down and slid the tip of his cock into her perfect, pink, porcelain slit.

Georgia swallowed and prepared herself. She could feel his cock. His girth and length impressed and terrified her, like a crazy bull, stomping and snorting behind a too small of gate to contain it.

"For the ceremony to work, you need to repeat this phrase," he kissed the side of her neck and playfully pushed the tip of his member into her but not penetrating completely.

Dizzy in a seducing head cloud, Georgia agreed. All she could think about was having him enter her. She wanted him in.

"Ready?" he asked.

"I'm ready."

Dr. Cherry reached over to his discarded clothes and found his trousers. Pulling out the pink mirror, he returned to Georgia's blissful looking face and kissed her eyelids.

"Keep your eyes closed and repeat after me, my darling."

"Okay," she felt his tip getting pushed further into her. "I'm ready."

"*Annan ruumiini Pamelalle uudestisyntymiseksi,*" Dr. Cherry held the mirror over Georgia's face and thrust deep inside her dark labyrinth.

Georgia gasped. The frenzied craving of wanting him to enter her, feeling his cock inside her, she opened her eyes and found herself looking straight into Pamela's hideous haunting dead face. She screamed a high pitched shrill.

"Say the words," Dr. Cherry fought to keep the mirror in place. "Repeat after me, remember the ceremony."

Georgia stricken with fear could no longer feel the pleasurable sensation. All she could feel was a growing malevolence and enmity for every living creature.

"*Annan ruumiini Pamelalle uudestisyntymiseksi*," Dr. Cherry said with urgency. "Say the words, Georgia. *Annan ruumiini Pamelalle uudestisyntymiseksi.*"

Insanity had begun to take over Georgia's mind. The wraith in the mirror had entwined the two images and Georgia's eyes turned a dark, ebony lifeless color.

In a trembling stupor the host muttered slowly the words that Dr. Cherry had been barking frantically over and over.

"Annan ruumiini Pamelalle uudestisyntymiseksi," frozen with fear, tears fell down Georgia's face as she finished the last of the ritual.

Dr. Cherry removed the mirror and ravaged her body.

Thrusting deep inside her, the old rhythmic instinct of life and lust consumed him.

"God, you are so sexy," he groaned with a gratifying buzz.

Pamela found Dr. Cherry's perspiring face and cupped it in her hands.

"You were always a love sick puppy dog," her husky voice startled Dr. Cherry as it was nothing like Georgia's sweet, delightful soprano voice.

"Pamela," Dr. Cherry hesitated, "You've come back to me." He finished in a loving tone.

"Does this poor girl know that you were using her?" Pamela's black soulless eyes looked down at her new body and grinned. "Damn, this body I will have fun with."

"I picked the best for you, my love," Dr. Cherry kissed her hard nipples playfully.

"I can hear her thoughts," Pamela closed her eyes. A sadistic pleasure came over her, "It's like I am two women now. Two women with insatiable appetites," she coerced Dr. Cherry on his back and straddled him.

"What is she thinking?" he asked.

"She wants to fuck your brains out."

"Goodness," Dr. Cherry laughed slightly. "For just losing her v-card she sure wants to get her freak on."

Pamela sat upright started sucking on her own finger.

"Mmmmm, everything is intensified when you are feeling it for two," Pamela continued to lick and suck on her fingers. Unaware of the change overcoming her body, Pamela's distraction hadn't noticed how her host's body had turned an ash-grey color. The blonde beautiful hair of Georgia had transmogrified into white, wiry hair that frizzed out.

"Touch yourself," Dr. Cherry prompted and allowed for the diversion to let him reach for his trousers, once more.

Pamela stopped sucking on her fingers and sensually touched one of her breasts.

"I've never been with a woman before," Pamela let her head fall back and took in the arousal.

"What is Georgia feeling?"

"She wants me to," Pamela caressed her body down with traveling hands to her backside. "She wants me to . . ."

Her blackened fingertips slipped between her round bottom and searched for the puckered hole.

Grabbing a vile of holy water out of one of his pockets, Dr. Cherry opened the lid and slowly sat upright.

"She wants to experience everything I see," Dr. Cherry whispered in Pamela's ear. "Don't disappoint her. Give her something dirty to remember."

Pamela breathed deeply and pushed her rotted finger nail into her butt.

"Oh, fuck," she cried out erotically and pushed another finger into the hole. Deeper. Harder.

"That's it, slut," Dr. Cherry bit her bottom earlobe, furthering the seduction. *"Juo tama pyha cum ja kuolla narttu."*

He grabbed Pamela's mouth and forcibly poured the holy water down it. Pamela thrashed violently. The blessed elixir seared into Pamela's throat. Her black eyes pierced Dr. Cherry's very soul as she felt the purifying pains of a righteous death.

Keeping his hands over her mouth, tightly closed, he kept the holy water in.

"Georgia, send this bitch to hell," he ordered.

Screaming into his hands, Pamela scratched fiercely at Dr. Cherry, maiming his chest and face.

"Georgia," Dr. Cherry yelled between frightful banshee screams. "Take back your body and get her out."

The chaos intensified as Georgia gained control of her body and in a gross, distorted facial expression tipped back her head and dropped her lower jaw. The hellish black essence expelled out of Georgia's mouth and vaporized into the air.

"Fuck me, that anal was so disgusting," she collapsed into Dr. Cherry and cried horribly. Her body shook with violent spasms of chill and fright.

"I'm so sorry, baby" He held her tightly. "If I would have told you everything, I'm not sure you would have gone through with the ritual."

"So it worked then?" she said between tearful sobs.

"Yes, sweetheart."

Georgia noticed the pink mirror on the soiled wool blanket and reached for it. With shaking fingers she held the mirror up to her face. Just her reflection looked back at her.

"Oh, thank god," she let the mirror drop to the ground and continued to let Dr. Cherry embrace her.

"You were perfect," Dr. Cherry kissed the top of Georgia's head. "It's all over."

Georgia's breath started to slow down as her traumatized body relaxed.

"Professor?" Georgia asked softly.

"Yes?"

"Why was your dead wife haunting you in the first place?"

Dr. Cherry smiled to himself, "Because, I developed an addiction to one of my female students."

Georgia's stomach turned sick, "Which student?"

"That would be you, dearest." Dr. Cherry whispered into her ear and nibbled on it. "I couldn't have her until my wife was out of the picture. So I cut the line to her brakes."

An Ogre in Blessing
David Turnbull

Blessing was a curse. An ulcer on the stinking orifice of Alaska. Built on shifting gravel and silt, held together by creeping mildew and apt to tumble in on itself any minute. It had pitiful sanitation and was such a cesspit of depravity and disease that Van der Hoon, the Dutchman who named the place, must have laughed till he puked.

The only reason Blessing existed was the gold rush.

It wasn't half as big as Dawson, nor anywhere near as prolific as Nome. But old Ven der Hoon had found a whole heap of gold in a creek nearby. Enough for him to retire back to Rotterdam and rest his miserable bones for the remainder of his live long days.

Desperate men came tumbling into Blessing. Desperate to panhandle their dreams into reality. Desperate to turn their blisters and chilblains into manicured fingers and perfectly clipped toenails. Blessing was supposed to be their respite from relentless toil in the freezing rivers. They came. They went. They came back again.

As a consequence, Blessing's fringes were an ever-changing jumble of listing canvas tents and ramshackle, thrown together shacks. At its heart was a half mile main street, wood and timber buildings either side, gaudily painted against the drab grey of the landscape, plankboard sidewalk with a treacherous mire of brown puddles and potholes running midway along its length.

Sourdoughs and panhandles filled Blessing up to the gunnels on some days and left it deserted and desolate on others. There was no rhyme nor logic to it. Gold fever was the making of a handful and the breaking of most. Either way, made or broken, celebration or consolation, when they were in town they mostly wanted to fuck till sun up.

I worked at the whorehouse.

But I wasn't no whore.

I was born pug ugly, see. Club foot, hair lip, nubbin for a left ear, squint in my right eye. Not exactly saleable commodity, as Bronwyn, the madam of the whorehouse, was fond of saying. I was the maid, the laundress, the seamstress, the cook, the general dogsbody. They paid me in tips and sips of brandy. Let me kip in a pokey little room up in the garret. I'd stuff my face while I cooked to save me going hungry when I was excluded because they was pissed at me. I sucked up their slaps to the face and kicks up the butt.

It was me what found the ogre.

The night before I found him, a drunken punter had broken the nose of one of the girls. Her name was Rachel. She told him he reeked like a piggery and he should take a bath before getting anywhere near her bed. Being drunk as the skunk he stunk like he didn't take too kindly to her suggestions. To make his point he punched her square in the nose with his ham hock fist. Knocked out a tooth into the bargain.

Bronwyn kicked him down the stairs. Two of the whores kicked him along the street. Almost gouged out his eyes. The doc came and reset Rachel's nose. Gave her a slug of morphine for the pain in her gum.

She was a mess. But she she'd fix. Men don't necessarily look at the mantelpiece when they're poking the fire. Well at least that what Bronwyn used to say. Except if the mantelpiece was me. Then they'd take one look and run like fucking hell before the tip of the poker so much as hit the cinders.

The sheets on the bed didn't fare so well. They was beyond fixing. They was soaked in Rachel's blood and ruined. Bronwyn said I should take them out back and set light to them. That's where I saw him. Back there in the alley, half naked in his raggedy clothes, big knees curled up to his belly, battered old satchel pressed to his chest.

First thing I noticed was that he was blue. Blue from the marbled veins that criss-crossed all over his grey looking flesh. Blue like the sky. Blue like the sky reflected on an icy lake. Blue like a field of lilacs poking up in the spring though dusting of snow.

I thought he looked dead. I ain't afraid of dead folk. Seen plenty in my time. Dead folk can look kind of beautiful. Like this one. All blue with the cold. Kind of angelic and demonic all rolled in one. I shivered from the chill in the air. Poor bastard must have frozen to death where he sat. That's what I reckoned.

I kicked him to be sure.

I used my club foot.

If I swing it right it packs a kick like a mule.

He groaned and turned around to look up me. His eyes were yellow, like he was jaundiced or something. The maw of his mouth looked impossibly pink. As if he'd been gnawing on a hunk of raw meat. He stumbled up to his feet, not dead at all. He must have been almost seven foot tall.

When I looked up at him, I knew he was an ogre come down from the mountains. I screamed. Then I fainted.

***

I came to on the couch in the atrium of the whorehouse.

This was where Bronwyn haggled with the punters before settling on price.

All the whores was gathered round. As was normal they was in various combinations of undress and underwear. The ogre was in the linen barrow, parked near the fireplace. He was unconscious again. He looked like a huge fish, all blue and limp, legs flopping over the rim of the barrow and his satchel sitting on his belly.

"How are you feeling?" asked Rachel, the whore who got punched. She smiled with her lips squeezed tight. I reckon it was to hide the gap where her tooth was missing. From where I was lying her nose looked pretty damned squint.

"I'm fine," I said. "You're the one what got her nose busted."

Rachel reached up and touched her nose, glaring at me like who am I to mention it, what with all my afflictions— my lip an' my eye an' my ear.

I changed the subject.

"You think he's an ogre what came down from the mountains?"

Bronwyn was stuffing her pipe with 'bacca. "I reckon he was a soldier at some point. By the look of all them stitched up wounds he's been in the thick of it on a battlefield. Botch job by some drunken army medic I'd bet."

I sat up to take a better look. She was right, amongst the blue marbling of his veins you could see the stitching scars. Dozens and dozens of them.

"Maybe he was in the civil war?" Suggested Maggie, who let the punters call her Pocahontas on account of being a quarter Kiowa. "Maybe he got himself blowed up by a cannonball?"

Bronwyn struck a match and sucked on the stem of the pipe to light the 'bacca. "War 'atween north and south is thirty years gone," she said from behind the fug of smoke that gushed from down her nostrils. "He don't look nearly old enough to have been for the Union nor the Confederacy. But there have been other wars. You girls know what men are like. Always coming up with a new reason to knock seven tons of shit out of each other."

The whores all laughed.

"Hombre don' look any age," said Maria-Ettie, the Mexican. "Don' look like no hombre I ever set eyes on."

"That's 'cos he's an ogre," I piped up.

"Oh, shut up, Lil," snapped Rachel. "You got your damned head in the clouds as usual."

"What are we going to do with him?" asked Honeylove.

I always thought her name was ridiculous. But she always swore blind that it was the name given to her at birth by her mother. Whatever the truth, it suited her. With her pink complexion, her wavy blonde hair and her pale blue eyes, she drove the punters wild. She was Bronwyn's favourite, because she could always entice men to pay double the fee for half an hour with Honeylove.

I saw Veronique glaring at her with a look so full of spite you'd have thunk she was spoiling to spike her broth with arsenic. Maybe she was. Veronique had been the favourite before Honeylove showed up. Now she was in a state of perpetual petulance. I'd lost count of the number of times she kicked me up the ass, just for the vindictive hell of it.

Jocelyn chewed on the stem of her pipe, the way she did when she was pondering. "Look at the size of him," she said. "If we had him as a doorman there would be no more busted noses."

***

We wheeled the barrow to one of the downstairs rooms. It took all of us to heft the ogre onto the bed. Maria-Ettie placed his satchel next to him on the mattress.

With her pipe clamped between her teeth, Bronwyn removed his scuffed boots. His feet were blue. His toenails were black. They looked dreadful. *He's an ogre for sure,* I told myself, somewhat smugly. *Them lot don't know what they're talking about.*

Bronwyn told Rachel and Maggie to take off the rags he was dressed in. They set about the task, giggling like they was school girls. When he was naked, we all just stood and stared. He was stitched up all over. Like he'd been randomly thrown together. A patchwork of skins—black man's skin, white man's skin, Chinaman's skin, injun skin. All of them mottled and faded to grey, streaked with the blue lightning of veins.

What's more, and this was the thing all our eyes were drawn to, he had no cock and balls. All there was where they should have been was crumpled furrows of green-blue flesh that had been badly sewn to a lopsided star shape.

"Poor bastard," said Bronwyn.

Maria-Ettie made sign of the cross.

"Never seen a man without a todger," said one of the other girls.

"I did," said Maggie. "I had a punter once. Sweet old Norwegian guy. Was on a wagon train that got raided. They cut off his dick and a left him to die. All he had was this ugly stump. Had to squat to piss."

"What was a man with no dick doing in a whorehouse?" asked Rachel.

"He had all his fingers," replied Maggie, grinning. "And they was in perfect working order."

The whores all laughed.

That was when I noticed that Veronique had her eyes on something else. There was a pear-shaped locket on a gold chain hung around the ogre's neck. She was eyeing it greedily. Everyone knew Veronique had sticky fingers, always stealing stuff from the punters, always denying it when she was challenged.

Bronwyn blew pipe smoke down her nostrils.

"At least this one won't be tempted to try and help himself to the wares."

She was referring to Cedric, our last doorman, an ex-circus strongman. He had this thing for Honeylove, like most men do. Ended up losing control of his wits and trying to bend her over the kitchen table. Bronwyn shot off his ear with that little gambler's pistol she kept up her sleeve, then she threw all his clothes out in the snow.

"You have to convince him to take on the job first," Rachel pointed out.

"I don't think he's going to take much convincing," said Bronwyn. "Way I see it he's either running from something or running to something. Whatever way round, he's clearly in need of a place to stay for a while."

"Should I go fetch the doc?" asked Maggie.

Bronwyn shook her head.

"My instinct tells me he wouldn't appreciate being examined by no doctor."

She turned to me.

"Remember that Scotsman who pegged it last July?"

I nodded.

"Where'd you put his suit?"

"In the linen closet," I replied. "Boots an' all."

"Go fetch them."

More pipe smoke came gushing down her nostrils.

"Stop gawping, Lil," she said. "Go fetch them."

***

Bronwyn's hunch was right.

The ogre didn't take much convincing to accept her proposal. When he woke up and she put it to him, he looked relieved. His big shoulders kind of relaxed as he sat up in the bed. He grinned and his teeth were dreadful. Brown and worn down to the gums. When he spoke, he had an ogre's voice. All low and gravelly and hoarse, like he had a dead man's words nesting in the pink of his mouth.

As part of the deal, Bronwyn put him up in the outhouse where there was a stained old mattress set on a wooden pallet that the drunks were sent to sleep it off on. If he was cold out there he never grumbled nor seemed to notice. I figured he was already blue, so what it did it matter?

A couple of weeks after he became our doorman, Bronwyn sent me there to change his sheets and sweep the floor. It was a blustery night and he was on duty, towering gigantically in the hallway, opening the front door when a punter rang the little brass bell. One look at him and they knew for sure they had to be on their best behaviour.

By then I was well and truly besotted by him. His blue skin, his yellow eyes, his black toenails. I had this daydream that we'd both run away and join a circus. Cedric had told me all about the circus. Reckoned I could make a decent living as a sideshow attraction. The Twisted Lady, or something of that nature.

If people would pay to see me, I was damn sure they'd pay to see an ogre. Me and him would travel around in one of them painted caravans. It would have big double hammock for us to cuddle up in. I didn't care that he didn't have the wherewithal to have sex. I'd seen enough sex, heard enough sex and smelled enough sex to have my fill for a lifetime. It didn't matter a jot to me that I never experienced it for myself, nor was ever likely to do so.

But I was curious as to how he went for a piss though. I remembered what Rachel had said about the old Norwegian and his stump for a cock and how he had to squat to piss. I couldn't figure out how the ogre would go, being all sewn up down there and all. It occurred to me that I'd never actually seen him eat or drink. Maybe it was on ogre thing? Maybe he didn't need to piss?

My thoughts were full of these notions as I stripped the bed. I knew in my heart that the circus thing was just a whimsy. It was never going to happen for real. But daydreams are daydreams and in my opinion, there's nothing wrong with being a dreamer.

It was when I was picking up the sheets that I noticed the satchel stuffed under the pallet. I froze, my curiosity niggling away at me. What was inside? What was so precious that he'd hold it so close to his chest when he was unconscious?

I got down on my knees and glanced over my shoulder. There was plenty of noise coming from the whorehouse. I didn't think I'd get caught if I sneaked a peak. I reached in, caught one of the straps and dragged it out.

Inside there were three items. A spent bullet, a tattered photograph and something large that was wrapped in a handkerchief. I looked at the photo. It showed a white man and an injun squaw, standing all formal, arms linked, like they was at a wedding or something.

I wondered if the ogre had killed them and eaten them alive. Maybe the bullet was from when they tried to defend themselves. Next, I unwrapped the object from the handkerchief. I gasped when I found myself holding the biggest gold nugget I'd ever set eyes on.

"You seen enough?"

I jumped so badly I almost dropped the hunk of gold.

When I turned, the ogre was there in the doorway of the outhouse, all blue inside the dead Scotsman's suit. I began to tremble. "I'm sorry. I was cleaning and I…"

"You heard about curiosity and the cat?" he asked, stepping inside.

I hurriedly wrapped the gold back into the handkerchief and dropped it into the satchel. I was crying. "You gonna' eat me, mister?"

He cocked his big head.

"Eat you?"

"You're an ogre," I said. "I found your gold. Maybe you're gonna' kill me and eat me?"

He laughed. I shivered. It sounded like the wheezing of someone on his deathbed.

"I'm no ogre," he said. "I was made this way. Dead flesh hung over dead bones. Constructed by the witchery of the Lakota Sioux. Roused by incantation. Animated by dastardly dark magic."

"An ogre'" I breathed. "They made you into an ogre."

"An assassin," he said. "Given life only to wreak hideous revenge. I tore men into bloody shreds with my hands and my teeth."

I saw the dreadful imagery in my head and felt my insides tremble.

The ogre looked at his big hands. The grey fingers curled and clenched. "I was supposed to return to those who made me in order that I would be disassembled. But I ran. And I am running still."

"Who were you?" I asked.

"You saw the picture?"

I nodded.

"I think the man was me."

He reached up and touched the locket.

"There's a lock of black hair inside this. I think it may be hers. I think maybe she was my wife. I think we may have been at Wounded Knee. On one side or the other of the massacre. I think the bullet may have been the one that killed her. Or even the one that killed me. I think, I think, I think. But I cannot remember…"

I knew about Wounded Knee. My Daddy had read an article about it to me from the newspaper. Three hundred dead Indians; men women and children, fired upon by the cavalry when they were supposed to be handing over their weapons. Twenty-Five soldiers dead as well. And plenty of injured on both sides.

I pushed the satchel back under the pallet and limped upright.

The ogre towered so tall above me that I had to stretch my neck to look up at him.

"Your secret is safe with me," I told him.

He sighed and his throat rattled.

"I wish I knew exactly what my secret was."

"Were you not cold when I found you in the alley?" I asked.

"I walked the Arizona desert and felt no heat," he said. "The chill of Alaska doesn't touch me."

"But you was unconscious from the cold."

"Sometimes death catches up with me and seizes me in a catatonic trance. It is when I am my most vulnerable. You saved me. I am grateful."

"You won't eat me?"

I gave him an ugly, hair-lip grin.

He grinned back at me over the brown stumps of his teeth.

"I won't eat you."

***

There were these three Irish brothers. The Doolins. Died in the wool protestants who'd emigrated from

Londonderry. Loud and boisterous, always spoiling for a fight. They had a claim they'd staked out thirty miles north of Blessing.

Whenever the Doolin boys came to the whorehouse they demanded two girls apiece. But they only ever wanted to pay the price of one. Bronwyn always objected. Having six girls tied up half the night and only getting half the profit into the bargain wasn't exactly her idea of good business. The boys would kick up a ruckus, threatening to smash the whole damn place to kindling and Bronwyn would end up conceding.

One night though, she put her foot down. She had to. Anybody in their right mind would have. The whole damn situation was an absolute disgrace. Scandalous. Farcical. Even by the down and dirty standards of Blessing.

It started when the Doolin's came riding back into town on their mule cart. They had fished a sizeable nugget out of the river. Sold it for top dollar. They were flush in their success and drunk on the notion of their preposterous proposal.

They was going to marry Honeylove, they said. All three of them. They wanted to buy her from Bronwyn and take her to their cabin as their wife. They was going to purchase a goose feather mattress. Each would have a night with Honeylove on a continuous rotation. She'd cook for them and keep the cabin clean.

They had the whole disgraceful thing thunk out and planned. Must have been discussing it all the way back to Blessing. Dermot, the elder brother, was doing all the talking. He'd shaved and splashed himself in cologne, as if he'd actually come courting. As if he was going to get down on one knee with a bunch of goddamn roses.

Honeylove was dressed in a red negligee and lace garters. She stood by the fireplace, wafting the musky French scent a Canadian prospector had gifted her, blonde waves of hair cascading down on her pale shoulders. As soon as Dermot Doolin recounted his proposals, her pink breasts started heaving. "She ain't mine to sell," said Browyn, packing her pipe with 'bacca. "Even if she was, I wouldn't hand her over to a pack of hyenas."

Daniel, youngest of three, stuck his hands deep in his pockets, then threw his head back and laughed. "Ye've got no choice in the matter, lady." Declan, the middle one, just stood there leering at Honeylove, reeking of whiskey, swaying slightly, huge boner swollen in his pants.

Dermot Doolin slammed a wad of bank notes down on the table.

'Ye t'ink this is a negotiation? T'ink again. We're takin' her and you're takin' the cash. All done and dusted. Nice and legit...'

Maria-Ettie plucked a pointed little stiletto from her garter and stepped in front of Honeylove. Rachel grabbed a poker and stepped in front of Maria-Ettie.

"Stand aside, bitches," roared Dermot, raising his hairy fists.

Bronwyn dropped her pipe, pulled out her gambler's pistol and took aim at Declan's head.

"Back off. Or I'll take out your miserable eye."

Both Daniel and Declan pulled the guns they had stuffed down the fronts of their pants. It seemed to me this had been part of the plan they'd talked through. "We'll shoot the feken lot of ye where ye stand," warned Daniel. He started to laugh like a lunatic, hopping from foot to foot. Declan swayed some more. His eyelids were drooping. He clearly couldn't handle his liquor. I didn't think he had enough wits left about him to hit anything if the shooting started.

I held my breath anyway.

Bronwyn didn't back down. Nor did Maria-Ettie and Rachel. Honeylove started crying, chin resting on her chest as she sobbed. That was when Veronique kind of shimmied up to the fireplace. "I'll go," she said, pouting a bit. She leaned forward slightly so the brothers could get a good eyeful of her cleavage. "I'll marry the three of you and come and live in your old shack. We can all share the same bed if you like."

The others looked at her as if she'd just lost all her marbles. Bronwyn's eyebrows creased as if she thought Veronique was having a joke, or maybe was up to something. Me, I reckon she said it because she thought by doing this she would somehow get one up on Honeylove.

Dermot swiftly rained on whatever parade she thought she was organising. He looked her up and down, sneered and turned to Bronwyn. "It's Honeylove, or nothin'." If he'd slapped Veronique on the face he couldn't have hurt her more.

She turned on her heels and flounced out of the room, accidentally bumping into Declan and almost knocking him off balance. Dermot held his hand out to Honeylove. "C'mon darlin' come away with us and we'll look after ye."

Bronwyn stepped up to him and pressed the gambler's pistol against his head.

"Back off, Mick," she went.

I heard Daniel cock his pistol.

Declan gagged like he was about to throw up his guts.

Everyone backed away from him in a manner that was almost comical. Dermot seized the moment and moved with such a speed that everything seemed to happen in the blink of an eye. He made a grab for Bronwyn's arm. She struggled and the gun went off. The bullet raked a furrow into the floorboards.

Dermot twisted Bronwyn's wrist and she dropped the pistol. Rachel raised the poker. Dermot slammed the heel of his hand hard into her face. She dropped to her knees, blood gushing from her nose, probably broke all over again.

Dermot grabbed the poker from her and made a swing at Marie-Ettie who only just dodged getting whacked on the side of the head. That was when the ogre stepped into the room, and I swear to god the floor shook and walls trembled.

It took him a single stride to cross the room and grab Dermot by the shirt collar. He yanked him up so his feet was kicking in the air like a string hung puppet in one of them puppet shows. When Dermot tried to hit him with the poker, the ogre snapped his wrist. The sound of the bone cracking made me sick to the stomach.

Dermot howled in pain and dropped the poker.

Declan threw up on the floor.

Daniel raised his gun.

The ogre swung around and used Dermot to knock Daniel to the ground. Still holding Dermot aloft, the ogre kicked Daniel into the hallway and threw both of them out into the street. He came back, lifted up Declan and showed him the same exit. Then he threw the wad of notes after him.

***

Bronwyn sent one of the girls to fetch the doc to come fix Rachel's nose. But he wouldn't come because he was seeing to Dermot Doolin's broken arm and because Daniel Doolin had sworn he'd fill him full of lead if he came within an inch of the whorehouse.

The girls did their best to stem the blood that was gushing from Rachel's nose. This time it was going to set squint, that was for sure. *Squint nose and gap tooth,* I thought as I mopped up Declan Doolin's puke, *serves her right for judging me.*

Some of the girls was consoling Honeylove. The ogre was all squashed up into one of the armchairs, big hands on the armrests. As I passed him with the mop and bucket, I felt my heart flutter in my chest. I allowed myself a secret little hair-lip smile.

That was when I noticed Veronique. She was in the doorway, leaning lazily against the frame. Her eyes were on the ogre. They were burning with the kind of spite and hatred I thought she only reserved for Honeylove. I think I might have plucked up the courage to say something had there not come a shout from the street.

"Hey big fella', come out here. I want to have a word with ye."

A whole bunch of us dashed to the window and peeked through the curtains.

Daniel Doolin was in the middle of the road, legs splayed, boots on either side of the wheel ruts that had been drove into the mud by the back and forth of wagons and carts, gun in his hand. His brothers were across the street in front of the saloon. Dermot mooching there moodily with his arms all trussed up in a sling, Declan slouched in a chair on the wooden boardwalk, nursing a whisky bottle.

Daniel waved his gun.

"Ye hear me, big fella? Are ye comin' out? Or am I comin' in to get ye?"

He pointed the gun at the window. We all screamed and ducked.

"Come out, ye yellow bellied coward!" yelled Daniel.

Had it been any other town than Blessing, there would have been a sheriff or constable to put an end to the nonsense. But Blessing was lawless. No lawman who tried to lay down any sense of order would have lasted till sun up.

The ogre rose from the armchair.

No, I wanted to yell. *Don't go out there.*

But I said nothing.

No one said anything, 'cept Bronwyn.

"You don't need to," she said.

"I do," was all the ogre said in reply.

The sleet began as he stepped into the road. Dirty sheets of it blown to darts on the icy wind. My Daddy used to read to me about the gunfights between outlaws and lawmen out west, in faraway places like Dodge and Tombstone. This seemed nothing like the romance of those accounts. Daniel Doolin, knee deep in mud and mule dung. The ogre towering before him, unarmed, marbled blue, stitching scars marking the mismatched territories of his patchwork flesh.

I tumbled out onto the porch with Bronwyn and her whores.

Across the street, huddles of booze filled men were congregating in front of the saloon.

It seemed to me that this was a standoff of a different hue.

On one side the prospectors, wrestling guilt about how frequently they deceived wives and fiancées waiting back home, resentful of having to pay for the privilege. Daniel Doolin their would-be avenger. On the other side the whores, hurt and angry at all the disrespect and insults they had to endlessly endure from these brutish men. The ogre their champion.

Part of me just wanted the ogre to step to one side and let them all run at each other, the whole miserable bunch of them, tearing and gouging with all their spite and bile. In my head I summoned up a vision of an imagined aftermath; bloodied corpses piled high on the muddy thoroughfare and me and the ogre, arms linked, gaily walking on them to keep our feet dry.

"Drop the gun," I heard the ogre say.

"Fuck ye," replied Daniel. "Arm yerself. Ye broke my brother's arm, so ye did—and yer gonna' pay."

The ogre took a step towards him, lashed by the sleet that was blowing in on the icy wind. Daniel raised his weapon and attempted to hold his trembling arm straight. The prospectors and the whores held their breath.

The ogre took another step, half frozen rain water gushing down his ugly face. Daniel curved his finger around the trigger and pulled. I let out a little squeal. The bullet hit the ogre on the shoulder. He staggered a bit, then carried on.

Daniel fired again. This one hit the ogre on the left wrist. His arm kind of swung limply backwards, spraying oily black blood. Then he carried on as if it was nothing. Daniel made to fire again. But he was too slow. The ogre was upon him already.

He snatched the gun from Daniel's grip, snapped off the barrel and tossed the two halves along the street. Daniel tried to back off. But the mud sucked at his legs and held him fast. The ogre clenched his big fist and brought it down like an anvil on the Irishman's head.

His knees crumpled as he fell unconscious.

Without a single word the whores slunk back into the whorehouse. They didn't even acknowledge their champion's victory. After a moment, the men bowed their heads and returned to the saloon. The two elder Doolins, one wounded, one drunk, lurched across the street to fetch their kid brother.

The ogre turned and headed for his outhouse.

I just stood there, shivering from the cold, weeping for the fact that the ogre had survived. It took less than five minutes for a couple of drunken prospectors to come creeping sheepishly across the road to ring the little brass bell.

***

The ogre lay on his bed in a death trance for two whole days. Bronwyn said I should tend to him because he wouldn't want the doc getting a close up look at how strangely put together he was. I said nothing. I knew a whole lot more that she did. But I'd sworn not to tell.

Bronwyn also said that the ogre would probably move on once he woke up. Said that the incident with the Doolins would have drawn more attention than he was comfortable with. Told the whores to get ready to be without a doorman for a while.

I hoped she was wrong.

I stitched his wounds. Both bullets had gone straight through and out the other side, so there wasn't no poking around to be done. I stitched them good. I was used to mending. Bronwyn always bought cheap sheets and they got torn frequently from all the hanky-panky that went on. I reckon my handiwork was a whole heap better than whoever else had stitched together the rest of him.

Most of the time he just lay there in silence. I dared to press my good ear to his blue veined chest. I couldn't even hear the slightest murmur of his heart. Once though, it seemed he was coming around. He thrashed about on the bed and started groaning and moaning.

I wondered if he was remembering what happened at Wounded Knee and the squaw that might have been his wife and whose lock of hair he carried around his neck in a silver locket on a silver chain.

When he fell still once more I snuck another look in his satchel. I honestly couldn't tell if the man in the photograph was him or not. At an angle it may have been. At another it may not. The squaw sure was pretty. If Bronwyn saw her, she'd have loved her.

I could see how she would have caught his eye. Back before they made him into an ogre he wouldn't have given an ugly little thing like me a second glance. But now. Now that he was a huge, lumbering ugly thing. Now there might be a chance. Or so I told myself.

I went on with my daydreams.

I imagined the ogre selling the gold so we could buy a painted caravan that was drawn by two pure white mares. We'd travel around with the circus; the ogre and the twisted lady. The horses would dance in the show. And at night I'd curl up in the patchwork nest of him as we lay entwined in the hammock.

I cried to think it might never come true.

***

The ogre didn't leave.

When he roused himself, he went straight back to work, perched on the little stool in the hallway, answering the bell, dealing with the drunks and the cheats who tried to get laid without paying. Maybe he should have left at that point.

The fact that he didn't meant that things took a dark and bloody turn.

It was me who found Honeylove's body. As usual I'd come down to the kitchen early in the morning. Most of the whores woke up with hangovers and it was my job to make sure that there was fresh brewed coffee on the go. It was still dark. Soon as I lit the lamp I saw her, all twisted on the floor in her blood-soaked negligee.

Her head had been stoved in, a big indent on her forehead, splinters of skull bone poking through the torn flesh. It must have happened in the early hours. The floor was tacky with puddles of congealed blood. No sign of a weapon.

This time I didn't scream. Instead, I went quietly and roused Bronwyn from her sleep. It was her what cried out and woke everyone else up. When she saw Honeylove lying there all bashed up she dropped down beside her, sobbing and hugging her limp head to her breast.

A commotion followed as all the whores tumbled into the kitchen, sleepy eyed and tousled haired. Bronwyn was inconsolable. Maria-Ettie knelt beside her and wrapped an arm around her shoulder.

"Who would have done such a thing?" wailed Bronwyn. "Who would have done such a wicked thing to such a beautiful girl?"

"One of the Doolin boys is my guess," said Rachel.

"More like the ogre," said Veronique, adopting her usual stance, leaning against the doorframe.

Maggie shook her head.

"Not the ogre. He ain't got the wherewithal to lust after nobody."

"I think she's got something in her hand," said Veronique, nodding at Honeylove's body.

Maria-Ettie reached over and plucked something from her pale, clenched fist.

She held it up.

The ogre's locket dangled there on its silver chain.

Everyone gasped.

At that moment I saw clear as day in my head what had happened. I'd noticed something strange when I was replacing the wicks in some of the corridor oil lamps the previous night. The ogre had just evicted a punter that Veronique had claimed was getting too boisterous. As he sat back down onto the stool, she leaned in and kissed him on his blue cheek like she was saying thank you. It was completely out of character. And that why it was stuck in my head.

That's when she did it, I muttered under my breath. *That's when she stole the locket.*

I had no doubt then that it was one of the Doolin's what stoved in Honeylove's head in. They was likely working on the principle that if they couldn't have her no one could. Veronique would have lured her to the kitchen. The Doolin would have been waiting there in the dark. When the deed was done, they'd have planted the locket.

"Remember what he did to Daniel Doolin with his big fist?" she was saying to the girls.

They all looked at poor Honeylove's fractured skull.

I looked at Veronique. A smug little half concealed grin had curved on the edges of her painted lips. I was about to confront her when Bronwyn rose to her feet. She had stopped crying and seemed to have composed herself a bit.

"Before anyone starts throwing accusations around, we need to show poor Honeylove a bit of respect. Someone go fetch the doc. Tell him he's needed in his capacity as an undertaker."

Veronique piped up quick as a flash.

"I'll go."

That convinced me even more. But she was too quick out the door for me to confront her. I thought maybe I should ask to speak to Browyn in private, let her know my suspicions.

But Bronwyn had other ideas.

"Lil," she went, "get a mop and bucket. The rest of you clean up Honeylove and then lay her down on one of the beds. Least we can do is make her look presentable."

The ogre was still asleep in the outhouse. I decided that the best option was to wait till I had the chance to rouse him and warn him of how he was being set up. At least then he'd have a head start. Some of the prospectors kept vicious hunting dogs. Toughened them up in a fighting pit they'd dug out on the edge of town. I reckoned with a start, the ogre would easily outrun them.

Four of the girls lifted poor Honeylove's body, a leg and a wing each. They shuffled slowly and edged out of the kitchen. I was left alone, mopping up all the dreadful blood she'd spilt. It was the chance I'd been waiting for. I dropped the mop and ran helter-skelter round the side of the whorehouse.

That was when I heard the commotion coming along the street.

I peeped my head around the corner. Veronique was on her way back, not with the doc as she'd been asked, but with a lynch mob. The Doolin's were at its head. Daniel Doolin was carrying the rope, huge smirk on his ugly Irish mug.

I ran for the outhouse.

The ogre lay silent on the bed, fully clothed, unmoving. Was he in a death trance again? He couldn't be. He needed to get up. He needed to grab his satchel and run. I shook his beefy shoulders. His blue eyelids seemed to flicker. When they didn't open, I slapped him hard on the face.

He grunted.

Came awake.

Stared at me with those mournful yellow eyes.

"Wake up," I cried. "You have to get out of here. They're coming for you!"

He sat up and almost instantly fell straight back onto the mattress. What was wrong with him? I knew what he looked like when he was in his death trance. This was different. It was like he was drugged or poisoned or something.

I grabbed his wrist and tried to haul him back up. He was far too heavy. Behind me the door crashed open. Veronique came barging in, the Doolins not far behind her, the doorway becoming crammed with angry prospectors.

"What did you do to him?' I yelled.

"What did I do?" she yelled back at me. "What did he do? That's the question, Lil!"

She turned to the men at the door.

"That's him!" She cried. "That's the monster that killed Honeylove!"

The men howled like they was a pack of hyenas. They were all at one time or another in awe of Honeylove. Now it seemed they all wanted a hand in avenging her. The Doolin boys moved toward the bed. I tried to get in between them. Veronique grabbed my blouse and slung me to the floor, tearing material.

She spat at me.

"You keep your ugly mug out of this, cripple!"

If the ogre could have come fully awake he would easily have fought them off, smashed down the flimsy wooden wall of the outhouse and made his break. But he didn't so much as struggle. He just lay there passively as they strung him up like a pig, dragged him outside and loaded him into the back of a mule cart.

"Murd'rin' scum," said Daniel Doolin and slammed his fist into the ogre's blue face.

Two mules hauled the cart through the mud of the main thoroughfare. The whole town came out to follow it, jeering and slinging insults at the ogre. Even the whores were there, Rachel, Maggie, Maria-Ettie and all.

It was like all the bile that Blessing had put in their bellies was being puked up in front of me. All the long months panhandling with nothing to show but pennies that were squandered on a loveless fuck. A boil had been lanced and the pus was oozing. They needed a scapegoat. Someone to take their anger and frustration out on.

The ogre was it.

I found Bronwyn in the crowd. The smoke coming down her nostrils mixing with the vapour of her breath in the cold air. "You have to stop this," I begged her. "You know in your heart it wasn't him."

Bronwyn stared me down. Her eyes looked cold and empty. She knew I was right. But she wasn't going to do a damn thing about it. She was a hard-nosed businesswoman through and through. She knew the men had worked up a bloodlust for a lynching. If she got in the way of it, her little enterprise was going to suffer.

"Needs must," she said and walked on without looking back.

They took him to a tree on the lower mountain slopes. On account of my bad foot I couldn't keep up. By the time I was near enough to see, he was already dangling with the noose tight around his neck and the dogs snapping at the circular sway of his feet.

After a while, they cut him down and dumped him under the tree. On the way back to Blessing, Maria-Ettie told me that there was a mean old grizzly that had been troubling some of the prospectors. They reckoned if the bear ate the ogre he'd have a full belly for a long time to come and leave them be.

I started to cry.

"What you blabbing' about?" asked Maggie, dress hem dragging in the mud.

"He was innocent," I wailed. "They hung an innocent man."

"Oh, shut up, Lil," said Rachel. "You've always got your ugly head in the clouds."

***

It was pitch dark when I walked out to the tree, wrapped in a blanket, buffeted by wind and sleet, dragging my club foot behind me in the mud. I didn't care if the grizzly was there. They'd hung an innocent man. I hated every damned person in Blessing, whores and prospectors. And I hated myself for not being able to warn the ogre in time. At that moment I'd have loved to slit my wrists and lay down stone dead on the ogre's barrel chest.

He was where they'd left him, beneath the tree, all blue and dressed in the Scotsman's suit. The noose that had been around his neck was gone. The Doolins was too mean and tight fisted to have left a good rope. But they'd been so full of themselves, the axe they'd used to cut down the rope stood forgotten, resting against the trunk of the tree.

I knelt down beside the ogre and pulled out what was hidden beneath the blanket.

"I brung your satchel," I said, tears frosting on my cheeks.

I jumped back a bit when his eyelids flickered and opened and he stared up at me with those yellow eyes, exactly the way he had when I found him that first day. My heart went into a joyous spin. "You're alive!"

He sat up.

"I doubt it," he said. "But you can't kill what's already dead, and that's a fact."

He rose full height and towered over me, still crouching there, holding my arms outstretched with the satchel in my shivering hands. He bent down, took it from me and grinned his hideous grin.

"How comes you didn't fight back?" I asked. "You could have easily knocked the whole miserable lot of them down. Every bastard one of them."

I stood up and pulled the blanket tighter around my shoulders.

"This is not the first time something like this has happened," he replied. "I learned a long time ago that it is best just to let them believe they've had their day."

"You was framed," I said.

"It was inevitable," he replied.

"I couldn't find your locket," I said.

"Try as hard as I might I still can't remember who she was," he said. "But it's you that came to me."

I gasped when he wrapped me in his monstrous arms and lifted me clean off the ground. He kissed me. Not on the forehead like a sister. But on the lips like a lover. Kissed me on my hair lip where no one had ever kissed me before.

He smelled of formaldehyde and orchids.

"I'm full of rage," he said when he put me back down. "About what they did to me. About how they treat you."

I bowed my head slightly and whispered. "I'm used to it."

The wind and snow howled around us.

"Time they were taught a lesson," he said.

"What are you going to do?" I asked.

He grinned hideously. "What I was created to do. Justice and revenge are two sides of the same coin, Lil. You deserve the same satisfaction."

"Me?"

"Pick up the axe," he said.

My mouth fell open. "You mean...?"

He nodded.

"But I've never done anything like that before."

"Just follow my lead," he said. "Take it at you own pace. It'll be painful at first. But then you'll find your rhythm."

The vision of bloody corpses piles high in the mud filled my head and again I saw the two of us walking on them to keep our feet clean

"Pick up the axe," he said again.

I picked up the axe. The shaft was so cold I could feel the flesh of my hand sticking to it. Soon it warmed up and felt hard inside my grip. My ogre set off through the swirling snow, heading for that accursed town they called Blessing. I followed with the axe resting against my shoulder, shivering with lustful anticipation as my pulse thrummed and pumped adrenaline.

It felt like we were about to make love.

Asmo and Honey
Vivian Kasley

Honey sat across from Asmo and studied his dark brown eyes. She'd been delivering her products, when he stopped her. He told her she was the most beautiful creature he ever laid eyes on. She smiled and invited him over for lunch and iced tea. She showed him her bee hives and they talked over peanut butter and honey sandwiches. When he leaned in for a kiss, she flinched.

"I'm sorry. I didn't mean to scare ya." Asmo said.

"It's alright. I just never...I never kissed anyone before." Honey cast her eyes downward and blushed.

"Never? I reckon you're kiddin', right? A girl pretty as you?"

"I never have. I swear."

"Well, I can change that for you, if you want? I won't bite." Asmo chuckled.

"Bite?" Honey gasped.

"It's a joke! It's a sayin'."

"Alright, then." Honey closed her eyes and leaned in. She felt his beard tickle her face. His lips engulfed hers, they were warm and sweet.

"How's that?" Asmo beamed.

"It was…nice." Honey smiled.

"So, tell me, is your name really Honey?"

"It is. My Daddy named me that. Mama thought it'd be cute, on account of their honey business and all. If you can believe it, my Daddy's last name was Bea. When they passed, I took over the business. Tending bees is peaceful work. I enjoy it."

"You're tellin' me that your name is Honey Bea?"

"It is."

"If that ain't the sweetest thing!" Asmo laughed and slapped his knees. He looked around the quaint living room. The couch was worn and made a noise whenever you moved. It was obvious she hadn't redecorated since her parent's passing. He noticed there was no television. "No Tv?" He asked.

"Daddy said they were the worst things that were ever invented. We mostly worked outside, listened to music, or read books. I wasn't lacking if that's what you think. I didn't mind being outside or losing myself in a good book. You can't miss what you never had. Mama always said that."

"Hey, no judging here. I'm just surprised is all. No siblings?" Asmo looked at the pictures on the bookcases and walls. They were mostly of Honey through the years and what he assumed were her parents, some were of family pets.

"No, just me. I always wanted a sister or brother, but Mama couldn't have no more after me. What about you?"

"Same. Well, I ain't got no siblings I know of. I don't much talk to my Pop, he's been locked away for years and my Ma, well, she ran off with some dude when I was small."

"I'm so sorry."

"It's no biggie. Life, ya know? So, Honey Bea, what do you want to do now?" Asmo's eyes burned into her.

"I…I don't know."

Asmo leaned in and kissed her again. She let him stick his tongue in her mouth this time, which he did slowly and then more hungrily. She dug her fingers into his strong back and moaned when he kissed her neck. Soon, they were pulling each other's clothes off like they were on fire and they made love right there on the couch. He kissed her forehead and she took his hand and led him to her bedroom.

They made love again and soon they lay side by side on her double bed. They were silent for a while and watched the dust dance in the afternoon sunlight that came through the blinds. She peeked over at Asmo, who noticed and smiled.

"I never thought my day would've gone like this." Asmo whispered.

"Me either." Honey sighed.

"Honey, how old are you? If you don't mind me askin'?"

"Thirty-five."

"I would've never guessed that. You have the fairest skin I ever saw on a lady. Like pure cream. Actually, with your strawberry hair, you're like strawberries and cream. Just beautiful, you are."

"Thank you."

"I have to tell you something. I should've told you before, well, before we did that. I haven't been able to tell no one in a long time. I've been running too long. You were just so beautiful and when you offered to have me over I just…I was just so happy."

"What is it? Are you married? You have someone else?" Honey sat up and pulled the sheet to her chest. Tears begun to well in her eyes.

"No! Nothing like that. It's something else. Something I'm afraid to tell you. And now that we, well, you know, I feel you need to know. I really like you, Honey. I know we just met, but I feel a connection. I wouldn't want to take this further or hurt you."

"What is it? Just tell me, I can take it! Was it me? Was I horrible?" Her lip quivered and the tears came.

"Oh, no darlin! No, course it's not you! Are you crazy? You were magical and wonderful! The best I ever had the pleasure of acquainting. That's why I reckon you know before anything else happens."

"Just tell me then!" Honey cried.

"I'm a…I'm a werewolf." Asmo said.

"You're a what?"

"A werewolf. A wolfman. A lycanthrope." He got off the bed and pulled his pants on. Waiting for her to throw him out.

"A werewolf?"

"Yeah. Do you know what that is?"

"I've read a book or two that mentioned them before. But they were fiction." Honey got off the bed and pulled her dress over her head.

"I assure you, it's real."

"I may be a bit naïve, but a werewolf? You're trying to make something up to get out of what we just did! You got what you wanted! Mama always told me to be careful and I was, till you! Get out!"

"Honey, I swear to you! I'm a werewolf and I've been runnin' for a long time. Men are trying to hunt and kill me!"

"So, you went grocery shopping? Why would a werewolf do that, huh? Why, did you need lunch meat? Why're you in this town anyway? I never seen you before today! You preying on me, then? Am I the stupid naïve small-town country girl that gets eaten by the wolf?" Honey shouted.

"I was passing through. I ain't got no money, so I went in the store to see what I might be able to fetch. I used the water fountain and I saw you, the most beautiful…"

"Shut up! Shut up! Shut up! I don't believe a word of it!"

Asmo came around the bed and tried to hug her, but Honey pushed him back. He tried again but finally retreated when she screamed. He grabbed his flannel and began to button it up back up. Before he turned to leave, she quietly asked, "What happens when it's a full moon?"

"I turn."

"Do you…have you hurt people?"

"I reckon I may've, but I can't recall what I've done when I wake the next morning. It's all a blur."

"How'd it happen?"

"All I know is, I was camping by myself in the woods a few years ago, and something attacked me. I was never the same since."

"Why didn't you report it?"

"Well, look at the way you reacted when I told you. I can't tell just anybody. That's why I've been so afraid. I don't wanna hurt nobody, it's just who I am."

"Then why did you come here?"

"I don't know. I suppose I couldn't resist strawberries and cream."

Honey smiled back and slowly walked over to him. She kissed his chest and breathed into his shirt. It smelled like grass, wood smoke, and his natural scent. She ripped it open and again, they made love. A few weeks went by and they made love like teenagers and talked late into the night about what their future could be. He helped her with the bees and they lived harmoniously without any more talk of werewolves. The whirlwind died down the week Honey knew a full moon was due.

She'd been keeping track on the same calendar she kept track of everything on. There were little moons in the upper right-hand corners showing their phases. She was hoping he would've mentioned something to her by now, but he hadn't. She planned to bring it up tonight over dinner.

"Asmo?" Honey asked.

"Yeah, Honey Bea? By the way this cornbread, is spectacular!"

"Is there something you should tell me? That I should know or prepare for?"

"Like what? What're you going on about?"

"Well, tomorrow's a full moon."

"Oh."

"Oh? That's all you have to say, is oh?"

"Well, I didn't realize is all."

"You didn't realize? Shouldn't you know this kinda thing, don't you get like, a tingle or something?"

"I've been a little distracted by a certain female as of late. Perhaps you cured me!" He chuckled. He wiped his mouth and took a long sip of tea.

"It's not funny, Asmo! What should we do? Is there anything I should do? Do you need me to tie you down or something?"

"Well, don't feed me any grapes or chocolate." He teased.

"What? Is that a joke? Asmo, I'm being serious!"

"Alright, alright! Look, I'll leave the house. I'll just need some money and an extra set of clothes."

"You can't do that! What if you hurt someone?"

"Better them than you, right?"

"Just stay here and I'll watch over you. We'll figure it together. I want to be there for you. I need to know how it happens. I…I love you, Asmo. That means I love every part about you."

"Me too, Honey Bea. You really are the perfect gal. Now can we just enjoy dinner and not talk about this anymore?"

Honey wasn't satisfied, but kept quiet for the rest of their meal. *Why's he being so easy going? He's going to turn tomorrow night! Why's he not more concerned? Maybe he's worried and doesn't want to worry me?* She waited until he slept and then went into her Daddy's old study and unlocked the safe. She found what she was looking for, brought it to her bedroom, and put it in her dresser drawer under the balls of socks.

The next day went rather quickly and by early evening, Honey could feel the sweat under her arms saturating her pink cotton shirt. She was scared. Asmo hadn't spoken a word to her at all about tonight, in fact he hadn't spoken much to her today at all. He fell asleep on the couch after an early dinner of fried catfish. She felt a deep pang of sadness as she left him lying there in one of her Daddy's old shirts and overalls.

It wasn't dark out yet, but it was getting there and the big yellow moon would soon be high in the sky. She went to her room and into her dresser drawer. The gun was heavy, but she knew how to use it. Her Daddy had shown her multiple times how to load, clean, and shoot a gun. She walked back to the living room, the gun was cool in her sweaty hand, and sat across from him. She waited.

Asmo moaned in his sleep. His back hurt from the old sunken in couch. He knew he had to go soon before things got too serious. *Perhaps grab a few things on my way out. Wonder where she's at? Maybe she fell asleep in the bedroom, good, makes it easier.* He forced himself awake, yawned several times and began to crack his neck and stretch his legs. It was dark and he didn't see Honey sitting across from him. He stood up and began to crack his back.

Honey heard him moaning and knew it had begun. His body was moving in the dark and she heard what she thought were his bones cracking. She stood up quietly and pulled back the hammer of the gun. She aimed it and spoke to the beast in the dark, "Asmo? If you can still understand me, it's me, Honey. I love you. These past three weeks have been the happiest I can remember. I just wanted you to know that. Say something if you can still talk."

Asmo heard her and froze. He didn't say a word. He tried to squint and see her in the dark, but his eyes hadn't adjusted yet. His mouth was dry and his stomach hurt. *Fried food always gives me indigestion.* Before he could stop it, a huge belch escaped, but he didn't even have time to say excuse me, before a bullet went straight through his forehead.

Honey heard him growl and she pulled the trigger. She screamed and dropped the gun when she heard him fall onto the coffee table. Her body was paralyzed. When she could finally move, she turned the light on and cradled his limp body in her arms. Other than the bullet hole in his forehead, he looked the same. She rubbed her face on his beard. *He must've turned back. My poor sweet, sweet, Asmo. I hope you're free now, my love.*

The shot had been heard by a passerby who was walking their dog and they called the police. They banged on her door and when she opened it, Asmo's body could be seen behind her. They held their guns on her, told her to put her hands up, then handcuffed her. She was unable to form words. She sat in the back of a police car shaking and sobbing uncontrollably wondering if she did the right thing.

One of the police officers recognized the dead man who lay on the floor. He had grown a beard on his face, but it was him. "No shit," he said out loud, before he went to get the detective.

"Isn't that the guy wanted for murdering those women in the Carolinas and Virginia?" the officer asked.

"Looks like him. If it is, she's done everyone a service." the detective said.

It didn't take long to make a positive ID. When Honey came out of shock, she explained what happened over a shaky cup of water. They assured her he was no werewolf, but he was a monster who preyed on women. They told her he was a serial murdering psychopath named, Asmo Ripley. She shook her head and insisted it wasn't true, she freed him. They told her she was really lucky and that no charges would be filed. They even told her she was a hero.

They recommended she get mental health counseling, but she refused.

Honey had stopped making deliveries for a while due to the constant attention she garnered when she went into town, but when the gleam wore off, she continued. Although, it was getting harder for her in her condition now. She rubbed her belly through his flannel, thankful for the little treasure inside. *My little monster, Asmo Ripley Jr.*

Husband of the Year
Aric Davis

1.

There are seven men buried on the back forty acres of Marie Hempford's land. Her husband, Jack Hempford, is not among them. He is buried at the Calumet Cemetery located flush in the middle of the Upper Peninsula's finger in Keweenaw County, surrounded by the steel waters of Lake Superior. Jack's death was one of circumstance: namely, the error that equestrian training and alcohol should be enjoyed simultaneously. The other seven died under far less natural occurrences.

2.

Marie Hempford walked into the Brass Cup with a smile on her face. Marie was a stout woman, though she carried her weight in such a way that it felt perfectly natural on her six foot frame, and was evenly distributed to the areas that men tended to observe most quickly. Marie's body, however, was never the first thing that anyone noticed about her. She was a beautiful woman, especially in the Upper Peninsula at the dawn of the 20th Century, but hers was a combination of beauty and size that would have made heads turn no matter where she chose to reside. Her hair was golden, and had a sheen to it that suggested a daily maintenance routine of great extremity. Her face was unlined despite her age and the sadness that she had endured, but her eyes were the sort to make even a tomcat look away.

The barkeep, Pete Weathers, noticed Marie immediately as she entered the Brass Cup, the sound of heels on the wood floor was a unique timbre in the establishment. It was not to say that women did not drink in the Brass Cup—they did, and with just as much gusto as their male fellows—but the arrival of a *lady* was a rare occasion indeed. Pete smiled jocularly at Marie as she took her usual place near the rear of the Cup and a good distance from the card table, and poured her the usual two fingers of whiskey. It had been eleven months since Marie last graced his bar, and he was happy to see her for both her pleasant demeanor and generous pocketbook.

"Here we go, Missus Hempford," said Pete as he set the whiskey down on the table before her. "Been a long time since I've saw you."

"It's been busy at the farm getting ready for winter," Marie said as she took the cup from the table, her wedding ring clinking against the glass. "Not that I'm complaining. Being busy with horses is a blessing from God most holy."

"As you say, ma'am. I've never been much for the ponies myself. Ceptin' at the race track down to Milwaukee, of course. Those are ponies that I find pretty damn interesting. 'Specially on the last quarter."

"They are a devious breed," said Marie as she drained her glass. "Which is why I would never bet so much as a penny on them. They are far too shifty of beasts to trust a wager on."

"Well, I've always been a bit of a wagerer myself," said Pete. "Can't explain except to say that my father was as well. God rest him." He pointed at her glass. "You want another one?"

"No," Marie said as she stood. "I'd best get my delivery and get on to the rest of my errands. Time and tide wait for no man, and they sure don't seem much too interested in waiting for women either."

"I'll get the hand-truck, meetcha out back?"

"And I'll ready the Abbot-Detroit and pull her around."

3.

Marie drove her Abbot-Detroit back to the hundred and sixty acres of Hempford land, packed with six cases of bonded Tennessee bourbon from the Brass Cup along with four cases of French Merlot. From Gwinnet's General there were two cases of cracker meal, two twenty five pound bags of flour, two pounds of yeast, a thirty pound bag of sugar, fifteen pounds of butter, ten pounds of lard, eighteen pounds of steel-cut oats, a case of ten gauge shotgun shells, and numerous other small but necessary packages. She had also purchased and loaded in numerous medicines and sundries from Allison Druggists, including aspirin, heroin, diphtheria and tetanus anti-toxins, morphine, cocaine, saltpeter, meningococci vaccine, laudanum, arsenic, several yards of surgical thread, a case of fifty syringes, and a small vial of powdered pennyroyal. Finally—and strapped to the back of the Abbot-Detroit due to the dearth of space in the car itself—was a box filled with equine remedies, an electric wand, large gauge hypodermics, and other veterinary medicinals provided by Doc Evans from the town clinic.

4.

It took the better part of a day to unload the car of its goods, but when the work was done Marie headed to the barn instead of to her sitting room. Her ten gauge Browning was bent over her arm, the double barrels broken open to show the exposed chambers. Strapped to her waist were a pair of knives that had been purchased by her father and gifted to Jack when they were married. The blades were sharp enough to shave the hair from a hogs back, and took much of the work out of breaking down a beast; so long as they were well maintained. That maintenance was just one of many tasks that Marie had inherited after Jack's passing, and she was at least as skilled in the work as he had ever been.

Marie walked past the horse barn and the pig pits behind it. The stench of the hogs attacked her nostrils long before the sty was in sight, but as she rounded the corner she smiled. The chosen animal was just as plump as ever, and looked at her with that dull intelligence that suggested a mind that was crossed between swine and man. Marie considered that for a moment as she looked at the massive beast and loaded the gun. How many times had she seen such a light before it disappeared in one of these animals? Never in a chicken, there's was a sensibility that didn't seem to realize the hour at hand until the deed had been done and their headless corpse began death's sprint in the yard. For pigs and horses it was different. Like when Marie had been forced to put down Collette, the mare that Jack had been riding before his accident. Jack was still moaning in the yard, but Marie's first instinct had been to the broken-legged beast.

The horse screamed in her mind, the shotgun snapped into battery, and the pig stared at her in bold defiance.. The gunshot crackled across the field and a murder of crows departed from their roosts in a maple in the back forty.

"Now the work starts," Marie said to the fallen pig.

5.

He knocked three times. That mattered, three was a lucky number, and Marie fixed her hair one last time before she walked to the door and opened it. She felt the usual blast of nervous anticipation as the air pushed by the door whooshed past her, and she could smell him on it. Tobacco, leather, the scent of a man. She smiled and blinked, the man smiled back.

"Silas Eberdeen," he said as he extended a hand. She took it and he smiled at her, then bent and kissed it. "You are even lovelier than I ever could have imagined, Mrs. Hempford."

"Marie," she said softly as she looked over his shoulder to be sure that they were alone. "Please, come inside."

"Well, yes, of course," Silas said as she moved aside to allow him entry, then slapped the door shut after him. "I reread your letters on the train. They were just as charged as they were when I first received them…You have a gift with words."

"How were your travels?"

"Exactly as you suggested," said Silas. "I traveled by train up from Indiana, then purchased a ferry ticket to get across the lake. From there it was thumbed rides and the kindness of my fellow man to deliver me, though I was forced to walk these last few miles."

Marie smiled. Silas was a tall man—this was important—and he stood over her by four inches. He was a healthy man as well, stout of arm and broad of chest, with just a little bump of a stomach under his overcoat. His hair was brown and so were his eyes, his lips curled slightly in a smile. There was a light to his youthfulness as well. Silas was ten years her junior but looked much younger, he seemed to have avoided the pitfalls of life that added wrinkles and tears via daily pains and sufferance.

"You are very handsome," she said as she wrapped her arms around him, and he shuddered against her embrace for a moment before he grabbed her back.

"Mrs. Hempford…"

Marie planted her lips onto his. There was little pressure at first, and then she was pushing into him, dominating him until he kissed her back just as hard. They flailed at each other's clothing, buttons and belts and tiny hooks released in tandem until she led him to the bedroom by a hand, the only sound his accelerated wind.

6.

Marie sat next to the bed. Her eyes were locked on Silas' ring finger, the dent and clean skin there confirming what she had known all along. She shifted her gaze to his face and then allowed her eyes to roam over his body. He was a specimen, and his boasts of ardor and endowment were made both plain and true against the rumpled sheets. His skin was tan, his breathing relaxed, his arms and legs bound to the posts of the bed by leather straps constructed from Collette's bridle. She held her palm open to see the treasure she'd recovered from his boot: a simple silver band with the initials S.E. and A.E. carved into its interior. She smiled to herself, watched as the beam of light from the open window began a slow race up his cheek and finally settled on his eyes to stir him. She watched this wakefulness with a feeling not unlike those which had been experienced hours earlier, a deep longing that laid low in her belly and extended to her every extremity.

Silas twitched first. His arms and legs fought the restraints. Slowly his eyes opened. He opened his mouth and twisted his head. He saw his bondage and battled it for a moment, pulled tightly enough against the bedframe to make her question the integrity of it for a moment, and then finally laid still. He rolled his head to face her as if he had only just seen her for the first time, and somehow he smiled.

"My love. I don't know what game you've decided to play at but—"

There was more but she ignored him. These were words that she'd heard seven times before, and just like those other seven times the eyes betrayed the mind. He was saying sweet, dutiful things, as though they were caught up in some great and mysterious confusion. But in his eyes there was a familiar fury.

"You are married," she said, and at once his sputtered words stopped.

"My Marie, things are not what they seem, I was—"

Marie held the ring up to the light.

"This was in your boot."

"It is not mine."

"You are a better lover than a liar," she said as she set the ring onto the nightstand and then began to strip out of her clothing. Silas' eyes bulged as she dropped her skirts to the floor and let her blouse fall upon them.

"Please untie me," he said, but his voice was small as she crawled onto the bed and began to tug at his penis. He whimpered, his manhood limp in defiance of her.

"You are mine," Marie said as she took him in her hands. She smiled. "And this can take as long as it needs to, but the sooner you learn the rules, the better."

"The rules? What rules? What are you doing?"

"There's only one you need to know right now," she said as he battled the restraints and came to life despite his struggles against her desires. "See? You are mine."

7.

Marie pounded the sledge into the anvil, flattening the ring between the irons until it was a coin. Next, she took an awl and hammer and pounded a hole through its center. If she looked closely she could still see the "A" from where it had been marked on the inside of the band, but the rest of the letters had been destroyed. She stared at the transformed ring for a frozen moment, then untied her necklace and laid it flat on the workbench.

The necklace was made of leather and it bore seven similar coins upon it. They were gold and silver and even one of cheap metal that she was unable to identify. They were pocked from their rude flattening, thicker and thinner in differing spots. Some the awl had been needed to allow the leather passage, others had a natural hole from where a finger had once occupied space. She worked slowly to untie the leather, then felt each coin after the other, their smoothness defined by both material and length of time spent rubbed against her chest. She laced the new ring onto the ornament, then pulled it back around her neck and tied it once more. She shuddered, clasped a hand to her breast and squeezed her left nipple hard enough to bruise, and walked back to the house.

8.

Marie sat next to the bed, her ardor spent. Silas was quiet. His hair was dirty and the sheets needed to be changed, and that meant that a discussion was needed. Whether he liked it or not.

"Please let me go," he said. "I won't tell anyone what's happened here. I won't, and no one would believe me even if I did, you're a proper lady and—"

She slapped him, the noise a rifle crack in the bedroom, and he shied from her a like a dog with a freshly trod upon paw. She turned to the window as a pathetic whimper escaped his lips. Snow was falling. Not much yet, but soon the world would be a frozen one and her stores of food and supplies would need to be taken far more seriously. That she had enough to survive a normal winter was never in doubt, but normalcy itself could never be guaranteed.

"Do you ever wonder what might happen if it never stopped?" Marie asked.

"What? What do you mean?"

"The snow," she said after a pregnant breath. "What would happen to us if it never stopped?"

"Please let me go. Please. I won't tell a soul what happened. People are looking for me, they—"

"Your wife?"

"Yes! Yes, Anne will be looking for me! If you let me go then she'll stop and I'll never come back here. You have my word!"

"If she's looking for you it's because you abandoned your vows," said Marie softly, "but she might be happy to have you gone. You go around on her I bet, get loose with the fists after drink most likely as well. Most men do."

"I would never—"

"There are three rules," said Marie. "You know the first. You are mine. There is no discussing the matter, it is as plain a thing as the falling snow outside. Would you like to know the second?"

"No. Yes."

"Then say the first one."

"What?"

"Say it. Say the first rule."

"You are…I am yours."

"Good boy," she said as she patted his leg and admired the taut muscles there, even as he recoiled from her touch. "The second rule is almost as simple. I eat three meals a day, and I expect to be serviced thrice daily as well. If you will not then I will stop feeding you. If you believe that you cannot, well, there are certain remedies to help persuade a man in such a state."

"And the third?" Silas asked quietly, his voice drowned from fear.

"The third rule is simple as well. If you try to escape I will kill you. That is not an idle threat, I will do it without even a moment of hesitation. I live a comfortable life and have no desire to disrupt it."

"You're a monster. You—"

"If you can adhere to the first two rules then I will allow you certain privileges. You might be allowed to take supper with me, for example, or even allowed out of bed for a few hours. The choice before you is simple. You can accept these rules and expect to be released at the end of winter, or you can die where you lay."

"You can't do this."

"The winters are long and hard here. No one is going to come and check on the property or me until it is done, and probably not even then. You don't know the area and you will undoubtedly freeze to death even if you were able to escape. You might not like it, but you are soon going to come to the realization that at least until spring you are going to need me a lot more than I need you."

9.

Two weeks before Christmas Marie's experimentation finally paid off. A combination of cocaine, whiskey, and stimulation from the electric wand proved to be enough to get Silas ready for Marie. Even when he was least willing.

10.

Marie stood in the blowing snow, chopping wood with Jack's old axe. She liked the work and enjoyed being out of the house. Silas was in bed, sleeping off his labors, and she could smell the smoke coming from the chimney even in the crosswind. The axe made a satisfying "chunk" sound as it divided timber, and Marie worked quickly through the last three logs that she'd decided to add to the pile. The several cords of stacked wood was more than enough to see them through the holidays, but splitting wood when it was least needed was a lesson that she'd learned as a young girl.

When the wood was split and stacked, Marie trudged to the horse barn and let herself inside. Old Ross and Bugle stamped their feet in anticipation as she walked towards them. She could hear the horses as they whinnied and begged to be released as the wind reminded them of the world outside of this barn. She did as they asked, one after the other, letting Bugle run free followed by Old Ross. The horses tromped into the snow without hesitation, and Marie watched them as they traversed the field while a smile spread across her face.

11.

Silas' right arm was free from the restraint on the bed, and he was clawing at the left, enough so that his fingers had become raw. His heart was still racing from what she had forced him to choke down. The strap to his left arm came free a few moments later, and then Silas was at the straps which bound his legs. He could see her through the window as she watched the horses, and he laughed as the first strap came undone. That laughter turned to exuberation as the second buckle was released, and he slowly stood from the bed. His legs shook as they found the floor, his body sore from the disuse of the past few months in a way that he had never known before. He fell to a knee, struggled back to his feet, and then staggered to the door. He was weak and he knew it, and as he looked through the kitchen window he could see the drifted snow.

"You leave this place and you'll die," Silas said to the empty room as his eyes hunted for a weapon. He moved on dull legs as he began to search the kitchen, his energy already faded from the exertion and adrenaline of his escape. He tore open drawers as he searched for a knife but there was none to be found, save for a few meant for spreading butter or lard. He slammed shut the last of these drawers and then set about in a search of the cupboards. He found plates and bowls, but finally took pause when a cast iron frying pan revealed itself on a hook next to the stove. Silas hefted the pan, he felt the weight and power in his hand and smiled, then turned to the window to see that Marie was no longer visible.

"God help me," Silas implored as he lifted his head to the heavens, but there was no answer to be found there, just the roof and whatever came after it. Silas looked again to the pan in his hand, then back to the bedroom. "Supper is in two hours," he said to himself, the recollection also vivid that Marie would be at him for a pre-meal romp. He looked again to the window and then back to the pan, before he headed to the bedroom with the handle of the skillet tightly gripped in his fist.

12.

Marie entered the bedroom in a negligée that she had ordered from the Sears and Roebuck book. She loved outfits like this. Lacy, dainty things that could take her back to her wedding night and her marriage to Jeff. He was a panty-man and an amateur photographer to boot, and though she found these predilections to be bizarre at first, she quickly warmed to them. Now, everything was as it should be. Silas was in bed, she was in the mood, and she had plans to make a supper of ham and biscuits.

"That's a good boy," she said as she looked Silas up and down. "You're stood to attention already."

"I've been looking forward to seeing you," said Silas.

"I can tell. You seem to be getting used to our arrangement."

"We can talk about it over supper," said Silas. "But first…"

Marie fell upon him and the bed like a lion diving for an antelope on the Savannah. She crushed him under her weight and she loved how small and powerless he felt beneath her. She quivered as she reached for him, anticipation bloomed red desire on her cheeks and hastened her breath. She felt a blast of air as she guided him and slipped, then turned to see his arms were free from the straps and he was swinging a skillet at her. She gasped as he found entry and grabbed for her hair. The pan came back with a rush of wind as he attempted to clap hand, pan, and head together, and so she dove towards him. Their domes collided as she fell, the crown of her forehead connecting with his nose in an explosion of violence. He shrieked, the pan fell to the floor, and as he grabbed for his nose Marie punched him dead center in the face. Blood sprayed in a fan. Silas screamed and tried to buck her from him. Marie held his arms flush, threatened his nose when he tried to fight, and rode her way to afternoon glory.

13.

When Silas woke the pain in his face ripped him to consciousness. He blinked at tears that fought their way to his cheeks and rolled to his sideburns. His arms and legs were immobile, his head a fog of pain and confusion. And then he saw her. Marie was dressed as though a ball were planned. She wore a Kelly green velour dress with lace sleeves and collar. A glass full with brown liquor sat in her right hand, and he could tell by her flushed cheeks that it had not been her first taste of the day.

"You slept for a long time," Marie said finally. "All the way into the new year."

Silas ignored her, rolled his head to look at the window and the world outside. The sky was gray, the ground white, and the air between them so full of flurries that he couldn't see the trees at the edge of the property. A shudder ran through him. It started at the pain in the center of his face and raced down his body in tributaries of fear that coalesced in his belly and extremities.

"That's a normal thing," she said.

"Nothing about this is normal."

"I set your nose," she said, as if he had never spoken at all. "I gave you heroin to calm you so that I could make sure it came out straight. Possibly a bit too much. You slept for better than a day and a half. I thought that might be the end."

"Why?" Silas croaked. "Why set it at all? Why didn't you just kill me for trying to escape?"

"Some lessons are taught so that others can be avoided," Marie said. "If you'd have not tried to escape, I wouldn't have needed to show you that I can handle myself and hurt you. I could have done so outright if I'd wanted to, but I didn't. That was a kindness meant to both save you the trouble of injury, and to keep your loins as fully functional as possible."

"A kindness."

"Yes, and now the time for kindness has passed."

"You dirty bitc—"

"You can pick," said Marie, and when Silas looked at her he could see that she no longer held a glass but instead a pair of bolt cutters. "Toe or finger."

"Fuck you!"

"Toe or finger," said Marie, "but if you won't choose I'll take one of each."

"God please help me!" Silas screamed. "Please! God! Please!"

"Last chance," said Marie, "and best choose quickly. I will take both."

"Toe," Silas said. "You do it you—"

And then there was pain.

14.

Silas hobbled into the kitchen. Marie had found a walking stick for him in the barn and it was tucked under his arm as he made his way to the table. His nose was a constant complaint, the missing toe itched and burned in equal measure. He felt as if he were waiting to be awoken from some impossible dream of pain and fornication and cruelty, but he knew this was no dream.

Instead of acquiescing to his pain Silas began to set the table. Marie's back was to him as she worked at the stove. She hummed and stirred, and she never once turned to see if he was considering another attack. He stared at her like this for a moment, frozen by indecision and fear, and then arranged the forks, knives and napkins.

"I'll be having wine," said Marie, back still to him. Silas could picture her on the ground, bloodied and prostrate as he stood over her panting, but the fantasy was gone as soon as it had arrived.

"Yes ma'am," said Silas as he went to get the glasses and a bottle of red.

"You're doing fine, Silas," she said.

As much as he tried to fight the words, they escaped his lips with nary a struggle. "Yes ma'am. Thank you."

15.

The farmhouse and barn were islands in a sea of white. Silas had given up on the cane while in the house but he needed it as he trudged after Marie in the snow. Even with the walking stick it was hard to stay upright, and the soreness in his foot was far more deeply rooted in cold. The pain of it was bitter and felt as though it were chasing up the nub of bone that she'd sutured a flap of flesh over. That was old pain, though, and if there was one thing that Silas had learned in these last few months it was that old pain could be dealt with, while the fear of fresh and new damage was far more injurious to his mental state. New pain could come at any time, and she knew exactly how to dispense it. Worse, he knew that she enjoyed it, that it made her voracious for more and more cruelty, and that one day she might not be able to stop herself. Two mornings prior she'd whipped him, and though she'd stopped after just a few lashes, he'd seen something in her eyes, something even worse than when she'd taken his toe.

Silas made it to the barn a few steps after her, and got to work feeding the horses as she yanked the door shut behind them. Bugle and Old Ross stamped their hooves and shook their heads as he dispensed oats and carrot tops. When he was done Silas stepped back to watch them for a moment, the horses bobbed in unison as they worked at their meals. He shifted to the side to take the pressure off of his bad foot, and then he felt Marie. Her breath was hot on his neck and so he was still even as his heart raced.

"You've been doing better," she said, and Silas nodded.

"I am yours."

"Good boy," she said as she patted his head a couple of times, her touch almost motherly. And then she took the walking stick from him.

"Marie?" Silas asked as he stumbled, then caught his footing next to Old Ross' pen. "I need that to get back to the house. I can't keep my balance in the snow without it."

"But I don't want to give it back to you."

"Then I shall go without."

Marie nodded, her face solemn. She smiled, then dropped the cane to the hard packed dirt.

"Finish the work here and then come back to the house," Marie said, and then he was alone in the barn. Silas watched the door. He was sure that she was going to come back, that it was all some trick, but the longer he was alone the more he began to realize that she really had left him alone. His eyes pored over the tools and farming implements that adorned the wall, but as he did so, an ache began to rise up from the missing toe. It was a song of pain and it was breathless in its threats. Giving a last look to the wall of potential weapons, Silas got back to work.

16.

When she was finished with him she strapped him back into the bed. Silas helped and offered up each limb as she affixed him in place. When the work was done she stood and dressed herself, then walked to the window. His eyes followed her.

"The weather will turn soon. Then the snow will stop, and the world will grow gray and ugly instead of gray and forbidding."

"That's good," said Silas, and Marie turned to him and nodded.

"It is. Spring is the time of change."

Her hand fell to her necklace and the rings there, she caressed them in turn. Her fingers stopped on the ring that had once been Silas and Anne's but was now hers as much as he was. She smiled at him as she rubbed it, then let the necklace drop to her chest as she walked from the room and closed the door after her. Silas watched the door, sure that she would return to surprise him, but it remained closed.

Silas began to pull at the right strap, the one that had once allowed him freedom from this hell. His efforts were not to loosen the buckle, however rewarding that could have been. Rather, he yanked at the strap itself. The bedframe was solid, the leather strong but supple. After a few minutes of effort he relaxed his arm and felt the give in the leather offered by the constant nightly stretching. Not much. Not yet. But soon.

17.

Marie was drunk. Silas was flying on a cocktail of cocaine, whiskey, and heroin. His body felt numb and flush, bent and broken and made whole all over again. He was nude and so was she, the pair of them sat in the room like a couple of newlyweds that had only recently discovered sex and the hollowness and joy that could come with coupling. Marie sipped from a wineglass. Silas sat in a stupor. And then she was moving to the door and was back to the side of the bed in the blink of an eye.

"I read about something," she said. "About the men of Borneo."

"The men of Borneo," Silas said, her words a mystery whose answer he desperately wanted to avoid. "The men of—"

"Islanders," she said. "Fierce headhunters called the Dayaks or Ibans or many other names. I read about them in *National Geographic*. They're a fascinating people. They're covered in black tattoos of animals and things for the animals to eat."

"For the animals to eat."

"Yes, to a Borneo headhunter the tattoos are as real as any other living thing, so they must have something to eat," explained Marie. "Even the women are warriors there, and they take heads and get tattooed as well. But you know what they love the most about their men?"

Silas shook his head and looked to his arm. He was strapped into the bed again but couldn't remember when it had happened. Worse, she had moved between his legs and was painting his member with something red.. She dropped his penis and then took something from the bag next to her on the bed. Something shiny that looked like a small dumbbell. Then she showed him a needle. A big one.

"When a Borneo headhunter becomes a man, one of the elder women in the tribe pushes a needle through his staff and then attaches a piece of jewelry to it. The practice is said to be quite painful, but the women love it. They even have a saying: that without the jewelry having sex is like meat without salt."

"Please no," said Silas.

"You are mine," said Marie, and then there was pain.

18.

The snow was melted in all but the deepest of piles, the sun was shining in the window, and Silas could move his wrists in the straps enough to turn them. Birds sung in the trees, and he could hear her footsteps in the kitchen. Instead of coming to him as she did every other morning, however, Silas heard the rear door to the house open and then shut. He heard her footsteps on the back porch, and then the house was silent. He sat up in bed as much as the straps would allow and looked to the window. He caught just a glimpse of her as she walked to the barn, and then she was gone. He worked at the leather, pulled and relaxed his arm, then slipped it free from the buckle. He stopped and lay in silence for a moment, terrified to go further and terrified not to stop.

"This is what you said, remember?" He hissed to the empty room. "When she breaks routine that is when you'll need to act."

He was still despite the words.

"She is going to kill you, either by happenstance or on purpose."

Slowly, Silas released the strap from his left arm, then bent to remove the bonds on his legs. His member ached from the still-healing wound there and he ground his teeth against the pain as he worked the leather.

"She is going to kill you," he said as he stood.

"She is going to kill you," he said as he slipped from the bedroom.

"She is going to kill you," he said as he walked into the kitchen and peered through the window there. Marie was visible at the far end of the property, a shovel and pick in her hands.

"She is going to kill you," said Silas as he grabbed at his groin, his hand came away dotted with blood. "She is going to kill you."

Silas watched as Marie began to dig at the far end of the property. Silas tore himself from the window, then began a frantic search of the kitchen. Just as before there were no knives, and now even the cast iron skillets and other heavy cookware were gone. Silas pounded a fist on the counter and looked back to the window. She was still toiling at the earth. He looked to the closed door across the room, the one by the bathroom. He spun back to her, then back to the door.

"She is going to kill you," Silas said, and then he walked to the door and opened it.

Marie's bedroom was different than he'd expected. He'd assumed a feminine touch, if not a torture chamber. Instead, the room was utilitarian in nature, masculine by default. There were pictures on the bureau of Marie with a smiling man, and Silas stared at it for a moment before he recalled his purpose and desperate need for armament. He ran back to the window, saw that she was still at work, and then bolted to the room again. Silas flung open the closet, began tearing down dresses and hatboxes and skirts and blouses. The room looked like some insane boutique's sale, but there was nothing to be found.

"She is going to kill you," he said to the empty room and to the pile of clothes. "She is going to kill you."

19.

Silas ran from the house and down the worn path in the driveway. He was dressed in ladies clothes. Frilly lacey things, topped with a housecoat. There was once a point in his life where he'd have preferred death to being seen in public in such accoutrements, but those days were gone. Now he was running down the packed earth of a still frozen country road without shoes nor even an ill thought of what being seen in such a state might mean for him. Even an asylum would be better than Marie Hempford's house of horrors, even being jailed for lewdness.

Suddenly there was a sound behind him. A car. Hope. Silas began to wave his arms wildly over his head. The car slowed as if the driver were trying to make sense of such a sight, then sped up. Silas flailed in the road as it drew closer, right up until the car pulled alongside of him and he saw the familiar pilot and the twin shotgun barrels pointed at him.

"Get in," said Marie.

Silas quavered. The words were stuck in his mouth. He stared at the shotgun, the blackness of the barrels impossible to comprehend or argue with.

"Get in," said Marie. "Can you imagine what the neighbors might think if they saw you in this condition? They're only a few miles up the road, and you look like you just escaped a brothel!"

Slowly, Silas made his way into the car. Marie kept the gun pointed at him as she turned the car around. He could grab the gun. He could fight. He could do something. So he sat and wept as she drove back to the Hempford land.

"You saw me out there," Marie said. "You thought I was digging a hole. You know you can't dig when the ground is this frozen. Or at least you should." She shook her head as the shotgun bounced on her knees. "I was filling it in, you old fool. I thought this time might be different." She took her free hand from the wheel and caressed the necklace there for a moment, her fingers fell to his ring last and squeezed it, as though she were trying to pinch some memory from the ruined metal.

20.

Silas died quickly—though not without some measure of violence—and was buried in a half filled grave alongside his predecessors.

21.

Wanted:
Disconsolate Widow Seeks Strong Man for Farm Work
and Possible Romance in Northern Michigan
Hearts Divided Suffer in Solitude

This comfortless relict seeks to hire a man with a strapping back and gentle disposition to help with work on her horse farm in Northern Michigan. She has no interest in a gentleman of leisure nor does she wish to find a man of ill-humor or with children of his own. The swain must be vigorous of attitude when it comes to farm work, but also understanding of the emotions of this lonely dearheart. Please send letters of inquiry or interest to: M. Hempford Post Office Box 217 Calumet Michigan 49913 and the matron will respond in kind.

Reign, Reign
Jonathan Walter

The chorus of hissing rain and howling wind rose to its crescendo, and April Kramer prayed the madness would climax with it. She needed the madness tonight, because redemption would be messy. It always was.

The conditions were right: a stifling hot July night, high humidity, and the man masquerading as her husband smiling at the sky hours prior, no doubt anticipating a tryst with his mistress, who'd be arriving soon—at least, so April hoped.

She was ready for her, or *it*. At least it had been predictable over the past two years: rolling in on the eastbound thunderheads from late spring to early autumn, always arriving at night. But the affair ended tonight. She'd rescue Reid just as he'd rescued her.

She glanced at the clock: 1:29 am. She knew sleep would evade her, her thoughts wandering, her eyes flitting obsessively between the slanted ceiling and the clock's digital readout.

Waiting.

Reid lay gently snoring beside her in bed, fingers limp at his sides, just beyond her reach—like the rest of him. Those fingers used to intertwine with hers, wrapping them in a warm embrace before squeezing three times to signal, *I love you*. The gesture had been their love language, their code. Three squeezes expressed all that needed to be said. It suited them, after all, she the damaged introvert and he the no-nonsense pragmatist. Sappy words weren't their thing and never would be. But even the silent signal that passed between them had been marred by this interference, this complication, which had also soured her relationship with the rain.

She'd been instilled with a love for driving storms at an early age. It wasn't just the storm itself that made her pulse race, it was the build-up: the pregnant clouds floating on the horizon like an armada, the damp ozone wafting up her nose, the prickle of thunder hanging in the air like a promise. As a girl, she'd slip on her father's galoshes and parka, feeling small but cozy, and wait on the driveway for the heavens to unburden themselves. She'd pace in circles and murmur her own altered nursery-rhyme lyrics:

> *Rain, rain, come today,*
> *Go away another day,*
> *Little April wants to play,*
> *Rain, rain, come today...*

When the rain did come, she'd spin in place and stomp through the little streams that formed along the edges of the street. She'd imagine herself a giant, a being with the power and size to alter the course of rivers and reshape lakes. Then she'd lie on her belly and watch her rivers circle into tight whirlpools before spilling into the abyss of the nearby storm drain.

She reigned over her kingdom alone—the way she liked it. Her father's only rule was to heed the flash of lightning, which meant game over. But she had never heeded those flickering warnings, waiting until her father boomed along with the thunder for her to come inside. Her ignorance of such warnings would be a repeated pattern throughout her life.

***

1:31 am

The first warning in the series of bizarre events that led to this point fell on her like a raindrop preceding a downpour. Almost two years ago in August, Reid was caught in a thunderstorm during his early Saturday morning jog in the secluded Cuyahoga Valley. He despised getting wet, watched his analog barometer like a hawk—an unusual habit for any man in his early thirties with access to weather data on his phone—and would forgo his jog at even the slightest chance of rain. The anomaly blindsided him. At the time, April thought the deluge a stray remnant of a system that had passed the previous night. Now she knew better.

It had been around eight o'clock that morning, and she had been curled up on the couch, sipping her coffee and browsing Instagram when Reid trudged into their little Cape Cod home soaked and dazed, as if walking off the effects of a fender bender. In truth, April had thought it cute: his dark curly hair matted down like the fur of a wet dog, his saturated T-shirt draping from his coat-hanger shoulders, the usual cocksure look in his brown eyes replaced by a meekness she hadn't seen since he'd first asked her out on a date.

She even thought it charming when he plopped down next to her on the leather couch, soaking clothes and all—

which, in hindsight, should have sent warning signals racing up and down her spine. But to her, Reid was just being Reid. His sense of humor was unfiltered and irreverent, sometimes veering into dark places, but his easy smile could disarm the devil himself.

Reid hadn't smiled—another missed signal. He just sat and stared at the blank TV screen, and she assumed the silence was his theatrical way of drawing out a lengthy joke that would surely end with a worthy punchline. There hadn't been one of those either.

She asked, "A little wet out there, huh?"

No reply.

"You okay, babe? What happened? You clearly got the worst of the tsunami."

This did get a response, though not a verbal one. Reid leaned forward and extended his arms out in front of him. They were still beaded with glistening rain. He remained that way for a long time, running his gaze up and down his wet forearms and hands, as if seeing them for the first time. He then looked down to survey his sodden clothing, his brow furrowing, mouth working as if uttering a wordless prayer. Odd, though not as strange or unexpected as what he mumbled next, before rising to his feet and shuffling upstairs to their bedroom.

"Stable up there."

***

1:35 am

She rolled onto her side and studied her Reid, her love—the loyal man who stayed. He was taken soon after that *stable* couch-soaking incident, but she hadn't known it. He'd been lying next to her, just as he was now, snoring gently as always, matching the rhythm of the pattering rain. And, as always, her bladder woke her up around half past two. After a quick trip to the bathroom, she returned to find his side of the bedsheet pulled down to reveal his torso. He'd been fully covered when she'd first gotten up, and she hadn't pulled his side of the sheet down when she'd risen. But she didn't have time to ponder that warning signal. A shudder rippled through Reid's body and he stiffened. Then his hips shot upward, his back violently arching to the point she thought his spine might snap.

She was frozen as he spasmed. His eyelids fluttered, his lips parted in a hedonic smile, as if in the throes of sexual climax. Then a trembling hand found her fingers. It was her true Reid—at least part of him. He gave her hand three hasty squeezes before his body went limp and collapsed back onto the mattress.

When she attempted to describe the seizure to Reid the following morning, he raised an eyebrow and smirked, as if to say, *you been using again, hon?* Though, at her insistence, he visited his doctor later that week, and even agreed to the precautionary neurological exam and blood test. He received a clean bill of health.

***

1:39 am

His spasms soon became extensions of every nocturnal storm. When it happened a third time, she swung a leg over his writhing torso, grabbed a fistful of his T-shirt and whispered urgently into the crook of his neck, "Babe, I'm here, I'm here. I'm *right* here!" But he hadn't been able to resist the pull of whatever was seizing him. His shaky fingers found her knee and gave it three weak squeezes before falling limp.

Her breath caught then; the tiny hairs on the nape of her neck standing up as a gentle wind rippled past her.

The color purple filled the corner of her eye, solid in the middle and blurred at its edges. Hurried whispers invaded her ears—feral and incoherent—but the voice was familiar.

Even as Reid lay stiff beneath her with his mouth ajar and his head thrown back, some part of him was in motion, carried off by that purple gust into some unknowable plane: his voice…*him*. She knew it to be true. A fleeting moment, an infinitesimal time slice inside the blink of an eye, but it happened. Then, as fast as he'd gone, he returned, fingers twitching and chest rising again, plunging back into the arms of sleep. It was then she knew he was leaving.

***

1:40 am

She soon realized that the rain and the night were the two essential ingredients for these bizarre episodes. The storm that arrived in late August that year promised to offer both. Maybe she could *prove* what was happening to him?

She was ready that night, lying awake as she was right now, thoughts racing, her iPhone resting in her palm. When the first tremor rattled Reid's body, she shot upright and pressed the phone's Home button to wake its camera application. Nothing happened. She hammered at the button, heart pounding as her husband writhed and contorted. Still nothing.

A minute or so later, her phone *did* awaken, but not to the bright screen showing her and Reid's wedding photo, which she used as her wallpaper. Something else lit up on the screen: the color purple. It clouded over the glass like ink spilling into water, eventually filling the screen from edge to edge. The purple light began to brighten and dim in sequence, pulsating as if it had its own heartbeat. Her mouth went dry. Something stung her palm. The phone had become cold as ice. She dropped it onto the bed and watched in disbelief as it swelled with the strange light. She was too numb to accept her husband's groping hand. *Am I hallucinating?*

Moments later, when Reid fell to the mattress like a spent cartridge, the phone turned back on as if nothing had happened.

The opportunity for proof washed away with the rain, but it wasn't just the night that bore these terrors. She'd learn soon after that they extended into the daytime hours too.

***

1:42 am

It was a Sunday in September. She'd lumbered up the stairs from the mudroom to the kitchen, arms weighted with brimming grocery bags, when she found Reid staring at the tap running into the sink. His hands were stuffed into his pockets and he was repeating, "Symmetrical, stable," between bouts of giggles.

She watched in silent horror as he said the mantra over and over again while watching the water circle down the drain, as if observing a magic trick. When he finally sensed her presence, he cast a sidelong glance and brought a hand to his mouth to stifle the laughter, but his chest still hitched in barely-contained mirth.

April dropped the bags, darted over to the sink and shut it off. Turning to him, she asked, "What the hell has gotten into you, Reid?"

He stared into the basin, hand clamped over his mouth, watching the remaining water gutter down the drain. When she pressed him further for an explanation, she only got a puzzled look. It wasn't until he turned to exit the kitchen that she noticed he'd pissed his running shorts.

***

1:45 am

An unrelenting winter descended onto Northeast Ohio that first year, and the spell began to fade with each passing week, frosting over like the window panes themselves. Eventually, she began to wonder if she'd exaggerated the events in her head. Had the hell she'd put her body through for all those years affected her mind? Or maybe the affliction had run its course like a bout of the flu. Maybe it was over?

They fell back into their usual cold-weather routine: Sundays huddled up on the couch, binge-watching Netflix, Friday nights indulging in Chinese carry-out and copious amounts of Pinot Noir, and of course, work and sex in between.

After a time, it wasn't clear what was work and what was sex; their reignited efforts to conceive had come to feel like a second job. Aligning their love-making with April's ovulation had accomplished nothing. More frequent sessions in the bedroom hadn't helped. Having Reid's sperm evaluated hadn't turned up any concerning issues either. The results showed that nothing was wrong with him—biologically speaking.

April had known she was the issue long before Reid was tested. In hindsight, they should have just saved their money. The problem was the endless torment she'd visited upon her body: the drugs, the comatose nights that escaped memory, the sallow mornings during which she discovered total strangers in her bed, the days that assigned pain her constant companion, tempered only by a cheeseball or another chase of the dragon. Her actions, her error, her shame—she knew it to be true. She'd wrecked their ability to conceive long ago. She'd never hear little footsteps patter down the hallway and into her bedroom. No, the only pattering she'd ever hear would be from the rain hitting the roof above.

She still prayed she was wrong, because Reid, more than any other man she knew, deserved to be a father. He had been the man with the courage to ask out the broken woman, the train wreck whose skin hung too loose about her twenty-nine-year-old face, whose once lustrous red hair had grown grey at the roots and frayed at the ends, brittle and dry, like kindling awaiting a flame.

A month into their courtship, Reid had found her overdosed in her apartment bedroom, half-naked and petting the carpet, pupils the size of pinpricks, a syringe and a length of rubber tubing at her side.

Reid stayed. Not her father. Not her stepmother. Not her stepbrother. Not any of the other worthless men. Only Reid, who'd nearly gone into debt to help pay for her stay at the treatment center. Reid, who'd lifted her up and had gotten her clean. Reid, who'd encouraged her to wear high heels the night they'd exchanged vows at the beachside gazebo in the Virgin Islands, despite her already being a good two-inches taller than him. Reid, who loved her, past demons and all.

***

1:51 am

Now she would lift him up. Because the man next to her wasn't clean. He was battling, and he needed her. The three squeezes he continued to give her each time he was taken all but confirmed this in her mind. Her imagination or some inflamed scar tissue from her former life had nothing to do with this—she knew that now. Her husband was reaching out. But Reid's battles were not the type that could be helped by a treatment center. There were no support groups to join. No hotlines to call.

The driving rain slowed to intermittent taps, like skeletal fingers striking tuneless piano keys. *The calm before the storm.*

This past winter should have been the calm before the storm—the previous winter had been—but this thing had managed to penetrate even that brief reprieve. It was getting worse. The February occurrence convinced her that she couldn't just hope these events would cease. They wouldn't, and she had no one to turn to. Who would believe the fantastical story from the former junkie, the liar and thief? Who would believe that an unseen force was luring Reid away like some nocturnal paramour each time it stormed between spring and autumn? The thought alone sounded preposterous to her.

She would get no support from her estranged family, who'd given up on her long ago and lived two states away. She would get no support from the internet, which had no answers in its reservoir of information. She would get no support from Jillian, her friend and fellow administrative assistant at the family medical practice where they both worked. Not when Jillian didn't believe in anything she couldn't see or feel. It was just April. And Reid would spill through her fingers like water if she didn't act soon.

***

1:53 am

The final straw occurred on Valentine's Day—a Friday. She'd left work early, called China Wok for an order of some Spicy Wonton and Crab Rangoon, and stopped at the store to pick up not one, but two bottles of their favorite red. She thought she'd surprise Reid—who worked from home on Fridays—with a late afternoon snack and maybe a romp upstairs. Instead, he'd surprised her.

She knew something was off as soon as she opened the storm door to the mudroom. The floor was much wetter than it should have been. While there had been a scrim of snow coating their tiny yard that day, the driveway and sidewalk were clean, making it odd that Reid would have tracked any wetness in with him.

And why was he outside anyway? she thought, running her gaze over his flip-flops, which looked hastily kicked off, the indentations in their rubber soles puddled with water.

She heard a faint buzz. It came from somewhere inside the house. She mounted the stairs to the kitchen, crossing into the snug family room, heart thudding in her ears, sneakers creaking over the floorboards. But her own sounds were drowned out by the staticky *hiss* coming from the bathroom, which couldn't be from the running shower—this sound was much too loud. It resembled the noise that made her pulse race as a child, the melodic whir of heavens quickening.

Rain.

The door was closed. She didn't want to barge in on him. Reid was already sheepish in his bathroom habits; the room was a rare oasis of diffidence for a man who had few filters. He was most vulnerable here. Would she make things worse by interrupting whatever was happening beyond the door? Would she do more harm than good?

But what if he hadn't barged into her bedroom the night she'd lent her veins to the needle? What if he hadn't pulled her into the bathtub and let the frigid water rain down on her? What if he hadn't called Kevin, his close friend and police officer who'd arrived later with the Narcan despite being off duty?

He could have cut his losses with the woman he'd only known a month and hadn't yet taken to bed. It had been in his power and his right to move on. He could have called 911 and let the ambulance take her away; wipe his hands clean of her. But he hadn't. He'd allowed her to save face on one condition: "No secrets," he'd said to her as she'd shivered in the tub, her stupid eyes gazing at everything and nothing. The secrets ended that night. And a year later, he put a diamond on her finger. Redemption was messy, but she would make things clean again. It was a debt she owed and intended to pay.

She didn't call out to him through the door as it would have done no good. The chill on the back of her neck told her so—a rare warning signal that struck home. She set down the wine and the cooling takeout. She stepped to the door, inhaled, and eased it open, into the deafening roar of rain, only to find the bathroom dark and... *dry*.

The iPhone, nestled in the cradle of a small portable speaker on the edge of the sink, cast an ethereal glow about the small space. Its screen featured a photo of rippling water puddles with text above it reading: *Rain Downpour*.

The blinds were drawn over the frosted bathroom window, the lights off, the shower curtain closed.

"Reid?"

Nothing.

"Reid, it's me. I'm home early."

She waited. Her head felt light, her mouth dry. *Is he dead?*

She didn't want to see what was on the other side of the curtain. She wasn't ready to confront the situation. But then again, Reid wouldn't have been ready to resuscitate the heroin addict who was supposed to be freshening up before their third date.

Tonight's a date night too.

She pushed down the fear and, with a shaky hand, pulled the curtain aside. The phone's pale blue glow washed over her husband, who was lying in the tub, a black sleeping mask pulled down over his eyes. Lumps of melting snow clung to his chest and stomach like oversized spider sacks. He was fully clothed in his athletic shorts and T-shirt. Clear water filled the tub to his pelvis. An empty mop bucket lay across his knees. There was something else—something about his leg that her brain couldn't process. Everything about him was still except for his lips, which were pulled back in a tight smile, murmuring the same two words over and over again:

"Symmetrical, stable, symmetrical, stable, symmetrical, stable, symmetrical, stable…"

Her legs buckled. She flung a hand to the wall to steady herself, but she was already staggering backward, out of the bathroom. A minute later—or maybe it was five—she found herself sitting on the floor of the family room, palms planted on the cold wood, trying but failing to force her quaking elbows to stabilize. She sat and stared into the dark maw of the open bathroom, the droning rain sounds fading into the background, replaced by the beating of her heart through her temples.

Her chest heaved. Her breaths were ragged. An odd sound penetrated the thrum in her head. Someone was crying—no, *sobbing*. Reflexively she glanced about the family room but didn't see anyone. Of course, why would she? She was alone, always alone, and now maybe forever alone.

Alone, April. You're alone.

The dawning realization washed over her, the black abyss creeping ever closer to invite her back in. She was the one sobbing.

She stayed on the floor for a long time, shouting at the voices in her mind, willing them to retreat.

You know how to make it better, they purred. *You know where to get it. You have the cash now. You no longer have to resort to those terrible things you used to have to do.*

She squeezed her eyes shut and pushed the voices further away; concentrated on keeping them there, tiny spiders clinging to the wall at a distance, but never truly gone. They would call to her for as long as she lived.

She was alone, but so had Reid been when she'd relapsed. He hadn't collapsed into self-pity when he'd found her. Instead, he'd doused her with water. She would douse him with something now: *the truth.* She staggered to her feet, wiped her eyes, went back into the bathroom and flicked on the light. Reid needed to finally *see* what this was, this addiction, which he somehow never saw.

He didn't see his nocturnal seizures, those sighs of wind that rippled his soul only to be forgotten by morning. He didn't fully see his bizarre behavior by day, either. The morning he'd come in out of the rain and slumped down onto the couch, it had been as if he were bewitched. But his extending his arms in front of him showed her that he was aware *something* had happened. How could he not be? How could someone who loathed getting wet not be aware that he was soaked from head to toe? It wasn't until after he'd declared whatever it was *stable*, trundled upstairs and changed his clothes, that he'd come back downstairs as Reid, concern flitting in his eyes. He'd asked her if he'd blacked out. She'd told him yes, he had.

He didn't know—he couldn't have known. Not the Reid she knew, who would drag all skeletons out of the closet, exposing their ashen bones to all. Secrets were antithetical to all that he was and bullshit enjoyed a very short stay in their home. Had their positions been reversed, he'd confront her, and wouldn't relent until all the skeletons were laid bare.

This would be the intervention. He would *know*—the moment was now. Grabbing her phone, she woke it without issue, opened the camera application and toggled it to Video mode. She selected the Record button, held the phone over the bathtub and panned the camera over him for a full two minutes, then stopped the recording. She walked out, leaving the light on, and scooped up a bottle of Pinot before striding into the kitchen, where she uncorked it, and poured two glasses. She returned to the family room, set the glasses on the coffee table, and waited on the couch.

When he emerged from the bathroom twenty or so minutes later, looking sodden and bewildered, she called to him before he could sneak upstairs. She wondered in that moment if it was from shame that he slinked off after these events, or if it was from something else. She thought of a cheating husband, skulking home late, wearing the scent of another woman, wanting to rid his skin of it as soon as possible.

But he didn't skulk off. He paused at the foot of the stairs and turned to her. She raised an eyebrow and patted the couch cushion beside her, summoning what sensuality she could. He hesitated, but then shuffled over to the couch like a child who'd been caught playing in a mud puddle. She knew he wasn't fully back to himself, because the man she'd married would sooner swallow antifreeze than sit on a couch in wet clothes. Nevertheless, he only glanced down at his clothes and then back up to her as if to say, *You serious?*

"Come on, it's okay. I'll make it worth your while," she said, patting the cushion again.

He dropped onto the couch beside her. She handed him his glass of wine and clinked it with her own.

"Happy Valentine's Day, babe," she said.

He returned the sentiment with a murmur.

"I have something to show you." She indicated her phone where it rested on the table.

He dropped his eyes to his wet clothes. "Can't it wait?"

"It's fine. It's certainly not the first time."

He knitted his brow at this, but then shrugged. "Okay."

She snuggled up next to him then, ignoring the chill from his wet clothes, and played him the video. But she didn't watch the video, she watched him. At first, he just squinted at the screen, as if scrutinizing the minute details of a fresco. But thirty seconds into the video, a small smile began to play across his lips. It grew from there. A giggle escaped his mouth. Then laughter spilled out, droll and unfettered. He leaned back and bit his knuckle, trying to plug the laughter. But plugging up one thing caused something else to escape, like a bizarre game of whack-a-mole: tears. He was crying. Not from sorrow—*joy*. The tears ran down his cheeks, rolled off his chin and dropped onto his lap where they disappeared into his soaked shorts. His wine glass slipped from his fingers, fell to the floor and shattered. He didn't seem to notice or care.

April couldn't feel her face—all the blood seemed to have abandoned it—but she could sense her mouth hanging open as her husband cried tears of joy over this video of himself—this profanity. Something pressed into her gut then. It was sharp and hot, a knife blade held to a flame. *Anger.* It was as if he didn't care. He didn't care how this behavior affected her. Hell, he didn't even seem to notice her in that moment.

The words erupted from her mouth. "Reid, goddamn it, what the hell is this? How do you explain it?"

He clamped a palm to his chest and shook his head, unable to quell the laughter.

"Reid, if you love me at all, explain it! No secrets, remember?"

He just shook his head; brought a hand to his eye and flicked away a tear.

She lowered her voice. "Reid, *please*. You can tell me. What happened to you during that jog? What happened to you that day at the sink? What keeps happening to you at night? What happened to you just now? Tell me."

He continued to shake his head, but something else glimmered in his eyes. Her Reid was in there somewhere—she knew it. The laughter hadn't fully taken his eyes. Was it a plea she saw in them? Was he battling?

The laughter died down to hitching giggles, the intervals between them widening. He tried to stammer out words, and more giggles escaped before his lips could form syllables. But the spaces eventually widened enough for him to utter two words, which were no more coherent than *symmetrical* or *stable*:

"My majesty."

***

2:01 am

She shifted in bed. She'd gotten nowhere with him that day. Like the other times, he'd quietly reverted back to being Reid, silent as a maple leaf turning over after the rain. He'd extended his arms out in front of him, studying his glistening skin, and then got up to go change. Later, he complained that he must have blacked out. She'd allowed him to believe this narrative and hadn't dissuaded him from another call to his doctor. Redemption was messy.

But the video held the truth, the evidence. She thought of showing it to Jillian, but felt that doing so would be a betrayal to Reid. What if he'd recorded her when she was doped out of her mind? Even if he'd saved her, she wouldn't have spoken to him again. She thought about setting up a meeting with a psychiatrist—alone—but knew there was something else happening here. There was a power she needed to better understand, a power she would not come to know until May, when she had witnessed its coming. The storm was its mighty chariot, the night sky its arena to roam. Because it *did* come from the night sky.

***

2:04 am

It had been a Saturday morning this past May, and they were about to leave for their monthly shopping trip to Costco. April had misplaced her membership card and had gone back into the house to rummage for it in her other purse. When she found it and came out to the driveway, Reid wasn't waiting in the running Jeep as she expected; he was standing down on the driveway apron, visible in profile, hands in his pockets and rocking on his feet. His eyes were closed, his head cocked with an ear to the cloudless blue sky, the trace of a smile on his lips, as if listening to the urgent whispers of a lover. The Weather Channel hadn't forecasted the savage storm that would arrive forty hours later, but Reid had. He'd known his mistress was coming. And then, so did she.

The prelude to the occurrence had unfolded as expected: damp air heavy with charged static, the sweet scent of rain drifting in from the west, dense clouds crowding out the violet sky. They'd gone to bed early that night—at her insistence. The wind was already picking up when Reid collapsed onto his pillow. He was snoring in minutes.

She set her phone alarm for 1:45 am, ensuring it was on silent vibrate mode so it wouldn't wake Reid. As it happened, she didn't need it. She didn't sleep a wink that night, wide-eyed and listening to the rain's steady drumming on the roof like an approaching army, earnest and ominous. She turned off her alarm and rose before the stubborn minutes could reach midnight.

She crept downstairs. Her items were waiting inside the front foyer closet: a parka, a pair of rain boots, a camp chair, and an umbrella. She made a half pot of coffee, poured it into a thermos and headed to the foyer, where she slung on her gear and eased open the front door. She stuffed the umbrella into the crook of her arm, grabbed the thermos and chair, gently closed the storm door, and stalked out into the driving rain. Flashes of lightning flickered in the distance, but she paid them no mind—her father and his warnings couldn't be further away. She set up camp in the same spot where Reid had communed with his mistress, two days prior. And she sat, watching the shapeless sky above the dusky streetlamp light, willing the minutes to slog by.

She decided not to open the umbrella, not wanting to obscure her view of whatever she might see—if she saw it at all. One-thirty came and went. The rain picked up around two o'clock, whipping at her parka hood, insistent at an angle, spraying her cheeks. Lightning flickered. Thunder rumbled. Her heart rumbled with it.

At two-twenty, she leaned forward in her chair and squinted harder into the driving rain, eyes fixed above the roof. It was difficult with the rain pelting her face, but her gaze remained unflinching. Ten minutes passed. Fifteen. Nothing. She fished out her phone and glanced at the time: two thirty-seven. She exhaled, and shifted in her chair. A prolonged quiver of lightning held the sky alight for an unnaturally long time. She froze.

Then it happened. It darted in from the west, silent as a night owl. It stopped abruptly high over the roof, on a dime, as if God had pressed *pause*. Her breath paused with it. It was suspended, caught in the flickering canopy like a splinter, oblong in shape and carved from deep shadow, unknowable in scale from where she sat. She didn't blink. She didn't move.

Then it bolted forward at a speed impossible for her eyes to track. A throaty rumble followed, accompanied by more flickering light, blinding like a camera flash. The light ebbed and guttered out moments later. *Gone,* as if it had simply vanished, there for maybe three seconds, but no longer. She realized she was holding her breath and gasped.

Did that just happen?

She fetched her breath and blinked rapidly, concentrating on the place in the sky the thing had just vacated. A slender ribbon of vapor, lighter than the surrounding night, hung like an umbilical over the roof. It tapered off where the thing had paused in its furious race through the electric dark.

Am I going crazy?

Maybe her eyes, raw from overexertion, had seen something her mind wanted her to see. But it had to have been real. What was happening to Reid was real. Was *he* the vapor trail? Was the vapor part of him? Did that thing just take him? And if so, had it already returned him? Had this entire event occurred inside the space of a heartbeat?

She tried to imagine what Reid's body would look like up in bed. Would his muscles be tensed, his back arched, his teeth bared? Or had he already collapsed back down onto the mattress, arms and legs slackening as if in post-coital repose? Guilt overtook her. Either way, he'd already reached his hand out to her. And it would have found nothing but the cold sheets.

I'm sorry, my love. Redemption is messy.

She wondered if her mere absence might have changed the dynamic of this thing's relationship with him. But what was it really? Abduction? And how could it be abduction if his body never truly left? How could it be abduction if he seemed to look forward to these visitations? Her thoughts raced but found no answers in the slanting rain. Minutes later, the lightning returned in earnest, tossing angry shadows over their home. Was the lightning its to summon? Those jagged bolts its to throw? The thunder its to clap?

***

2:08 am

She stirred and pulled a pillow over her eyes, but it was no good. She brought her knee up to her chest and ran a finger over the tender bump on her shin, the bump that had once belonged to Reid. She thought back to the video she'd taken of him in the bath, when it seemed there were no answers. But there was one. It was tiny and obscure, but it was an answer.

Not long after she'd seen its coming, she'd worked up the courage to watch the video again, thinking there might be something she'd missed. As much as she'd wondered *why* it was all happening, the other troubling question in her mind unexpressed but always there, had been, *how?* Not just how it had first taken him that dawn in the park, but how it continually came back to him. How did it know him? And how did it follow him to his home? Was it watching him? Had this thing marked him?

When she'd discovered him in the tub and recorded the video, something had caught her eye, wedging a foreign thought into her brain, but she'd been too distraught to register its accompanying warning signal. Like an elusive fish, she caught it her third time through the footage. It hadn't been the bucket resting atop Reid's knees that had made her pause when panning the camera over him, it had been something else that signaled to her: a small teardrop-shaped bump, visible on his left shin beneath the clear water. It wasn't the resulting round bulge of a mosquito or spider bite. It wasn't a wart, a tumor, or some kind of pus-filled infection. Reid treated his body like a shrine and would tolerate no such blight or affliction. She didn't know how long it had been there, but suspected it had been there since that morning jog.

To confirm this, she went back and looked at older photos of Reid, who had a habit of wearing shorts, unseasonable weather be damned. She swiped through dozens of photos saved on her phone, focusing on those taken before the jog. She found pictures from their vacation in the Outer Banks. No bump. She scanned through photos she'd taken of him three years ago as he competed in the Akron Marathon. No bump. She thumbed through hundreds. Still no bump. It wasn't until she'd gotten to more recent photos that the bump appeared. She found a shot of him sitting on a fallen tree they'd come upon during a hike, sixteen months ago. He was leaning forward, forearms resting on his knees, wearing his usual self-assured smile.

She zoomed in on the photo until it became a mosaic of pixels, and panned to his left shin. Even at this grainy resolution, the bump was visible. The light slanting in through the foliage from the left kissed its raised surface, casting a thin shadow crescent on its opposing side, describing a teardrop. She considered searching for more evidence, but it was enough. She knew. In fact, she thought she'd known all along. He'd been implanted with something.

***

2:11 am

She turned and faced him, her Reid, her love, the loyal man who stayed. The man who'd redeemed her. She whispered into the dark, "Tonight is the night I redeem you, my love. I'm so sorry for what I had to do to you."

She'd cut him open four hours ago. He hadn't felt a thing—or so she hoped. The ground-up Lunesta tablets she'd mixed into his glass of Pinot had made him drowsy faster than she'd expected, causing him to slump next to her on the couch, his eyelids drooping in the flickering candlelight.

It was just past nine o'clock, and dragging him up to bed was an ordeal, even diminutive as he was. Her arms burned as she guided him up the stairs from under his armpits, coaxing his clumsy feet forward and upward, his body like an oversized marionette made of meat. But the real work began after she eased him down onto the mattress. She lowered herself to the floor, reached under the bed, and pulled out the small bag of supplies she'd stolen from work. She'd surprised herself with that blatant theft, that act of recklessness, a disquieting reminder that the muscle memories from her using days were still alive and well. *I'm desperate*, she'd told herself at the time, and had rationalized the act in the same way she'd justified stealing money from her stepbrother years ago for another dance with the needle.

A deep rumble sent a shudder through the house. Reid didn't budge. She poured the local anesthetic ointment onto a small cloth and applied a liberal amount to the bump. Then she waited, watching her husband and listening to the rain pelt the eaves above. Fifteen minutes later, she pulled a little scalpel and a bottle of sterilizing agent from the bag. She strapped on a headlamp, poured the sterilizer onto another cloth, wiped the scalpel clean and waited ten more agonizing minutes to ensure the numbing effects took hold.

When ten minutes had passed, she glanced up to find he was still snoring gently, lips parted, innocent.

I'm sorry, my love.

She turned on the lamp, leaned over his leg, and set to work. Making a small incision along the inner edge of the bump, she drew a bubbling red crease. Blood raced down the angular contours of his leg and she chased it with gauze to keep it from spilling onto the sheets. She dabbed at the wound and leaned closer. Taking a deep breath, she used the tip of the scalpel to ease open the upper flap of skin. The dark object glistened in the cold lamplight. Tiny blood ribbons decorated its surface. It was as if she had opened an eyelid to reveal the black and blood-shot eye within. It gazed accusingly back at her.

She maneuvered the scalpel tip into the flap, careful not to cut Reid further, and began to ease the object out. Minutes later, she watched it slip from his leg and bounce onto the powder-blue sheet, stippling it with red specks. She grabbed tweezers from the supply bag with shaky fingers, plucked up the tiny object, and let it drop into the sterile cloth. Wiping it thoroughly, she used the tweezers to hold it up to the light. As expected, it was roughly the shape of a teardrop; thick and round on one end, tapered on the other. Its surface was black as obsidian. She grazed it with the tip of her forefinger. It wasn't as smooth as it looked, its surface coarse as pumice, textured and intricate. Studying it closer, she rotated it in the light and thought she could see slender golden conduits snaking in and out of its black exterior, like meandering rivers. *Gold?*

Reid stirred and snorted. Her breath caught. He shifted and reached down to his leg. She froze, praying he didn't feel it or turn onto his side, which he sometimes did. He did neither. He swatted an agitated hand just below his kneecap and let it fall back to his side. Thinking the anesthetic would last a while longer, but not wanting to press her luck, April abandoned her inspection and set to work closing the wound. She found needle and thread in the bag and worked fast to suture it. When that was done, she flicked off the light, put the supplies back into the bag and knelt to slide them under the bed. She'd return them to the office on Monday: no harm, no foul.

"No secrets," he'd said to her when he'd doused her with water. *No secrets.*

What is your secret, Reid?

She didn't slide the bag under the bed. Instead, she grabbed it, along with the tiny object wadded up in a cloth cocoon, and headed downstairs to the kitchen. She poured a generous measure of bourbon and numbed her leg.

***

2:17 am

A sizzling hot poker pressed into her leg, but she welcomed the pain. It was real, absolute—the truth. But would it be worth it? Would it still come? Or had she just removed the robin's egg from the nest, condemning it to abandonment?

Either way, there would be no secrets after tonight. Tonight would be madness, messy, but tomorrow would be clean. Every day forward would be clean. And if this thing came, April would *know*. If it didn't come, Reid would no longer belong to it. Something was going to happen, even if that something was nothing but throbbing legs and bloody sheets. *This is the tipping point.*

But the thought of this climax didn't make her pulse race. It did just the opposite—her heart slowed and her fingers unclenched. She'd done it. One way or the other, he would no longer be under its influence. Her eyelids became heavy and soon closed.

***

She dreamed of an owl with three heads. It was perched atop a power wire, gripping it with human hands instead of talons, its crimson plumage striking beneath a grey sky. Its middle head faced her, the tufted tips of its horns like antennae. It stared at her indifferently as its other two heads spun atop wide shoulders.

She stared back at it for a long time, watching its breast rise and fall with the gentle sway of the wire. It cocked its middle head and spread its massive wings, which were out of proportion with the rest of its body. Dozens of syringes spilled loose. Then, hundreds, thousands. The creature rose into the sky, beating the air with its airplane-sized wings, fanning the syringes in all directions, blotting out the grey canvas. The syringes rained down upon her, slamming into her arms, shoulders, neck, and face. Their cold needles sunk into her flesh and thrummed like fishtails. She screamed.

Then, clouds. They were coming toward her, slow and deliberate. They weren't floating in aimless vagrancy like typical clouds, but controlled, as if pushed toward her by some unseen hand. It didn't feel unnatural, it felt *right*—ordained. Gone were the needles, the owl, the power wire. It was just her and the approaching clouds. Her heart sped up as they drew closer. *Closer.* Her legs weakened, her eyes widened as they neared and their details emerged. The clouds' billowy shapes were not random, but hectic fractal patterns, intentional in their design—severe, sacred, symmetrical. They were almost on her now, light quivering within them. Purple and white currents hustled through networks of golden conduit. They pulsated with life, stability. There were eyes inside. So many eyes. And they were all gazing down upon her with… love.

They love me.

The clouds were above her now, swelling with light older than time itself. So bright. Her blood vessels pulsated with the light, matching its rhythm. She needed to see the clouds more closely. It was a need more acute than anything she'd ever felt. She wanted her eyes to detach themselves from their sockets, sprout wings, and soar up to meet the clouds at their incredible heights. For she knew her heart would swell to the size of the sun if she could just see them; get *inside* them. They would put the lightning in her eyes. Her new heart would pound like the thunder. She'd become the matriarch, the storm, and would wash over all: demon and angel, daughter and son, old and new. She would sweep away all malice and sorrow. When that was done, she'd seep back into the Earth. She'd go under root and rock, into river and sea, before the sands of time and the songs of birds, and seed it all to begin anew. She'd render it all clean, stable, and symmetrical.

Overtake me, she thought, eyes hot with tears—tears of joy she never thought possible.

But she knew it was just a dream. She could still sense her body lying in bed, the pain in her leg becoming more insistent. She was back in her bedroom. *I am dreaming. Is that what this is? Is it all just a dream?*

But it had to be real; it was unlike anything she'd ever experienced. It wasn't just her imagination, or some tumble into a vivid whiskey dream. It was real, but now fading fast. *Fading.* She stirred. She wanted to go back, had to go back, had to will herself to—

Something pressed into the pain of her leg. She gasped. A warmth spread about and around the wound, expanding and then contracting into a single, focused shape, thin and austere. It lingered at the wound for a moment, and then began to move across her leg like a finger. But it wasn't on her leg, it was *inside* it, tracing every nerve, every vein, every artery, from toe to hip.

She couldn't move. But the finger did, somehow switching to her other leg, where it took careful measure. It then moved up to her sex, paused and remained there a long time, examining the hurt in her womb. There was nothing sexual in its touch. It had become curious and cautious, a child exploring the ripped seam of a doll. Then it resumed its calculated routine, moving up to trace her intestines, her stomach, her lungs. She didn't breathe as it shifted from her torso to her left arm. It didn't take long for it to find the wretched elbow crease, that old rail yard, the station where the poison began its journey. It walked about those red tracks, inspecting the wreckage, the hell.

It crossed back into her torso and arrived at her heart, where it unfurled and lay a gentle hand about it, feeling her rhythms and undercurrents. It remained there a long time, calculating, understanding. And then it was down her right arm and then back up again, into the arteries of her neck, the optic nerves behind her eyes. Finally, it arrived in her head.

There, it spoke to her. It spoke to her mind in a voice without words, a voice she'd always known, but had been lying dormant inside her all her life. It was a voice that transcended all, its reign absolute, older yet newer than time itself. It was the storm, its power implacable, beyond manmade contrivance or whim, that which summons the elder to eternal night, that which urges the infant down the canal and into the pale of day. Its language was phonetically impossible, but understandable; feminine, maternal, and sacrosanct.

"My April, you need not do it this way," said the voice.

She didn't think she could reply. Like her body, her thoughts were stiff with fear. But she thought, *Are you God?*

The voice replied, "No, my April. You are God. You are moving flesh. You are my majesty."

She thought of Reid. *Why? Why are you taking him?*

"It is his time to go to the Stable. All go to the Stable in time, my April. Some go sooner than others."

I don't understand. Why do you keep taking him from me?

"You will know in time."

When will that be? When will I know?

"In time."

Why can't I go now?

No reply.

Please take me. I want to go now. No secrets.

Several moments passed. *They left.* She would never know. Her husband's secrets would remain and she'd forever be on the outside looking in. No redemption.

Don't go. Please. Please ta—

"It can be your time if you wish," said the voice. "But all who go to the Stable must become symmetrical. You are asymmetrical, my April. We are all symmetrical here. In time, you will become symmetrical too."

I-I don't under—

The finger pressed into her head with force. She gasped. An orb of purple light grew to overtake her vision. Her eyes shot open, unseeing. The light was overwhelming, all-consuming—euphoric. Her bones became buoyant, her organs warm liquid. She was being pulled out through her forehead. She was only dimly aware of her body; its arching back, its fingers clawing at the bed sheets.

Oh God, I'm leaving. I'm leaving my love. Oh, Reid. It's so incredible.

Before the last of her was pulled up and out of her husk, she summoned all her will, all her strength, all her love, and sent it down to her right hand. She walked a stranger's trembling fingers over to where Reid lay, found his hand and gripped it.

She squeezed three times.

Other HellBound Books Titles
Available at: www.hellboundbookspublishing.com

Spells in Waiting

For as long as she can remember, Lauren Merriweather has fought to separate herself from her mother - by focusing on school and developing her healing powers. Like her mother, she's a natural-born witch, but unlike her mother, Lauren is not a killer driven by hatred. But, when a fight with her rampaging mother drives Lauren to seek relief in alcohol and mindless flirting, her world is twisted violently out of her control.

Lauren's attraction to David is as immediate as it is undeniable - to the extent that she forgets about the spells that have, until now, kept her from getting close to a man. But, David Fredricks is the government operative investigating her mother for murder, and he and his partner have determined that Lauren is their best lead.

As far as David is concerned, Lauren and her mother are both witches, and that makes them little better than monsters. Lauren's allure doesn't change the fact that her mother is a vicious serial killer, and he's prepared to do whatever it takes to stop her.

An interrogation goes too far, and Lauren finds herself bound to David in a way that neither of them could ever have imagined - and her very survival depends on her trusting the same people who stole her identity.

The Waning

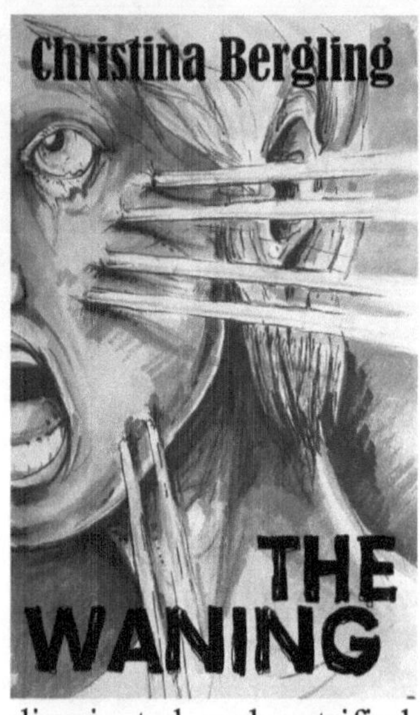

Beatrix woke up in a small metal cage, Lost in the darkness, a persistent dripping sound her only company.

She was celebrating a promotion that was the culmination of her entire ruthless, driven career; a promotion that would cement her status enough for her to take her relationship with her girlfriend out of the lesbian closet; Beatrix had finally made it.

And then she was here, disoriented and petrified in a blackness she could not define. Yet the reality of her Master may be even more terrifying than the crushing darkness and enveloping isolation. He appears as an ominous shadow in the doorway of her cell, never speaking. Instead, he teaches Beatrix the language of pain and torture, of submission and obedience, of domination and possession

With each passing day, the fight and hope in Beatrix begins to shrivel and wane. With each savage beating, her survivalist instincts rise up to overwhelm the person she was. With each dehumanizing condition, she begins to forget who she was and the life from which she was ripped.

Can Beatrix ward off the psychological breakdown of her Master? Can she resist the temptation to survive and thrive through submission? Either Beatrix will succeed at surviving and escaping the torments of her Master or her Master will succeed at breaking her completely and reforming her into his design for a human possession…

Flanagan

"Straw Dogs meets Fifty Shades - heart pounding, gut-wrenching, sexy as all hell and with a twist you'll never see coming!"

Meet the Sewells, your typical, all-American couple; happily married for ten years, respected high school teachers, still crazy about one another and with a secret, shared dark side.

During their annual Spring Break vacation to recharge their batteries and reconnect as a couple, they are waylaid by a perverse gang of misfits in the one horse, North Texas town of Flanagan.

Taken hostage as the focus of the gang's twisted games, the Sewells are brutalized into performing increasingly vicious physical, sexual and emotional acts upon one another, until events take an unexpected turn - triggered by an unintentional death.

As their circumstance descends into the worse nightmare imaginable, the Sewells find themselves involved in an altogether different situation...

Take Me

Adriana Santos, a fearless, idealistic young police officer on beach patrol, interrupts the sale of a young Mexican girl into slavery.

Adriana goes undercover to break up the human trafficking ring, a mission complicated by a the vicious serial killer 'Juan the Ripper'" who stalks the streets of central Texas and brutally murders young Mexican prostitutes.

In Corpus Christi, Adriana is kidnapped, her partner left for dead. She struggles to establish a relationship her captor, both feeling a strong mutual attraction.

In her quest to help the girls that are held captive, Adriana causes trouble with her captor's ruthless boss, and despite their disagreements, she and her captor must learn to work together to survive.

Depraved Desires 1

A mind-blowing collection of the very darkest erotica from the very best minds in the business!

Desires - we all have them, even if we won't admit it. Some are considered normal, and probably healthy. But what about the others?

Those haunting stirrings within that rail against societal norms and the bounds of decency?

Depraved Desires delves into the writhing depths of carnal appetites and sin, peeling back the veneer to reveal tales of wanton lust and supernatural depravity...

The terrifying prospect of knife play; a cosmic liaison; a classy party that turned out to be more than a hired call girl ever expected; or when a sinister fantasy becomes reality - all will shock you.

Whether your desires drive you mad or your madness drives your desires, delving within these pages will take you to places where those itches live, the ones that demand to be scratched.

Graveyard Girls

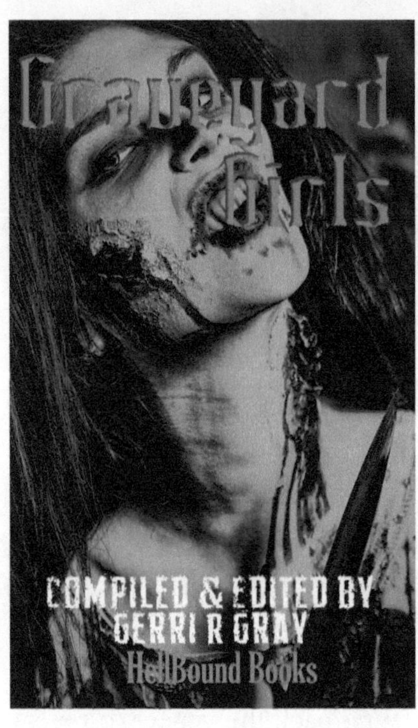

Female authors + Horror = something spectacularly terrifying! A delicious collection of horrific tales and darkest poetry from the cream of the crop, all lovingly compiled by the incomparable Gerri R Gray! Nestling between the covers of this formidable tome are twenty-five of the very best lady authors writing on the horror scene today!

These tales of terror are guaranteed to chill your very soul and awaken you in the dead of the night with fear-sweat clinging to your every pore and your heart pounding hard and heavy in your labored breast…

Featuring superlative horror from: Xtina Marie, M. W. Brown, Rebecca Kolodziej, Anya Lee, Barbara Jacobson, Gerri R. Gray, Christina Bergling, Julia Benally, Olga Werby, Kelly Glover, Lee Franklin, Linda M. Crate, Vanessa Hawkins, P. Alanna Roethle, J Snow, Evelyn Eve, Serena Daniels, S. E. Davis, Sam Hill, J. C. Raye, Donna J. W. Munro, R. J. Murray, C. Bailey-Bacchus, Varonica Chaney, Marian Finch (Lady Marian).

**A HellBound Books LLC
Publication**

http://www.hellboundbookspublishing.com

Printed in the United States of America

www.ingramcontent.com/pod-product-compliance
Lightning Source LLC
Chambersburg PA
CBHW062017190726
48284CB00012B/424